DAMAGED GOODS

A DETECTIVE INSPECTOR WHITE CAPER

JACK EVERETT
& DAVID COLES

BARKING RAIN PRESS

Damaged Goods: A Detective Inspector White Caper

Edited by Ti Locke (www.urban-gals-go-feral.blogspot.com)
Proofread by Dr. Julie Spergel (www.barkbks.me/JulieSpergel)

Barking Rain Press
PO Box 822674
Vancouver, WA 98682 USA

www.barkingrainpress.org

ISBN Trade Paperback: 1-935460-92-7
ISBN eBook: 1-935460-93-5
Library of Congress Control Number: 201493755

First Edition: January 2012 (Published as *The Tourist: Damaged Goods*)
Second Edition: November 2014

Printed in the United States of America

9781935460923

Dedication & Acknowledgements

This book is dedicated to our children,
our grandchildren and our great grandchildren.

We would like to thank Dr. David Harrison
for his help with psychiatric questions and answers
regarding the problems suffered by
our character, Robert Cleghorn

And our thanks go to our editors,
Ti Locke and Julie Spergel,
for their sharp-eyed culling of
our typos and other errata.

Chapter 1

For the better part of three weeks, Robert had battled against the wilderness that had been his brother's backyard. Now only selected specimens of saw palmetto and wild magnolia were left among the scarred but proud southern oaks that would form a cool canopy over the lanai. Where the ground dipped below the water table, clear pools had formed and water hyacinth flourished. At least some shape, some form, was materializing from the five-acre lot on which Alan had built his dream house.

The house was sited so that the front door opened onto the eleventh green of the Pelicans Dream Golf Club and the back windows looked out over Lake Kissimmee. The house represented the aspiration of many successful men: golf, fishing and boating; a millionaire's lifestyle without necessarily having to be a millionaire.

Alan, thought Robert as he carried dried up cabbage palm fronds to the shredder, *you're a very lucky man.* A beautiful home, three cars and a golf cart in the garage and a pile of money in the bank. Then he thought of Stephanie, his one-time girlfriend. Alan had poisoned her mind against him while he'd been off in Iraq, stolen her while Robert's back had been turned. At least she was away when he'd arrived: it had made things easier. Off on a holiday in England, his brother had told him.

Robert ground his teeth and managed to bark his shin against the wheelbarrow, he cursed and his thoughts collapsed. A few of the right connections, that's all it took, he thought, an ounce of luck and it could have been Alan cleaning up my backyard.

Another two hours passed while Robert played the if-only game as he worked with the spade. The Florida sun burned his back to a deep mahogany color and the smell of hot earth filled his nostrils. He could feel the soreness beginning and reveled in it the same way he did down at the gym when his muscles struggled with the last few reps.

He closed the valve; the water, almost level with the edges of the pit, started to soak away the moment he turned off the hose. Robert went back to the ten-year-old oak to be transplanted and squinted up at its twenty-foot height, little more than a black silhouette against the bright pale blue sky. The ring trench around it was already three feet deep and all that remained was to cut the deep tap root which still anchored the tree. Choosing the side with the most shade, Robert started the final excavation leaving a ball of damp earth clinging to the roots. The sharp blade of his spade connected with the last root and he sank the edge into the gnarled wood again and again until, suddenly, with a small pop, it parted.

Robert stood back and eased his aching muscles, looking up at the big tree which swayed a little. It swayed a little more and all at once began to lean. Suddenly galvanized, Robert dashed around the tree and put his shoulder to the trunk. He pushed with all his might, but he might as well have tried to stop a moving truck in its tracks. Slowly, inexorably, the tree pushed him out of the way and continued to fall towards the house until the upper branches crashed through the picture window of Alan's study, spraying glass everywhere.

Robert could hardly believe it. He simply stood and watched as the oak settled itself a little and broke yet more wood off the sill. He closed his eyes and shuddered. When he opened them again, his brother was already striding across the scorched grass and his expression was thunderous.

"You bloody fool," he said, struggling to find suitable words but palpably failing.

The two brothers shared the same red hair and hard features, differing only in the twenty pounds of extra weight the five-years-older Alan carried and maybe two, three inches more in height. He looked from the damaged window to Robert and back again.

"Why did I ever let Connie talk me into giving you a job? Eh? You're a foul-up, Rob, a total foul-up. You know that?"

Curiously enough, being called a foul-up did not upset Robert. He knew he had been stupid or rather, that he'd had a hell of a bad break just there and Alan was justifiably mad. What made Robert mad just then was being called Rob. He'd hated the diminutive ever since he'd been a toddler and... Alan should have Goddamn well known that!

"You've never amounted to anything," Alan continued, getting into his stride, "and you never will. Twenty-five jobs in five years—half of..."

How many? wondered Robert. There'd been one or two certainly, maybe three and that accident he'd had that played havoc with his memory... "Hogwash!"

"...and five of them Dad got you. What?"

"Twenty-five jobs. That's bullshit. How'd you expect anyone to listen to you when you talk bullshit like that?"

"Twenty goddamn five. Dad ran out of friends willing to do him a favor trying to find you work. You broke the poor old man's heart, you know that? And our mother's, too."

Alan's eyes fixed on the smashed window where about half the oak tree's canopy had managed to force its way into his study. His tone had become level, almost a monotone as he recited what he had obviously rehearsed in his mind over the years.

"Never the same after that car crash you had with Old Billy's Chevy. Watched mom and dad go downhill all through the court case, lie after freaking lie you'd told them Rob, and when it all came out, they just started fading away. You were away for five years and it took them all that time to die…"

"Three years. And it's Robert."

"Dead they were when you came back, dead and buried. You wouldn't even come to the funeral, would you?" Alan turned away as he looked back at the damage.

"Hell, Alan, you want to lay the sins of the world on me? Think hard now, anything else you can dredge up and blame on me? They died of pneumonia. Was a bad winter and I didn't know they'd died. I was… was away working and didn't have time to call them, is all."

Alan turned at last and seized his brother by the arms. "You killed them, Rob. You and nothing else." He increased the pressure and pushed his face closer. "You're a murderer, Rob. You should never have come back from New Mexico or wherever it was you said you were. They'd still be alive if you'd stayed away."

"Let go of my arms, you asshole."

"Why? Hurting you, am I? Pathetic weakling. Always was, Rob."

Robert sucked in a great breath of warm air. He could feel the tingling beginning, deep down around his stomach. "Just let go, Alan. I don't want to get mad at you, you're family. I'm trying to keep that in mind."

Alan laughed and his grip slackened a little. "Keeping it in your tiny mind?" And he squeezed his fingers tightly again, emphasizing how he was the senior and in his own mind, the stronger. "Rob, the Incredible Hulk, eh?"

The tingle in his nerves had spread to the whole of Robert's chest now. He was hyperventilating; his eyes would not focus properly. Somewhere at the back of his brain, Robert—the real Robert—had withdrawn, hiding from what he knew was coming.

Clasping his hands together into a wedge, Robert struck upwards, breaking free of Alan's grip as though it had been a child's. He brought his locked fists down, striking viciously at the bridge of Alan's nose, filling his eyes with stinging tears so he never saw the third blow. Using the side of his right hand, Robert delivered the blow his unarmed combat instructor in the forces had called the meat cleaver. It smashed Alan's larynx to pieces, filling his throat with blood and pulverized tissue. Alan was already dead from massive shock, otherwise the blood and debris in his paralyzed airways would have asphyxiated him very quickly.

Robert's attack had lasted one-point-three seconds. Long enough for him to extinguish a life, not long enough to analyze his actions or to change them. The moment had been too brief even to think in terms of regret; it had happened at an almost cellular level, an instinct for killing drummed into him in training and one he'd used during the heady days of fighting in Iraq—and since, working for his shadowy organization.

Bodies though. That was the difference back here. Getting rid of bodies. He glanced about furtively, his eyes sliding over the newly dug pit, the garden shredder, and then to the gleaming expanse of water across the yard.

Alligators. Robert remembered the 'gators, swimming or sitting on their tails or whatever they did out there in the lake. Take a leg off. Take your arm off. He had heard it said in the local bars a dozen times. Take a whole damn body if it was left for them. Robert nodded to himself. *Yep, stands to reason, no one—nothing—objects to a free meal.*

Robert went through Alan's pockets, removed his watch, wedding ring, and checked the back pants pocket for a billfold. Instead of weighting the body, he laced a few dead branches together and heaved his brother's body onto them. He waded out into the shallow margins of the lake and pushed the makeshift raft ahead of him. Looking back, he saw that he was out of sight of the golf course, and the shore was pretty overgrown at this end of the lake. It was unlikely that anyone would spot dearly beloved Alan's remains from there, so he shoved the branches out toward a dense patch of weeds some thirty feet or so from the bank. His luck held. Just short of the weed patch, the branches came apart, and the body drifted onward, partly submerged and almost unnoticeable.

As Alan's body disappeared, the incident faded from Robert's mind. There were no regrets, no attacks of morals; his brother might never have existed as he waded back to the bank and across to the house.

Nothing to keep him here now.

His few possessions were in the guest room, his pickup parked out on the driveway; he could pack everything up and just go.

Robert made up his mind to do exactly that. He went into what Alan had called the great room as the screen door banged behind him. He noticed the five leather suitcases waiting by the hall door. Alan was going to England.

He stood there for several seconds as curiosity got the better of him and he shuffled over and tipped the nearest bag on its back to raise the lid. He was distracted by a small collection of leather document cases on the telephone table beside the suitcases.

Robert picked the top one up. It held a passport which, when he opened it up, held a photo taken some years before: red hair, pale blue eyes and that almost naked look the eyelids had because the lashes were so fair. The angular cheek bones and the sharp, straight nose had been overlaid in Alan's present day appearance by a layer of soft flesh. The likeness was, Robert realized, very, very close to his own. Especially the hair and that blunt, almost square chin.

Even then, Robert didn't realize what his subconscious was setting up for him as he checked the other wallets. There were business class air tickets from Orlando, a thousand English pounds, an Avis car rental arrangement, credit cards and Alan's driver's license. It was almost as if the plan emerged fully fleshed in the forefront of his brain.

Ten thousand pounds in travelers' checks—more than fifteen thousand dollars, he realized—that was what clinched it. Some holiday his brother had been planning! His brother had been paying him a hundred bucks a week to clear the wilderness from the lot—plus room and board, of course... which wasn't much, compared to *this* sort of money.

Robert put the things back on the table and went through the hallway to his room. He stripped and showered as he built mental lists of things to do. He made a call to a local builder and left instructions for the tree to be moved and the damage made good, using his brother's name. It would not do to give the local police reason to be looking around when everyone knew Alan was going away.

Robert made himself some lunch and sat in the long kitchen on the west side of the house. Who knew he was here? He'd kept to himself when he'd been out drinking: smoky, dark bars, corner tables, discouraging conversation and watching the chicks doing their bit from the corners of his eyes. Not wanting to associate with anyone who might report him to them...

In fact, the only person who could place him here at the house was Stephanie. He'd overheard Alan talking to his wife the morning before last and telling her that he, Robert, was here. She was staying with relatives in... somewhere. He frowned, looked at the ceiling, somewhere in... in Yorkshire, England. The address would be in Alan's documents; he had been going to see her... before.

Correction! *He*, Robert was going to see her. No, he mustn't think like that: he, Alan, was going to see her. That was the way it was.

Shortly before "Alan" was due to leave for the airport, Robert, now dressed in a smart worsted suit, went outside and parked his pickup behind the left-hand door of the four-car garage. He locked the garage, carried the suitcases out in pairs to Alan's Mercury and locked the house up. He headed for 27 North. He popped a Jerry Lee Lewis CD into the player and thumbed the volume, humming along and singing the words. Fifteen minutes later he stopped at the first Walgreens he came to and purchased four bottles of ibuprofen and on impulse, a pair of rose-tinted sunglasses, similar in every respect to the prescription glasses Alan wore for driving. He made his way onto I-4, then the 417, and resumed his drive out to Orlando International Airport.

Inside the terminal he checked his bags and glanced at the clock, sliding the glasses down his nose a moment before readjusting them. The time was 3:15, the temperature 92 degrees outside. Inside it was a pleasant air-conditioned 72. He walked through the arch leading into the departure lounge with a spring in his step, barely noticing the steel framework of the metal detector at the entrance. Smoothly, Robert brought out Alan's passport and handed it to the female official. She took two seconds to open it to the photograph and hand it back to him. If she had glanced at his face it was so briefly that there was no chance of her seeing the tense line across his forehead or the bunched muscles at the corners of his jaw.

In fact, it was only later, when he was sitting in his seat in business class, his coat folded away in the overhead locker, that a perceptive observer would have noticed how the muscles of his forearms gradually relaxed and the white flesh on his knuckles returned to the color of tanned skin. Even then, the watcher would have put it down to takeoff nerves.

Robert would have made one hell of a poker player if he had had a tad more patience. With relaxation came the expected headache which he knew would be followed by a continual nagging feeling—a feeling he had forgotten things, important things. He grinned ruefully and swallowed two ibuprofen dry—the legacy of war, he told himself.

CHAPTER 2

The room in the Leeds Civic Hall smelled of old leather, of polished wood and stale smoke. The monthly meetings between the four men always occurred here. Grimes—Chief Superintendent Grimes—preferred the meetings to be away from the Ridings Regional Crime offices and it was his pipe which was responsible for the ever-present smell of tobacco smoke. He continued to smoke in his office even though the antismoking law forbade it. No one would say a thing, he reckoned.

Grimes glanced from one man to the other from beneath bushy eyebrows while he struck the tenth match of the session. "Appointments." The match flame bent over as he sucked on the pipe, igniting the strands of tobacco before he tamped them down to a smolder with his thumb. "A vacancy for the post of inspector."

"Yes." Chief Inspector Allenby nodded. He was in his late forties, his steel-gray hair contrasting with a florid expression. "You'll recall that Inspector Walker had a stroke. We have to fill his position."

"That's right," said Grimes, as though Allenby had passed a test. "How is he?"

"He's off the critical list now, sir, though I'm afraid he's never going to make it back to the office."

"Have we seen his wife?" Grimes asked and then continued without waiting for an answer. "The Ferremore murder. Wasn't he on that case?"

"Yes and yes." These meetings were a waste of time but Allenby held his face expressionless. Grimes could have asked all this on the phone or better yet, got his secretary to check. "We've given the case to Inspector Foreshaw. He'd just finished up on the Allied Shores fraud thing."

"Seems a logical choice. So, a replacement then. Do we have someone in mind?"

"I have someone in mind; however there's a short list of two. You should have had the details." He looked out of the window where a pale sun was shining. It had been raining earlier, and the sunlight illuminated the streaks where rain and city dust had mixed on the glass.

Superintendent Flowers appeared tired of Grimes's style too; it showed in his voice. "In the green file," he said wearily, "Inspector Jamieson from the Edinburgh force and Inspector White from the City of Birmingham. Both of them have exceptional strengths although they are in different areas."

Perhaps Grimes noticed the antipathy and realized he was outnumbered for he became suddenly brisk. He opened the file and although perfectly conversant with the contents, held onto authority for a few seconds longer as he glanced through the two applications and the attached comments.

"All right then. Jamieson. Thirty-four, married, children. Sergeant at twenty-six, inspector by thirty. Criminal Investigation Division—CID. Drug squad. Commendation for bravery and others for good work. Good solid man." Grimes had come up the hard way; predictably, he had a lot of respect for Jamieson. He dropped the pages onto the scarred table top. "Here's White. Got a photograph too." Grimes looked at it a moment, a young dark-haired man with questioning eyebrows and an intelligent gaze. There was a suggestion of a crooked smile on the wide mouth. He turned to the C.V. "Cambridge graduate, first in, em… in psychology. Also something or other in computer studies, applied maths. Fast track entrant at Police College, came out second in the group." Grimes looked up as he dropped the second set of papers on top of the first. Thirty years old, four years in uniform.

"Fast track," he said. "What do you think, Joe?"

"White for me, sir," replied Flowers without hesitation. "No doubt about it."

"Fast track. Academic. Whiz kid." Each one an indictment from Grimes.

"He's from a working class background, sir. He's also very bright. We need him."

"Experience." Grimes stabbed the papers with his forefinger. "Has he got enough experience?"

"Maybe I can say something?" It was the first time Jordan had spoken that afternoon. A nod or the shake of his head had been sufficient up to the present. Chief Inspector Jordan was quite a few years younger than Grimes; he was a slim man with a neat moustache. He got on with Grimes during business hours but socially, they moved in different circles.

"Feel free," said Grimes, lighting another match.

"I've spoken with White's superior officer, a Superintendent Evans."

Grimes answered the implied question. "Don't know him."

"He's fuming. He doesn't want to lose White; told him he'd be getting his extra pip inside two years. Make him the youngest Chief Inspector in the force."

"And what did Inspector White say? Didn't want the promotion?"

"No." Jordan rubbed his nose. "I'm reading between the lines here, what I think is he wants a better challenge. He's known for his lateral thinking, but he's too constricted in the West Midlands."

"Call him Sherlock, down there," Flowers smiled as he said it.

"What was that?" Grimes looked up.

"He's got a nickname in the West Midlands. They call him Sherlock."

"Do they? Well what's the vote on this one?"

Grimes was the only dissenter. The Superintendent nodded at the result and stood up. "Well, let's hope he lives up to your expectations. Eh?" he said, already distancing himself from the possibility of a bad decision.

The meeting wound to its close, and they stood up, gathering papers.

"You know why he has these meetings here, don't you?" Flowers kept his voice low, so that Jordan would not overhear him.

"Why?" asked Allenby with a grin, standing and stretching as the door closed behind the two senior officers.

"Poet's day."

"Pardon?"

"Push off early, tomorrow's Saturday. Gets a free cup of tea here and a fast get-away. Big deal when you reach Grimes's age."

I don't know if I had some sort of inkling that this was my last case here, as DI Stewart White. Certainly, for some reason, I was leading it rather more recklessly than usual.

It had been a fine warm day turned now to a cool and showery evening and the concrete storm drain—dry at six o'clock—was three inches deep in muddy water.

Nevertheless, the drain—some six feet in diameter and located about three feet above the river's surface—afforded an excellent view of the nearby railway bridge. Four men, members of the Birmingham Armed Response Unit, stood just inside the drain; no doubt at least three of them wished fervently that they were elsewhere. I grinned at Sergeant Darren's discomfort *and* it was information from his *snout*, Leigh, who had brought us here, news of a huge load of drugs expected to change hands at about ten that night.

I knew how each of my officers felt, and even sympathized with them. I'd have felt similarly if I'd been expected to stand around ankle deep in water and water-logged rubbish on the strength of someone else's expectations.

Desperate situations required desperate measures, however, and Leroy "King" Richards was about *the* most desperate—not to say ruthless—of the racketeers we had in the Midlands underworld at the moment.

I'd followed Richards's career for the past two years, knew it by heart: every deal, every beating, every murder; there was just no kind of hard evidence to back up this common knowledge. The man flaunted his wealth and power, he was driven around the city by a squat, Neanderthal-like chauffeur in an imported Lincoln Town Car, he wore enough bracelets and finger rings to buy me a pension for life. Richards entertained in the grand style, frequenting gambling clubs and restaurants with a succession of women who wore the most exclusive of designer clothes and jewelry.

The police had lost count of the times he'd been stopped on almost any excuse and searched. His two houses and his penthouse had been turned over both officially and clandestinely. Clean, nothing: no records, no drugs, no inexplicably large amounts of cash, no weapons.

Richards's sidekicks had been brought in and interrogated. They told one story, and that came from the gaps and silences rather than the words—no one had anything to say about the King. Richards inspired such a degree of unhealthy fear that, without exception, no one who worked for him would consider even a whispered hint to the police.

I knew it all. I knew how Richards never involved himself personally with any of the deals he made; all of them were contracted at one or two removes from himself. Yet young Everett Leigh had brought him this unbelievable tidbit of information. I'd flatly disbelieved it at first, until "Earwig," as his *snout* was called, came back the next day with an explanation.

Two situations had occurred simultaneously, it appeared.

The drug squad had been squeezing the pushers mercilessly over the past months, so much so that supplies on the street had all but dried up. Few of the regular army of pushers and dealers could get hold of stock and those that did had to tread warily because competitors were happy to negotiate with knives and brass knuckles for their merchandise.

The second development had to do with a new Dutch supplier who would deal with no one except the boss. Richards badly needed stock and if he wanted to remain at the top of the muck-pile, he had little choice other than to meet the supplier and do a deal before any of the competition could make the connection.

Tonight was a chance in a lifetime—or perhaps, a career. The buy was estimated at about four million, cut that for street consumption and the King was looking at twenty million; say, a ten million profit after expenses. I'd acquired a bit of a reputation for getting things done and I wanted to add Richards to the list of busts so much it hurt.

Sergeant Darren Hill—Daz or sometimes, Dazzler to his friends—stood to my right. Daz had his Smith & Wesson .38 drawn and was ready for whatever came; he had been for the past half hour. His feet were never still and again I smiled; without actually pacing up and down, he was managing to wear out just as much shoe leather. The King's bully boys carried an assortment of weaponry, favorites were sawn-off shotguns and Daz had seen the kind of damage they caused if they got in with the first blast. At thirty, he was a veteran and he handled himself well. His only fault, if fault it was, was too much nervous energy at this stage of a rumble—keyed up to breaking point by the time the action started.

"Reckon they're coming, Skip?" he asked as he reached round and tightened up one of the Velcro straps on his flak jacket.

My eyes stayed where they were, fastened on the bridge. A damp breeze brought the smell of old mud and decaying things across the water. "Does it matter, so long as we're here? You're drawing overtime. What more do you want?"

"Overtime? I'm doing this out of the goodness of my heart, Boss. I don't like the waiting. You know I don't like the waiting."

"Call the other teams; see if they've seen anything." It didn't need doing. If anyone did see anything they'd call in and say so. It gave Daz something to occupy his mind though, and that was what mattered.

I could hear him pulling his phone out of a pocket and then the slight rustle was lost behind another noise, a soft thumping sound that carried across the water. All four of us tensed and strained to locate the source. Several shapes materialized under the railway bridge; a powerful torch flashed on and off.

"Forget the phone call, Daz. None of our lads'll miss that. It's a boat of some sort, coming up river; wait for it to stop before we go in."

All was silent except for the rhythmic thump and four lots of heavy breathing. The vessel came into view: a canal boat—the sort used for holiday cruising. "Got the loudhailer, McGuire?" I asked in a low voice.

"Right here, sir."

A sliver of moon showing between the clouds was enough to strike highlights from the cabin windows and metalwork. A canal narrow boat, they were all over the canals around Birmingham but I didn't recall seeing any here on the river before and wondered where it had come from.

It was slowing, the engine was idling now and the craft coasted in towards the bridge. As it passed the hideout, the engine switched off and it glided onward silently until someone jumped off the bows and carried a rope ashore. There were three swift hammer blows as a peg or a stake was driven into the ground and the rope secured to it.

"Loudhailer please, McGuire. Remember, no firing unless they start it." I put the hailer to my mouth and pressed the switch. "This is the police." I could hear echoes coming back. "Everybody stay exactly where you are." It was a vain hope; however, proper procedure had to be observed.

The men beneath the bridge and on the boat's deck froze for an instant and then exploded into movement. Curses filled the night. The typical bark of a shotgun blasted out, the first of many and a signal for chaos to begin. Clouds of luridly red smoke from several shotguns lit the darkness and the sharp crack of police rifles added to the din.

Suddenly, the dark recesses were lit by the light from a police car's headlights and a spotlight. The noise of the firearms diminished as their owners dove for cover and began to look for ways out of the mess.

I led my boys out of the drain and along the bank to cut off the drug dealers retreat. They fired several shots as they went, discouraging any shotgun wielders from targeting us. Then we were there. A man fell into the river, blood from a neck wound unnaturally bright in the spotlight. I ignored him, hoping someone else would see to a rescue because straight ahead of me was the man I was really after. *God, how I wanted to snap the cuffs onto his wrists.*

Richards, both looking and feeling less like a king than usual, ran from the bridge as a line of police appeared on the far side. He certainly wasn't carrying a gun and when he saw my group coming, he stopped and looked at the river, figuring the percentages. It took only a moment; he jumped, disappeared below the black surface for a second or two then reappeared, making a rather scrappy attempt at a crawl.

In the darkness, the current was swifter than it appeared to be. Richards was being swept back under the bridge away from us. That wasn't good. There was no time for debate; I tore off the flak jacket and shuffled off my shoes.

Cold and wet or not, I went in after the drug dealer and caught up with Richards before he'd travelled twenty yards. The drug king was not a fit man—too much eating and drinking, too little exercise; he tried to fight me off but there was no real contest. He went under several times and came up coughing and spluttering. I got hold of his head and pushed him under, held him there until the struggles changed from fighting to frantic. I towed the bedraggled dealer back to the bank where willing hands took over.

Emergency blankets had already been brought from the cars and the thin Mylar-covered plastic was wrapped around us both. I stood up, clutching the thing around me, and looked the big Jamaican-born man in the eyes. He stared back; hate was the only emotion there, no fear, no disappointment. Just loathing and contempt.

"Have we got the stuff? " I asked without looking away.

"Oh yes, Inspector, tons of it. We'll have to hire a warehouse."

I nodded. "Great." I smiled at Richards, "You're nicked."

"And you're a dead man. You'll have bleeding nightmares about me, man. I'm coming for you an' I'm gonna tear your tongue out and stick it up your ass."

I chuckled. "Not the first time somebody's told me that. By the time you get out, chum, you won't have the strength to wipe your own ass, let alone do anything to mine."

I turned to Richards. "Get him out of my sight."

Stewart White Senior went into his kitchen at six thirty that morning, just as he always did, as he had done as far back as he could remember. Retirement hadn't changed his habit; he simply could not sleep after six o'clock in the morning.

The note which had been trapped under the kettle caught his attention as soon as he went to make his breakfast tea—as it was intended to. He pulled it out and read the scribble.

Dad, it read, *got him! Came home too late to wake you up so I'll tell you about it later. When* I *wake up.*

Stewart smiled to himself and re-read the note as he made the tea. He brought them both through to the sitting room, propping the note on the mantelpiece and putting the tea on the table next to the old swivel armchair. He lit the gas fire, turned on the TV and changed channels to the BBC. On the wall above the fire a photograph of his son at sixteen looked down at him. The boy was wearing a white amateur boxing strip across the knuckles of his gloves. A Latin motto ran along the base of the photo: *festina lente*, a suggestion which had always struck him as ludicrous. How did a boxer—or anyone else, for that matter—make haste slowly?

Stewart was proud of his son; even their disagreements had brought about something worthwhile although it was a hard thing to see at the time. He had wanted the boy to be an electrician, get a solid trade behind him which would stand him in good stead for the rest of his life. No such thing. Despite the rows between them, the boy was determined to be a policeman, for God's sake. Still, look at him now.

Rows and arguments didn't matter—the fact that Stewart Junior had stayed on at home with his father when the mother died said it all—but just lately, there had been hints his son wanted to lead his own life.

He got up, found his glasses, and put them onto look more closely at the snapshot. There were things there he'd overlooked before or maybe he had forgotten them despite looking at it every day for years. The rounded chin and the deep-set blue eyes—faded now in the photograph—came from his wife; Marie had had those same electric blue eyes. His own misted a little as he remembered... remembered all those years they'd had together.

He looked back at the picture when he could see again. The strong nose—now that had been his own father's, like the brown and crinkly wayward hair, hair like that went back in the White family to before the Great War.

Stewart sat down again and finished his tea. Nearly cold, he would have to make another, or maybe the lad would be down soon.

He looked back at the snap. "Damn," he said aloud, "Got that job though, the little devil." *Leeds.* He said silently, to himself. *Moving out anyway, that was definite.*

Stewart's only regret was the lack of family. *No wife, no children.* It saddened the older man a little. *What's going to happen to the family name if he doesn't buck up and produce some grandchildren?*

He got up and made his way through to the conservatory, picking up a tin of dog food on the way through the kitchen and leaving his tea cup at the side of the sink. Pip, his son's Jack Russell, saw the tin and capered around him with approving barks. Stewart stooped, groaning as the twinge of arthritis in his knees hit him, and he spooned out half the tin's contents. He pulled himself upright again.

Leeds. He thought again. Maybe he'd find a girl up there and marry her. He couldn't force his son to provide him with grandchildren, still, you never knew. *I'll have to think up something to say, something really persuasive.* Persuasion almost always achieved better results than nagging.

Stewart smiled as he made his way back, locking the back door as he passed it. *He's a good lad – chip off the old block.*

All that effort to get the scum off the streets and the results had been disappointing. Richards was remanded for six months and eventually given a three-year term instead of the seven-to-ten that I'd expected.

He looked at me as he was taken down from the dock and mouthed "You're a dead man walking, White. Remember that." I doubted he'd give me a moment's thought after a week; he'd be too damn busy…

Still, three years. No wonder I was looking for a way up the career ladder—*somewhere* I could get results.

CHAPTER 3

Buck Gehrig regularly flew supplies across Lake Kissimmee on his way to a clinic in Sebring. The lake was like a brown-tinted relief map from fifty feet up. The various channels were as clear-cut as rivers and streams on land, shoals of fish, half a dozen basking 'gators and flocks of birdlife changed the appearance of the lake, day by day, hour by hour.

It was a beautiful early October morning and Buck's eyes were more on the scenery than his flight path. The odd patch of white caught his eye immediately. He changed course slightly so that he could see out of the right-hand window and banked the chopper slightly.

Human remains, clear as could be, shrouded in tattered white pants and shirt. Buck radioed in to his control and maybe a half hour later, Sheriff Merrick of Highlands County met the recovery team and the medical examiner on the bank close to the reported location.

When the body was brought back to dry land, John Merrick saw that identification might be difficult. The alligators had taken the limbs off and had chewed the head up some. Enough was left of the head to show that the corpse had been male, red-headed, and that was about it, except that the corpse bothered Merrick. There was something familiar, something he should be able to pick up on.

John stayed in the background, phlegmatically watching Al Ribart, the M.E., do his gruesome job. Al was a bit overweight, as was John himself though he rarely admitted it, and his florid face was hidden behind a surgical mask for the moment. Al turned the body over and speaking into a small recorder, made notes about the multitude of wounds. It was thirty minutes or so before he was through and clambered to his feet. He stripped off the latex gloves and the mask as he straightened up.

"Near as I can tell, John, he died sometime yesterday. The 'gators didn't get around to the body, too much. The stomach contents will give us a better fix and I reckon there's enough dental work left to ID him with."

"Did they kill him?" John Merrick nodded out to the shining waters of the lake; he screwed his eyes up against the glare coming off the surface. "The 'gators, I mean."

"Can't tell you that really. Not yet. I can tell you what he died of, *vagal inhibition*, the bones in his throat were crushed and he died of asphyxiation."

"I know what vagal inhibition is. Guy drowned in his own blood is what you're saying."

Ribart nodded, a little put out. "Yeah. I guess so. Could have been a 'gator, a slap from a tail could do that but I'd have expected some lacerations around the throat. More likely to have been a blow with something heavy and padded. Anyway…" He shrugged. "Let you know more when the bruising comes out, water's a damned nuisance in this sort of case, makes things swell—well, expect you know that?"

Merrick ignored the question. "How old would you say he was?"

"Over thirty." Ribart replied without hesitation. "Less than forty though. Tell you more after the autopsy."

"Yeah, well…"

John Merrick had known Al Ribart for the better part of ten years and totally respected his expertise despite the occasional needling. He had to call on his services almost every week nowadays and from time to time they'd share a drink and wonder what the world was coming to.

"Anyway, thanks Al. I'll call by the office tomorrow if that's okay. When will you be done?"

"Make it after lunch, John. Got that young girl they fished out of Lake Wales to do later today so afternoon will be about right."

The sheriff had driven over from the golf course to meet the recovery team. He had crossed into someone's property to get to them. He turned round and looked at the house behind them. "Whose place is this? Anyone know?"

"Guy by the name of Alan Cleghorn, Sheriff." And Merrick jumped. Bob Haskins was a long, lean man in his thirties with dark saturnine features. He'd been a Deputy for more than five years, took his job seriously, did it thoroughly. "Nobody home. Tried to raise someone when we got here. Realtor at Thwaites & Son."

Merrick knew Cleghorn, *had* known him. It had been a year or two since he'd last seen him though, not since John Merrick's wife had died, in fact. He had been buddies—on and off—with his son since school days. There'd been awhile when Merrick did little more than work at his job and hit the bottle in between; it had been a bad time, and when he came out of it a lot of his friends had moved on—Alan among them.

"Cleghorn. Reckon this could be him?" Merrick looked closely but couldn't see past the reality of the water-swollen torso and the torn flesh.

Haskins shrugged. "Couldn't say. Seen him around and I've a feeling that the guy did have red hair. Wore a hat most times though so I can't say for sure."

"Yeah, well, he had red hair all right, I know that but a guy gets half his face chewed off, makes him difficult to recognize. Follow it up anyway. Damned inconvenient when we can't fingerprint him—you know the routine. Seems to me he had a wife. Probably around somewhere; see her when she gets back, maybe she's at work or shopping. Get the other guys to go round to the neighbors. Oh, and see his business partners of course. Okay?"

"Sure thing."

"Call me if you find anything."

CHAPTER 4

Robert Cleghorn landed at Manchester at 6:10 a.m. He stumbled on his trouser cuff halfway down the aisle and had to adjust the oversized pants before he stepped onto the walkway into the airport. The majority of the passengers made their way to the *EU Residents Only* barrier; Robert was one of eight who carried an American passport. He followed the others to the queue for foreign nationals.

The immigration officer spent a full ten seconds examining the passport before he stamped it. "Purpose of visit, sir?" he asked as the stamp came down.

"Tourist. On my way to join my wife. She's English."

The officer put the stamp aside and raised his right eyebrow. "Funny way to be married, sir."

"What? Oh yeah, see what you mean. No, no. She lives in Florida with me. She's on holiday too, came over before me. She's visiting with her relatives."

"I see." He handed the document back again. "Weather's not what you're used to I expect, have a good holiday anyhow."

"Well, thanks." Robert took the proffered passport and made his way to the baggage claim, chilly and full of echoes at this time of the morning.

It took about ten minutes for his luggage to appear on the carousel and five minutes after that, he was wheeling the baggage trolley out of the main door in search of the Avis office. Only then did he realize what the man at the passport desk had meant. Beyond the concrete airport buildings, which covered the highway, it was dark and gray with angry clouds boiling across the visible sky. The outside temperature seemed close to freezing and the wind struck straight through the lightweight suit he was wearing.

He found the car rental place and a few minutes later, the formalities cleared up, he had the luggage stowed in the trunk and the keys in the ignition. It was a Vauxhall Insignia, a medium-sized car for England, a little on the small side compared with what he was used to.

"Left-hand side of the road," said the Avis girl, smiling and then, when his expression remained blank, added, "We drive on the left hand side of the road, sir." Robert nodded and looked doubtfully at the map she'd given him. "Just follow the signs. All the way to the York exit, here." She pressed a carefully manicured nail against a blue coded road. "And your destination is here. You did say Brideswell?"

Robert had found Stephanie's address among Alan's travel documents. He nodded.

"Maybe you should ask locally."

"This M62," he asked. "That's like the Interstate?"

"Very similar. We call them motorways. All the signs on motorways are blue and on trunk roads they're green."

"Yeah, well." It was becoming just a little too much for him. "Thanks."

"Speed limit is 70 miles per hour and… right, bye now."

Robert pressed the window button, shutting her off and carefully put the car in first gear. *When was the last time he'd driven with a stick shift? Years ago, a tractor. Ten years ago, maybe more.*

The motorways took some getting accustomed to. Entrances and exits seemed to flash by every mile, or even less, and the available lanes changed from three to two and back to three without apparent reason. Two near collisions almost occurred before he figured out how to change lanes properly. At last, he was able to settle down and head off east where the sky showed a lighter gray across some jagged mountains.

Robert drove for thirty minutes before he realized that he needed a bathroom and began to look out for billboards advertising gasoline. There weren't any, he understood at last. *What kind of a country is this? No gas stations—what did automobiles run on?* Eventually, he passed a sign, white on blue like the Avis girl had said, with crossed knives and forks and a gas pump. A minute later, he slowed down and was drawing into the parking lot of a service station.

The washrooms were clearly indicated past a small shop unit and opposite a bank of amusement machines where half a dozen youths were playing shoot-em-up and racing-car games. One window of the shop was filled with road maps and he went in and bought one, a better version of the one he'd been given with the car, and another for Yorkshire on its own. He put the money in his left pants pocket so it would not mix with his American change; he would have to put his own money away somewhere else. The maps went into an outside pocket of the coat. *Maybe there'd be time for doing the tourist bit later, after he'd sorted things out with Stephanie.*

He crossed the tiled floor to the washroom entrance, hurrying, aware once more of how cold it was.

Behind him, three of the game players stood watching him. One was a slim, almost thin boy in his late teens; he wore a torn anorak, woolen hat, and a grin which revealed a gold tooth. He spoke to a hulking figure at his side. "Chooty. Stand outside the bogs and make sure no one comes in."

Chooty did up the toggles on his scruffy sheepskin and nodded. "Got a fag?" The slim one offered him a pack; Chooty put his hand out.

"One, ya bagga lard. Jus' one." the slim one said. Chooty took just one, then took his own matchbook out.

"Not here!" said Smitty. "Wair till you're outside, idiot."

"Yeak, Smitty. I know the routine," Chooty said.

Smitty looked at the third figure. "Got your little equalizer there, Biff?"

Biff opened the front of his raincoat and half-pulled a viciously shortened and sharpened bayonet of World War Two vintage from a homemade scabbard. He didn't bother to speak. He pushed the hefty weapon back into its hiding place again and turned the baseball cap back to front on his head. He grinned. At six feet three, Biff was the tallest of the three, his bean pole frame made Smitty's figure look overweight. He was an experienced mugger, working motorway service areas at night and dimly lit subways by day. His eyes were bright; he kept blinking them—the effects of a recent sniff of speed.

"Okay. Usual routine. In quick, credit cards, money and out. Was he wearing jewelry? Ne' mind, we'll soon see. Show'm the blade when I signal. Maybe won't need to though."

Robert Cleghorn saw the two come in through the steamed up mirror where he was washing his face. They had trouble written all over them so he carried right on, drying himself on a paper towel as he covertly sized up the two men. A moment later, Robert leaned back against the wall, giving them his full attention. *Hard or soft?* He thought.

Not that it mattered.

The shorter of the two held out his hand and made beckoning motions with his fingers. "Give us your money and you won' get hurt." Smitty spoke softly and as clearly as he could. Some of these idiots couldn't understand his Lancashire accent. His dreadlocks flapped about his face as he stalked down the length of the washroom. "Come on, haven't got all day."

Biff moved out three feet or so from Smitty's right side, blocking any chance of an escape.

"And what if I don't? " Robert's tone was completely unconcerned, even a little amused.

"Freakin' Yank," said Smitty and Biff grunted. A flick knife appeared in Smitty's other hand, he held both of them out to Robert, the empty one and the armed one. "Cut ya balls off, won't we? Biff, show'm y'little friend."

Biff chortled, a high feminine sort of sound and pulled out his razor-edged bayonet.

Robert Cleghorn smiled, a grimace without humor. He had what he wanted to know and the tingling was working its way out of his belly, up his chest. His lungs felt as though he were breathing living flames.

He held out both hands towards the muggers, let a little of his inner tension show as a tremble in his fingers. He backed away, to the smaller boy's left and away from the tall skinny boy.

Smitty grinned and followed him, closing up. Robert backed a little more, pulling back his hands. He waited until Smitty was close enough to reach and without warning, lashed out with his right foot, smashing the mugger's left knee with a crack which echoed around the washroom like a pistol shot. Smitty screamed, the sound owed more to the boy's animal ancestors than to a human being. He collapsed in a dead faint and outside, Chooty grinned for all the wrong reasons.

Biff had watched it all happen but refused to accept it. He flung his bayonet arm up and charged, bringing it down in a slashing movement like he had seen on TV.

Robert stood sideways onto the boy and at the last second brought his left hand up in a blur. He parried the blade away from him as it came down, and seized the taller man's wrist in a lock. With a continuing sweeping movement, he turned the wrist inwards and the bayonet towards his assailant. The man's momentum brought him onward, the blade slid into his stomach and stopped only when the hilt was pressed firmly up against the thin abdomen.

Robert released the other's wrist and stepped back. Biff crumpled to the floor and looked down at the equalizer growing from his stomach. He opened his mouth to speak or to shout; he died before the word had formed. Biff tilted forwards and fell over on his face.

Robert turned to check the smaller one but heard footsteps approaching. A fat, dough-faced boy came in and stopped in shock, all three hundred pounds of flesh shuddering to a belated halt. The American cursed and, stooping down, tugged the bayonet from Biff's stomach. When he looked up again, the fat boy had gone.

Robert was already running on pure instinct; he didn't need to think about what to do next, his legs were running him out of the washroom in pursuit. He paused at the entrance. To the right was the parking lot—no movement, it appeared deserted. A passage to the left was the only other option. He turned left, running again, the bayonet hung from his right hand and clattered against the wall as he raced around a corner. Robert slid it up his sleeve, out of sight, and pounded up the steps which appeared ahead of him.

The steps changed direction twice and brought him out on a glass-encased bridge over the motorway. Thirty feet away from him was Fat Boy, laboring along and looking back over his shoulder every third step.

He was too far along though; Robert doubted that he could reach him before the boy came to the stairs on the other side and whatever was beyond. He let the bayonet slide out of his sleeve and hurled it at the fugitive. The blade struck Chooty almost square in the back, his body kept moving for a further three steps before he lost his balance and collapsed in an untidy heap halfway across the westbound carriageway.

Robert ran on across and bent to remove the blade and as he did so, became aware of the traffic passing twenty feet below. As each vehicle passed, headlights shone across him, spotlighting his face, reflecting on the gory heap at his feet. The sensation of dozens of eyes staring at him every second was curiously gratifying; it gave him a feeling of unsurpassed strength and immense satisfaction. He was so transfixed that it took every ounce of willpower from the saner part of his brain to urge him into movement as the sound of children's voices came to him from the still hidden end of the bridge.

He retreated, moving faster as the urgency of the situation came home to him. A few minutes later, Robert was again behind the steering wheel, driving east into the pale gray dawn. He stabbed at the CD player button and as Jerry Lee Lewis came into his head, Robert let the strident rhythm of the thumping piano take him home.

CHAPTER 5

On Tuesday evening, I went to view two of the properties I had selected from the lists from the various agents. The first was a two-bedroom town house on the outskirts of the city with rear views over a cricket pitch. The rooms seemed small, even empty. I knew immediately that it was not for me. In addition to the poky feeling it gave me, the place smelled of disuse and there was no character to it. Its nearness to the office had seemed in its favor at first; now I began to wonder if the reverse might not be true. I thanked the young man who had opened it up for me and left to see the second place.

I pulled the car into what had once been a graveled drive, now a little weedy and could do with another ton or two of stones on it. I checked my appearance in the interior mirror and winked a brown eye at my reflection before running a comb through my hair. *Pass muster*, I thought—and wondered what the real estate agent, Ms. Jackson, might be like.

The gable end was built with black mock-Tudor beams and in-filled with white-painted plaster. So it wasn't seventeenth century, but it still looked good and, peeking through a large bay window of small framed squares, I could see a well-lit, fully furnished room with an open fireplace against the gable end.

I knocked and when no one answered, tried the door, which was locked. I walked round the house, glancing in windows and looking at the garden. At the rear, the land fell away. The slope was filled with fruit trees, now devoid of leaves and just beyond what must be my boundary was a river. Not a big one, not deep but just big enough and deep enough. I imagined the trees covered in blossom in April, fruit ripening in August. I was already thinking my boundary, *my* fruit trees.

I wondered what kind of fish were in the river. No matter, I was hooked (as they would soon be).

When the agent did arrive, ten minutes after I'd returned to the front, I walked across as she opened the door.

"Don't bother getting out." I said and laughed.

The woman, well dressed in a lime two piece, early forties, was taken aback, her expression one of consternation. "Oh, I'm so sorry for the delay." She got out anyway. "Let me show you round at least."

"It's sold. You can't talk me out of it. What about the furniture?"

"Sold? Um, *you* want it?"

"Damn right."

"Well, it is for sale furnished or unfurnished."

"I'll take the lot. How soon can I move in?"

"It depends on your solicitor. He'll have to conduct searches, protect your interests. It usually takes about two months—if he gets a move on."

"He or she. Sure. Look." I gave her my nicest smile, the one that has forty-year-old female estate agents swooning in the aisles. "I need the place now. Get the owner to lease it to me until the sale's made. I'll use your solicitor if that helps."

Ms. Jackson shrugged and held out her hand. I shook it.

"Done?"

"Done. I do know the owner, I'm sure we can arrange something. You know, you ought to join my firm, sell houses for us. Here's my card, call me tomorrow."

"Thanks." I said and looked at the card. "Thanks, Carol."

That night I packed my suitcases except for the essentials—next day's clothes, toiletries—and then I called my dad and told him about the house. *I expect you up here for a holiday in the summer*, I told him. I think he was pleased, he sounded pleased but you can't always tell, there were all these gun-toting criminals up here in the north!

CHAPTER 6

John Merrick sat across the desk from Al Ribart in the coroner's office. The desk was one of those heavy gray steel things with the scars and cigar burns of many years' use on its surface. John leaned his elbows on the top and sat forward. "So what you got to tell me, Al?"

"Guy in the lake? Thirty-six to thirty-eight, overweight and he liked Scotch. Died between ten or twelve, day before you fished him out."

"That's awful precise. Two hours, close as that."

Al's lips stretched a fraction, but otherwise he ignored the observation.

"Vagal inhibition like I said, but not with something padded as I thought at first. No trace of any fibers."

"So then? 'Gators."

Al shook his head slowly. "One vicious blow to the larynx." He tapped his own Adam's apple. "Probably delivered by an expert."

"A human fist?"

"More like the side of the hand." Al made a chopping motion. "Martial arts, karate-type blow like you see in the movies. Found out who he is yet?"

John shrugged his shoulders minimally. "Best guess says he's Alan Cleghorn, owner of the house and the property where we found him. Moved in from Fort Myers a few months back. Funny, I used to know him some years back, gives you an odd sort of feeling—as though you could have done something? Anyway, we're trying to find who his dentist is… was."

"What about his wife?"

"On vacation I think. In Great Britain, I think she was English. He was due to fly out to join her; we haven't got an address yet."

"Seems you got yourself a neat little problem."

John nodded as minimally as he had shrugged. "At the moment, we're not even sure it *is* Cleghorn. Not sure where his wife is. Seems to me it might be a pretty big problem. Fortunately, since it's going to go international, I can pass it upstairs to the governor's office."

"If it's Cleghorn?"

"If it's Cleghorn."

"Better make sure before you trouble the big guy."

"Al, how many times you seen me shoot pool without chalking ma' tip? Hmm?" John Merrick may have been joking, but *if* it was Cleghorn, and he *was* pretty damn certain it was, he wanted to find the murderer.

CHAPTER 7

Wednesday and my third day in the new job, the day I was scheduled to shadow Sergeant Fearon and see first-hand the drug scene in Leeds.

It started badly. The day's correspondence was stacked on my blotter. How do these organizations get hold of names and addresses so quickly? No, I did not want another credit card, not even with a picture of goldfish on it, not even if I already had an overdraft. I was scraping the offending junk mail into the wastebasket just as Superintendent Flowers called on the internal phone, asking me to come and see him.

"Morning, Stewart. Sorry, I'm afraid you're going to have to go without seeing Sergeant Fearon's territory today. Just got a call from the *Nicies*."

I guess I must have looked puzzled.

"National Criminal Intelligence Services, NCIS?"

It clicked. "Oh, *those* Nicies." The government had set the Service up to combat organized gangs operating scams between the UK and the Continent. "Run by ex-police officers? Have I got it right?"

"Former police officers *and* the Customs and Excise personnel, I believe."

Almost right. "What can we do for them?"

"They tell me that a busload of Asian illegals are heading our way, second group this month. Our brief is to locate the bus which is currently northbound on the M1 and follow it, see where the passengers go. The last time, they simply disembarked and disappeared into the crowd. Anyway, I've agreed to let them have twenty men; twelve to mingle with the shoppers in the open air market—follow them on foot. The others, including you, will follow the bus by car in case they try something different this time round. Take Sergeant Fearon with you. She has a good knowledge of the local geography."

"Right, sir. Liaison?"

"You'll be picking up Inspectors Adams and Sowden from the NCIS at the railway station. Train is in at 9:25. Theirs is a watching brief only; be courteous, we've all got our jobs to do."

"Fine. Do we have a description of the bus?"

Flowers gave me a fax. *Cream with light green paneling, registration MLX 830.*

"And what exit from the motorway?"

"You want everything done for you?" He was grinning as he said it. "There are two unmarked cars following it now. They've got your car phone number and your cellular, they'll let you know."

I nodded. I seemed to have spent the morning nodding, so far.

"Shelly... Sergeant Fearon's waiting for you in the squad room."

I *almost* nodded that time. "Thank you, sir. I'll get off then."

"And good luck, Inspector."

Sergeant Shelly Fearon, looking every bit as delicious as the last time I'd seen her, was waiting outside my office as I returned. She had a full-length curly sheepskin coat on, in a mottled gray color. Her voice was husky with a bit of music in it. I really did find her appealing. Like I found most women to be, I suppose—when I wasn't in a relationship, anyhow. I have to be honest with myself, at least.

"Morning, sir."

"A good morning to you, Sergeant. How long does it take to drive to the railway station?"

"Five, ten minutes, sir. Depending on traffic."

"Very good." I checked my watch. "We'd better go then. I'll fill you in on the way unless you've already been briefed?"

"Yes, sir. I was catching up on some paperwork and Daisy—er, Inspector Flowers, told me what was happening."

I struggled to keep the smirk off my face and ignored Flowers's nickname. We walked out to the car and I asked if she'd done this before.

"Mmm," she said. "Three weeks ago. I followed the first coach load, but the *Nicies* weren't involved that time, not directly. They didn't come along with us. Shall I take the wheel?"

"I'd prefer to do it myself, Sergeant. You direct me while I drive. It's the best way for me to memorize somewhere new."

We got in and she directed me around the back of the shopping center (our offices were at the top) and down onto the southward leg of the traffic loop. "What happened that first time?"

"Nothing out of the way. We picked the coach up at the top of Dewsbury Road, that's where one of the M1 exits comes into the city. Turn right here and oh, bad luck."

The lights turned just as the traffic opened up a little and we were stopped for half a minute—long enough for a convoy of buses to clog up our route; signs directed cars straight on here, around a more circuitous route. When the lights changed again we ignored the sign and lurched along Boar Lane towards the station.

The sergeant continued. "Followed it down into the city and all the way to the market. It stopped, about fifteen or twenty men and women got out and trooped into the market. We had no instructions to follow the coach or to follow the occupants on foot." She shrugged. "Left here and follow the road round. Mind the taxis; there'll be a huge queue."

There was but there was a way around, right up to the main entrance. I pulled in and stopped.

"Shall I go in, sir?"

I checked the time again and shook my head. "In a while. It's only 9:20 now, we have five minutes before it's due. Presumably these people off the coach had someone waiting for them?"

"Presumably. There were only the two of us and nobody seemed to want to tell us what to do."

"Hmm. Well, I understand all that's been taken care of this time."

I checked the time again and was about to suggest she did her rendezvous thing when two men came out and stood uncertainly in the entrance. One of them had a neat little moustache; he was slim and was the shorter of the two, the other—six foot three, had a build to match his height.

"I think our friends have arrived. Train must have been early.

"Now there's a thing." She opened the window. "Excuse me, gentlemen. Meeting someone?"

They were. They got in and we introduced ourselves to each other.

"Stewart White." I reached round and extended my hand between the front seats. "And this is Sergeant Fearon."

"Alec Sowden," said the smaller man.

"George Adams," added the other with a pronounced Liverpool accent.

"Pleased to make your acquaintance, gentlemen." I indicated right and pulled away from the station entrance, then round to merge with the traffic coming out of City Square.

"Bear left here," Sergeant Fearon told me and a minute or two later, "left again." We made our way back alongside the river and canal and eventually came to a halt where the M621 and the M1 motorways ended.

"This is where the coach came in last time," I told our guests. "If they choose a different route in, we'll hear about it the moment it happens."

"Fine, Stewart," said Alec. "We've just a watching brief this time. You run it as you want to. If it goes wrong this time though, our superiors may want to do it differently."

That sounded like a veiled threat, but I let it go. "What do we actually know about the illegals?"

"Came through the Channel Tunnel last night in secret compartments built into six tautliners, eight to a truck. Must have been like sardines." That was George Adams's voice.

"Someone's making a lot of money if they were that organized," said Sergeant Fearon. "I suppose you want to trace their contacts up here. Is that why you didn't arrest them on entry?"

"Self-evident, isn't it?" Alec took the conversation back again. "These aren't your average Asians coming to live with relatives, oh no. These boys and girls are coming in to work for peanuts in sweat shops making fake designer gear. You're right though, someone's getting awfully rich. And we want them all."

One of those silences developed, where no one quite knows what to say next and then my earphone buzzed. The voice had a London accent. "Keep this brief, mate. That White?"

I acknowledged.

"Target just turned off the M1 onto the M62 westbound. You want us to follow them?"

"Can you stay with them until they come off the M62?" I started the motor and pulled out. "We're coming south on the M621 and we'll be ready to catch them at junction twenty which is their most probable route."

"Will do," confirmed the London voice.

"Inform us when they start to exit."

"They could come down the A62," put in Shelly Fearon.

I reviewed the road layout in the back of my mind. "It's a fairly long, straight road. We can catch them up if that happens." They came along the M621 as I'd anticipated and we pulled in behind, staying fifty yards or so back from them.

It was an older coach with a wide rear window. Three women sat in the center with a man on each side. The women all had the same hairstyle, plaited and tied with a blue ribbon. *Ultramarine*, I said to myself and laughed, *not blue*. When time permitted, I dabbled in oil painting and I sometimes found myself thinking in colors and form.

We left the motorway, turning onto busy streets and heading for the city center, round into a vaguely industrial area then over the river again. A maze of road works confronted us.

"You don't think he knows he's been tailed, do you? Trying to shake us?"

"You're getting paranoid. All this," she gestured toward the tangle, "is to keep traffic out of the center."

"I've seen the narrow roads in the middle, doesn't that discourage the traffic?"

"Don't get me started on that, Stewart... Inspector," Shelly said.

I grinned at the slip and concentrated on driving. The road passed under a railway viaduct, the arches spreading out to left and right, smoky black in places and covered in small business signs. The bus moved out to the center of the road in order to pass under the arches at their highest point and followed the road right on the far side. Just as we came up to the archway a group of cyclists swept out from the left, I had to brake hard and gave them a blast on the horn. One of them gave me the finger.

"Sorry about that." And we moved off again, shooting through the archway and looking for the coach we'd been trailing. A minute or so later, we picked it up again at a stop sign and I heaved a deep breath. "There. Thank God." We started off again and I ducked my head to look at the sky. I thought the sun had come out because those blue ribbons seemed to be a definite cobalt blue. I frowned. No, the ribbons were a different color of blue.

Apart from an interminable wait for a road roller to move out of the way, we followed the coach without further incident right up to the side of the open air market where it used a city bus stop to let the passengers disembark.

Some of the Asians had small bags with them—one carried a plastic Sainsbury carrier; most seemed to own just what they stood up in. Directed by the driver, they left the road and walked across and disappeared between the market stalls.

"Everything in order?" I asked, turning to glance back at the *Nicies*.

"Seemed okay to me, Stewart," Alec answered. "George?"

"Fine. No problems."

"Well, we'll see what the others come up with." I was referring to the men and women who had been waiting in the market crowd. "Meantime, we'll drop you off and see you later. Okay?"

After we'd left them outside the Beresford Hotel but before I pulled out into the traffic again, I turned to Sergeant Fearon. "Did you notice anything different this time? Compared with the last time, I mean?"

She thought a moment. "No sir." She shook her head. "Same route, same mess at that bloody viaduct, too."

"Hmm. Thought we'd lost them for a moment then." Well that was it for the moment. I checked my seat belt. "Tell me about these drug problems of yours."

"That's not the best way to put it." She grinned cheekily. "It probably needs a Sherlock to sort it."

Well, I heard the comment, though I thought I'd let it pass and pretend I hadn't.

It wasn't until much later that day that I heard about the business at the market. Our people had stopped twenty Asians who, the officers were prepared to swear, came off the coach. All of them were genuine passport-holding British citizens—someone had screwed up in style.

From the safety of my armchair that evening, I phoned my dad.

"How's it going, pal?"

"My reputation's preceded me."

"Nothing to be ashamed of."

"I mean the *Sherlock* bit."

My father laughed out loud, a sound that always cheered me ever since I'd been a child. It was something I hadn't heard all that frequently once my mother's health started going downhill.

"Your mum wanted us to call you Susan. For the whole of the nine months she carried you, she was adamant that you were a girl. Old wives' tales you know, carry the babe all around the body—that's a girl, all out at the front, a boy."

He laughed again, turned it down to a chuckle and I could see his face as though we were standing next to each other.

"Mum must have been a bit startled then, when I was born."

"I reckon."

Unlike many of Dad's tales, it was the first time I'd heard that one. Sort of brought me closer to my father, somehow.

"Anyway, I've always told you there's nothing wrong with blowing your own trumpet as long as there's something to blow it about. So next time they call you Sherlock, you tell 'em." His voice grew serious. "You've still got a lot to prove, pal. They'll be weighing you up, looking for signs of weakness—you know that, don't you."

"Yes, I do."

"Happens everywhere, doesn't matter whether it's the police station or a foundry. Don't show that it affects you, Son, put on a brave face as they say. They'll respect you then, even if you make the odd mistake—and you're bound to."

"I'll bear that in mind." Dad was a great believer in the stiff upper lip—which was all right in its place, of course.

"You do that. Now I won't keep you, these long distance calls are expensive."

That was shorthand for: *it's getting late and I want to get off to bed.*

"Okay Dad. Goodnight and God bless and..." I hesitated—stiff upper lip again, "...love you, Dad."

CHAPTER 8

Robert Cleghorn woke up to the sound of music. It was dark and the bed felt unfamiliar. It took him a moment or two to get his bearings. He pressed the tiny button on the side of his watch and peered at the twenty-four-hour display: 20:25. Twenty-five after eight. Just over four hours sleep, about average since he'd returned from Saudi.

The music permeated up from the bar below him. *The pub, that's right, they call them pubs over here.* He had found the place after leaving Brideswell, the sign outside had said "home-cooked pub food" and below that, "bed and breakfast." Despite it being three-thirty in the afternoon, the buxom woman behind the bar had been delighted to let him a room. Robert sat up and felt around for the bedside lamp and switched it on. He got out of bed and stretched.

It wasn't a large room, big enough for a double bed and a chest of drawers with a small closet and a bathroom off. *Good enough,* he'd thought when she showed it to him, pressing up against him as she'd opened the door. *Slept in far worse than this over the years.*

Robert showered and pulled fresh clothes out of his case. Suddenly remembering the difference in temperature, he pulled on a sweatshirt over the top of the tee shirt. In front of the mirror, he ran fingers through his still-damp hair and combed it back at both sides without a parting. His stomach rumbled. *Guess I could do with something to eat.*

The food, as promised, was home-cooked and good. Steak and kidney pie would not have been his choice back in the States; here however, with potatoes and carrots and peas which he was assured had been growing that morning, it tasted pretty good.

When he'd finished, Robert left two of the thick, gold-colored coins as a tip and went through the connecting door to the bar where the music came from. There were five or six people there at the bar and four youths shooting pool. Checking his watch again—just after nine thirty and still fairly early, he went looking for a phone.

The idea had come to him in those moments just before sleep when all sorts of thoughts slip through the mind. He was masquerading as Alan, why not continue, and take it to its logical conclusion? He could call the house where she was staying and ask to speak to Stephanie. He could tell her—as Robert—that he was in York and ask her to meet him somewhere.

He found a wall phone in the short corridor leading to the men's room. He pulled Alan's diary out of his pocket and opened it to find the number. It rang several times before being answered by a woman's voice, sort of bubbly.

"Hello, Amanda here. Sorry I'm not in; I'm touring the county this week. Please leave your message and a number after the tone and I'll get back to you. Bye." There was a long tone and then silence, waiting for his message. Robert hung up.

Amanda. He had no idea who she was; Stephanie had never mentioned an Amanda back when. If no one else had answered the call, the house was presumably empty, Stephanie away with this Amanda. *But she'd been expecting Alan to turn up. Why would she leave? It didn't matter,* he supposed, *just stick around a bit longer until she turned up.*

Robert returned to the bar and ordered a Jack Daniels with Coke. "Make that a double, will you?"

He took the drink across to the pool tables and watched the players; they were at the smaller of two tables, playing with red and yellow balls and a single black one. Two young men in sweaters and without a clue between them as to how to play held their cues with the ends stuck up in the air. They did not get down to sight along the surface and every third or fourth shot, the cue ball skidded off the table.

Robert had once been pretty good at the game, spending a lot of his evenings in bars, winning enough to keep himself in beers most nights. He shook his head and turned his attention to the other table which was American design. A banner hanging from the overhead lamp proclaimed it to be the only nine-ball table in York. At least this pair knew how to hold a cue and in fact, as he watched them, he began to realize they were quite good.

Reckon I could take either of them, though. Or both.

They were both dressed in similar fashion, denim jackets over black tee shirts with scruffy jeans and high leather boots. One guy, a little shorter than the other was fair haired with steel rings piercing his eyebrows, his ears and a nostril. The other one, darker and more heavily built, had black tattoos marking his forehead and face.

Robert Cleghorn shook his head, fascinated at what kids would do to themselves. He looked again and noticed that what he thought was a necklace was, in fact, a chain tattooed around the guy's neck and when he turned a little, there was a teardrop also tattooed under the left eye. *Quite the little artist*, he thought and suddenly became aware that *he* was being studied.

"Want a game?" asked the fair one, probably in his early twenties.

"Sure," Robert replied. "Haven't played in a while, might help to pass the time."

"Freakin' Yank," mouthed Tattoos behind the American's back and the blond one grinned.

"Table stakes're ten quid, best of three. Too rich for yer?"

Rich? wondered Robert and made the conversion. *Say twenty dollars. No problem.* "Fine." He shrugged and Blondie racked the balls.

The first game was scrappy. The cue was shorter than he was used to and the cue ball seemed to run a lot slower than he remembered. Robert won the game, only because his opponent miscued. Still, his brain was starting to remember the angles.

"Oh tough shit, Jimmy boy," said Tattoos. Robert turned and looked at the speaker and noticed another adornment he had missed before: a black line with stitch marks across his forehead and a metal screw head at either side. Just below the stitches were the words "open here."

"Yeah unlucky, kid."

Blondie—or Jimmy, as Robert had discovered—grinned, chalked his stick and broke the diamond apart with a hard stroke. The yellow nine ball flew into a corner pocket and again, the grins were exchanged.

"Looks like I was lucky that time, mate."

Robert shrugged and Jimmy picked up the cue ball and waited for Tattoos to rack the balls again. He broke again, this time none of the balls dropped despite flying all over the table. Robert walked round to have a closer look at the one ball that was banked and then at the nine ball sitting precariously near to the opposite pocket. He had not heard the other guy nominate his intended strike but he spoke up anyway. "One onto nine ball, top left." The one ball flew off the rail to strike the nine. The nine dropped in sweetly. Game over.

The two younger men seemed shell-shocked, as though a major plan had gone wrong. They glared at one another and then at the American. "Bit freakin' good, aren't yer? Or maybe just freakin' lucky."

Robert smiled, thin lipped and watchful. "If you can't stand to lose, that's tough, kid. If it's the money, forget it, I was only killing time."

Blondie came up to him and leered into his face. Robert held his breath against the other's beery exhalations. "S'not the money, sunshine. What it is, is I think yer a bloody hustler. Come in here to show us up, right?"

Robert shook his head, hardly believing what was happening yet knowing where it would lead if he didn't cool it. "Look bud, let me buy you a drink. I'm no hustler. And even if I were, I wouldn't be hustling for chump change." Robert was enjoying himself, watching the young men get angry. He put out a friendly hand, an offer to shake on it, but Blondie just knocked it away.

"Pig off, Yank. I want nothing from yer."

Robert Cleghorn shrugged, dismissing the abuse as drunkard's talk. He began to turn away and something heavy and hard struck him right on the back of his skull. The light turned brown and then black at the same time as the floor came up and smacked his chin.

Tattoos threw the broken pool cue across the table and kicked the American in the ribs. "Bog off," he said in a low, angry voice. "Bloody tourist." A second kick landed as the landlord—suddenly aware of what was happening—came running across.

"Hey," he shouted. "Get off him." The publican got hold of a beefy shoulder and tugged. "Muriel, get an ambulance for Christ's sake."

Tattoos wrenched free and he and Jimmy ran for the rear exit giving the finger to the furious landlord.

The ambulance took Robert to the York district hospital.

As he lay on the hospital bed he recalled an earlier time in Florida when he had been involved in another fight.

"Spineless geek."

Robert Cleghorn looked up at the tiny square of blue sky, which was all he could see of the outside world, from inside the cell. *Looked as though he'd been going to fight, he was a body builder for sure – all that muscle piled on muscle and he'd turned out to be as meek and mild as a four year old.*

Robert shook his head. One good thump to the side of the guy's head and he'd fallen over. *Must have been what, nineteen, twenty? Went home and told his Ma for Christ sake.* The sentencing would be tomorrow morning. It was going to be a long stretch; Robert could feel it in his bones, shut away like this for the next ten to twenty. He didn't sleep that night and it had nothing to do with the thin mattress and hard bunk he had to lie on.

The next day he had found it difficult to believe when they led him away, took the shackles off and gave him back his personals. He'd pushed through the small crowd of reporters and turned left before ducking away down a back street as soon as possible. A suspended sentence he'd thought and a very, very strong recommendation to leave town. Someone up there must like him, just a little maybe.

When he'd got home from the lockup, Dad was out at work, Ma would have been down at the clinic where she had a part-time job. He'd let himself in silently and gathered a few clean clothes together and rolled them up in a sleeping bag. He'd counted what little money he could find, fifteen dollars and a few cents. *Freaking useless.*

Alan would have some cash, never miss a coupla bills. He'd gone into his brother's room and pulled drawers open, riffled through their contents. Where'd he keep money? Under the mattress? A loose floorboard? And it was there, staring him in the face, in the bookcase between the two windows. A slim wallet stuffed between *Eighty Seventh Precinct* and *Psycho,* the authors – *McBain* and *Bloch,* he'd borrowed them often enough.

There must have been a hundred dollars or more tucked away in there, it had taken no more than a moment to slip five ten dollar bills into his pocket and put the wallet back. That was money—and as for transportation…

He looked out of Alan's bedroom, down into the neighboring yard, where Billy Garter's '57 Chevrolet was parked. Billy would be watching the ball game, a six pack on the floor at his side and a bowl of salted peanuts in his lap.

At the city limits he'd stuck his hand out of the window, three fingers folded, middle finger extended upward. "Screw you all!," he'd shouted at the top of his voice.

CHAPTER 9

The weekend came along and so did the keys from Carol, my friendly real estate agent. I guess being a police officer impressed some people; the owner had readily agreed to the lease. Perks of the job—cheap mortgages and the assumption that all officers were as honest as me.

The job had been relatively quiet since the market debacle. I'd met and spoken with most of the squad now and rescheduled the meeting with Sergeant Bell on Monday. I could relax and inspect my new place in a leisurely fashion.

A large oak wardrobe in the master bedroom was more than large enough for everything in my suitcases. I'd bought some bed linen during the morning and with the bed—another huge piece of oak furniture—made up, it was beginning to feel like home. The central heating had been on since I'd arrived too, and that slightly clammy feeling you get in an empty house was gone. Plus, the water was hot enough to try out the Jacuzzi in the modernized bathroom.

Jacuzzis are not for solo bathing and my thoughts slipped from one girl I had known to another. I suppose it was inevitable that I should think of Shelly Fearon. I killed that thought as quickly as I could; Shelly—*Sergeant Fearon*, I thought determinedly—was far too close professionally for me to indulge in daydreams.

How long had I been in the bathtub? I wondered suddenly; the ends of my fingers had become crinkly. What was the time? I climbed out and went back to the bedroom, checked the alarm clock. Must have been the better part of an hour I'd spent soaking in there.

I toweled myself dry and was slipping into a pair of old corduroys when I heard the thump of car doors closing. I glanced down through the window and saw Jack Shaw standing at the side of a white rent-a-van looking at the house. Someone else I vaguely recognized came round from the van's far side and joined Jack.

I pulled on a tee shirt and sweater as they were knocking on the front door. I ran down the stairs and flung it open. It wasn't Jack who was first to greet me, or his companion. A red-and-white ball of fur on a blur of legs streaked between them, paused a moment and launched through the air at me. I caught him and got a wet tongue all over my left ear.

"Pip!" I put him down and scratched behind his ears. "Wow, have I missed you, little feller." The dog rolled over so I could give his stomach the same treatment. I straightened up and shook my former sergeant's hand. "It's not that I'm not pleased to see you, Jack, It's just that after four years of having Pip around my feet, I've been getting a bit lonely this last week."

"Not a wink of sleep since you left him, your dad said," he told me. "Pip's been howling every night."

"Really? Hell, he hadn't said a thing about Pip on the phone. Didn't realize."

He laughed. "Joking. Actually, I think your dad's going to miss the little devil. Seemed a bit reluctant to let him go. He nodded at his companion, "Remember Martin Hall?"

I looked the other man in the face while Pip tried to pull at my trousers. "DC Hall. That murder case, the Patel murder. You worked on that with me."

"That's right, sir. And the ram raider robberies."

"So you did." He was talking about a gang who specialized in hijacking backhoes and using them to break into banks and building societies then tearing out the night safe. We caught them after I'd figured out which outlets were likely to be next and keeping them under twenty-four-hour surveillance. "Seven years for the brains of the outfit, five for everyone else. Right?"

Hall nodded. "And due out any time now with good behavior."

"Keep you lot out of mischief, anyway. Now what have you brought me? For God's sake, Pip, let me go." The dog looked up at me, deeply wounded.

"Everything, Stewart but how about a brew up first? The traffic on the motorway's bloody murder. I've got a throat like the Sahara."

"Of course, Jack. Let's go through to the kitchen and we can sit down. I'll show you round the place afterwards." They followed me from the hallway, Pip bouncing around my feet like an animated football.

"Must have cost a packet," I heard Jack say, speaking his thought aloud.

"Not as much as you think," I said. "Housing's a lot cheaper here than in Brum. Reckon my mortgage is going to be twenty thousand lower than it was for the flat I had. And I've got free country air here, too, that's got to be a bonus."

After coffee, the three of us carried packing cases into the house and into the garage, mostly books and painting stuff which I didn't want to put into storage. I picked up a bundle of ten twenty-pound notes from a bookcase in the dining room and handed it to Jack. "Happy with that? You and Martin can split it how you like."

Jack took the money and grinned. "Thanks, Stewart. Reckon that'll help with the electric bill this winter." He stood back and looked through the dining room window out to the fruit trees. "Nice place, I can see why you like it. You got a river down there?"

I nodded. "That's what clinched it for me. Bring Katy up in the summer and the kids of course. They'll love climbing around in the orchard."

"Nice of you to ask. I'll mention it when I get back and really, we've got to get back. Big darts match tonight."

I walked out onto the front drive with them. "Hey, I was going to show you round."

"Next time, Stew. Thanks anyway."

Jack and Martin climbed in. It had all been sort of false in a way. I knew Jack would never take me up on the suggestion to bring his family up, and he knew that I knew. Somewhere the camaraderie of the old team had gone; I was another step up the ladder of rank now, leaving him behind. It was sad.

"C'mon, Pip. Let's see if you can fit through the cat-flap in the back door. No need to put a tray down if there's a better way, right?"

I started to unpack the crates and boxes and put things away. That lasted until almost teatime when the doorbell rang. It was Carol Townsend, the real estate agent. She had a stack of legal forms and accepted a cup of tea while I put my signature in the places she pointed to. "You can't be a policeman," she said, "you're too trusting to be a policeman."

"That's the whole point. When you're a copper, you can trust anyone. Nobody dares to cheat, you see."

She grinned and looked around the room. "Hey, those are real paintings, aren't they? Not prints."

"I paint sometimes. When I've got the time and the mood's right—which isn't all that often, really."

"Landscapes. Ever do portraits?" She sat back and assumed a comfortable pose.

I shook my head. "Never very good at them. Noses. Noses never seem to come out right."

She laughed, ran fingers through her hair, tilted her head, and looked through the front window. "Looks like you've got another visitor. Another woman." A car door slammed. "Like wasps round a jam pot, eh?"

When the doorbell went again I excused myself and went out to answer it. It was Shelly Fearon with a pair of carrier bags. Carol had followed me out into the hallway and I could see her from the corner of my eye, sizing the black girl up. Shelly was doing exactly the same. It was funny but not something I could chuckle out loud at. I introduced them. They shook hands and Carol left, saying she had another client to see.

"Got those papers?"

She patted her bag. "All here."

"Thanks a lot." And I closed the door. "Well, Sergeant Fearon, to what do I owe this pleasure?"

"Well, you said you were moving in this weekend. I suspected you might not have stopped to eat so I brought you some home-cooked food." She hefted the two bags and I leaned forward to relieve her of their weight. She drew them back out of reach. "Just lead me to your kitchen table and, um, do you think you could call me Shelly? We're not on duty now."

I gestured towards the kitchen door and she preceded me. "Shelly." I said. "Thank you, it's a nice name. Call me Stewart, then."

"Not Stew?"

"Preferably not. Ah, and this," Pip slid through the cat flap as though it had been made for him and sniffed at Shelly's ankles, "is Pip. He..." Pip gave an extra sniff at her rump. "Does that. Sorry." The dog ran back to his basket and wagged his tail against its side.

"Hi, Pip." Shelly drew a large flask from one of her bags, "Now, what we have here is home-made soup. Tomato and green pepper." From the other bag came a package of newspapers which when the multiple layers had been removed, proved to be a foil wrapped dish. "My own recipe, this one. Jamaican hot pot."

"You're too good to be a policeman—person."

"You tell me I'll make a fine wife for someone and I'll crown you with it."

"The dishes are in that cupboard over there. If you like to choose what you want, I'll get the cutlery out and I have a couple of bottles in the fridge." I opened the door as Shelly selected dishes. "I've got an Italian Soave and a bottle of Chardonnay. Any preference?"

"Soave please. Don't you fellers go in for red? I thought it was sort of macho, you know?"

"Ah, well. You're probably right. About the macho thing. I think it's a bit pretentious, too. I like both, probably white a little bit more though."

There was some crusty bread to go with the soup; enough to clean the hot pot gravy off the plates too. "More wine?" I asked.

She covered her glass. "Thanks but no. I'm driving and there's something I want to discuss with you, sir."

I'd been about to pour a second big glass for myself but desisted. "Sir? What's on your mind?"

She leaned down and pulled a sheaf of computer listings from the carrier bag. She leaned down again; a wad of faxes came out this time. "These came into the office yesterday. I read most of the new stuff that comes in, just to keep tabs on what's happening. Just thought these might concern us."

I spread the paperwork out and leaning back, switched on a wall light. Daylight had just about gone and it was getting quite dim in the kitchen. The faxes concerned two murders and an injury case which had occurred at a motorway service station early Wednesday morning. One death had occurred more or less midway across the M62 on the foot bridge. The other had been in the gent's toilets on the eastbound side. The injury, too, had been committed on the eastbound side; the victim had been a heroin addict and not the most reliable of witnesses. The local police had interviewed him and apart from his name, Smales, had not got much information out of the boy.

Reading through all this—more skimming than reading—I said, "Looks to me like a mugging gone wrong. Smales and his mates hit the wrong bloke." I tapped the copy of his statement. "Oldish man he says. What do you reckon a youth like Smales would call old?"

"Thirties?"

"Steady on, Sergeant. I'm—Ginger hair, that's reasonably concrete, I suppose. Well dressed, funny accent. Midlands would be a funny accent up this way, wouldn't it?"

"Or Geordie."

"Kid says the oldster knew kung fu, I guess he'd call any kind of self-defense kung fu, all those Jackie Chan movies. But that jibes with the injuries to the lad killed in the gents, doesn't it?" Shelly didn't reply, just nudged the computer printout a little nearer. The printout detailed an incident on the outskirts of York. A red-haired tourist had been assaulted by two youths. Their descriptions followed and…

"You're assuming they're related? These two incidents?" I looked up.

She opened her hand, palm upwards. "The first one happened on the M62 Eastbound. York is thirty miles due east of here. The second incident occurred the same night. Both reports mention a red Vauxhall Insignia."

"Ouch! I missed that. And the red hair. Is it within our remit?"

"Motorway patrol answered the call from the service area which is well within our patch. York police were dealing with the second incident however when they went to interview the man at the hospital." Shelly leaned over the papers to spot the paragraph she wanted. I could smell her perfume—warm and… stop it, I told myself. "There, see?" She pointed. "He'd discharged himself."

I read on. The landlord at the pub had said the guest had paid cash in advance, and then there was the bit about the Insignia—similar to the publican's which was why he remembered. He had his own door key and the next morning he had gone, luggage, car, the lot, although neither the landlord nor his wife had seen him return from the hospital."

"Hmm. Why didn't you go to the Super with this?"

"They're still looking for the kids who hit him."

"Why didn't you go..."

"You're my boss, Stewart. Not my style to go over the boss's head."

I smiled at her. "Appreciate that, Sergeant Fearon. Loyalty's something I'm used to earning though, not having it given." I thought of Jack Shaw, a new boss, his old one gone. "I shall have to buy you a drink—something a bit stronger than this—as a reward." *Oh shit*, I thought. *What have I said now?*

"Why, goodness me, sir, I'm a married woman." Shelly failed dismally in an attempt to look demure. She gave up and grinned. "Our relationship is a professional one."

"Um. Well. A business drink is what I meant." Oh, dear! I did sound lame. Here I was responding to something that obviously wasn't there—in spite of all the warnings I'd been giving myself. She was just so damned attractive. And intelligent.

She grinned. "Forget it, Boss." And all at once she was bright and brisk. "Where do we go from here?" I'd been let off the hook.

"Issue a bulletin for that Insignia. Did the man at the pub get its registration? They usually ask for it." I re-read the relevant bit of the report. "No. Damn. So, a bulletin for the car, driver's description. Hey. Driver's American. That's what his *funny* accent was—look at the York report. And keep watching the faxes."

"I'll have to find out who's handling the murder with a view to taking over responsibility there. Don't want to rock any boats this early in my Leeds career. I'll call the Super when you've gone, got his mobile number here somewhere."

I made coffee and sat across that massive old pine table from Shelly, watching her and wishing she wasn't already married and also that I'd been a bit more subtle with the old come-on. It seemed that all my relationships hit the down track; I was too fast or too late or just too clumsy.

"What do you make of Sergeant Bell?" I asked, leaning back.

"How do you mean?"

"Good copper? I mean, I already know he's the archetypal dour Scot; at least, I've never seen him smile."

Shelly laughed. "Yes, he's dour and Scottish all right. He gets called Haggis a lot although not to his face." She lost the laughter lines and the brightness in her voice, as though she'd turned a light off somewhere. "He's meticulous though. Perhaps it's his specialty that makes him such a glum chum."

"Fraud?"

Shelly nodded. "Especially computer fraud. Computers can't be much fun anyway. Computer fraud—can you imagine? No, I feel a bit sorry for him. Sometimes."

I laughed, though I didn't mention the fact that I rather liked computers. I loved crosswords too, puzzles, schematics—maybe for the same reason. They were all a bit of a challenge—but I wouldn't have balked at saying I liked them. Why shouldn't I admit to being a computer buff? Funny. "I'm scheduled to see him Monday. Get to know what he's working on. I just wondered what to expect."

"He plays his cards close to his chest. Probably spend most of the time trying to size you up and wondering what to let you know and what not to."

"Do you think he's disgruntled because they brought in an outsider? I mean, he's probably got more years in than anyone else in the department."

"It could be, but he must know he never got considered for the position. It was never advertised internally. Anyway, he's been a miserable chap as long as I've known him so—no, can't be you, can it?"

"Well, whether it's me or not, I've got the job and I've no intention of leaving it. He'll just have to put up with me."

Shelly smiled, a professional sort of expression, and stood up. "Thanks for the coffee, Stewart."

"And thanks for the food, it was absolutely delicious and thanks for the company too."

"Ah. Now that's a secret. One of these days I'm going to give up being a copper and I'm going to market both the soup and the hotpot. Reckon it'll make me a fortune."

I grinned though inside I was hurting quite badly. It had been a long time since I'd met a woman as easy to get on with as Shelly and now I had to keep her at arm's length. "Call round any time you like."

She grinned noncommittally and started for the door. "Bye, Stewart."

"Cheers, Shelly. See you Monday."

When she had left, I got Pip's bowl out and scraped the leftovers into it. Pip made a fine garbage bin. It took him about ten seconds to finish what had been left and another two to lick the glaze to a nice shine.

I didn't ring Dad that night; it was on the late side and I didn't think his usual aphorisms would accord with the way I was feeling at the time.

I went up to bed and lay there thinking about the squad because I knew I wasn't going to be able to sleep for a while.

Women had that sort of effect on me. All my adult life I had been falling out of relationships almost faster than I got into them. Sometimes it was a basic incompatibility, the sort you don't find out about until you've known someone a while, more often than not it was because I was a copper. Surprising how many people never really trusted a copper, never felt able to drop their guard long enough to find out we're just ordinary people like themselves. Did they really expect me to nick them for being late with the car tax or burying a pet dog in the back garden? I didn't know; that was just the way it seemed.

Everybody, coppers and public alike: we're a pretty mixed-up bunch but I guess it helps to make the world go around.

As to the squad—I hadn't really thought about them at all and I was just about dropping off by then.

CHAPTER 10

Superintendent Flowers's new office looked out over the city of Leeds through panoramic windows. I prefer a little less glass in a room, though I had to admit it was a fine view. I gawked out of it like a tourist that fine cold Monday morning while I waited for him; he entered, closed the door and came up behind me all without my noticing.

"Morning, Stewart."

Startled, I nearly hit the ceiling. "Morning, sir. Gave me a bit of start there."

"I noticed. Sit down, will you?"

Flowers sat down and got a cigar alight before continuing. He waved it in front of him. "Filthy habit I know," he looked at the coiling smoke a little sadly, "going to have to give it up. These no-smoking laws will be the death of me. Now, where to begin?" He checked a hand-written list on his desk blotter. "Ah, yes. This business with the immigrants. Seems the *Nicies* are putting the blame on us for not pulling them in."

"That's unfair, Joe. Grossly unfair. What were we supposed to pull them in for if they had done nothing wrong?"

"I'm inclined to agree, but there it is. The Chief has told the Old Man that his men'll handle it next time. Got any thoughts on that?"

I shrugged. "I can live with it although it puts a slur on the squad. Anyway, I've an idea about this; it'll redress the balance if I'm right."

"Well, we can't interfere with them now. They have the authority to go it alone." His tone suggested he would brook no interference either.

I nodded. "Fine. Let them get on with it, Joe. There'll be no interference unless they cock things up. All *I* want is to know when the next bus load is due. Can you do that?" I kept my tone purely business-like, copying Flowers.

"No problem. They've got to let us know that, professional courtesy at least. Besides, they'll want us to keep out of the way."

"Thank you. I'll keep you up to speed on developments. What's next? The M62 business?"

"The murders. Yes. Funny business that. Huddersfield CID is handling it at the moment; they agree the perpetrator left the service area and appears to have moved east. They're prepared to fax us details of the interview with the injured laddie. Apart from the physical description, they've nothing to go on." Flowers leaned across his desk towards me and lowered his voice. "Between you and me, they're happy to get rid of the case. Still, if I give you permission to take this on I want your assurance it's not going affect the rest of the work of this office." He seemed almost conciliatory.

I nodded, knowing about his problems. "I can assure you of that and something else. I shan't enter into anything that'll jeopardize our work. I want to make my mark but not at the expense of everyone else."

Flowers leaned back again and tapped his cigar against the edge of an ashtray that looked as though it had been cut from a lump of volcanic glass. An inch of ash rolled into the bowl. "I'm glad you said that, Stewart." He grinned. "Bit melodramatic. What is it about these murders makes you want to get involved?"

I grinned back at him. "My entire career I've done things by the book..."

"Not what I've heard."

"By the book unless I've had a feeling and this one gives me a feeling, Joe."

He looked up at the ceiling. "A hunch is what they used to call it."

"Call it a hunch if you like, I get one every now and then and this is one I'll take bets on."

The Super stood up, signaling the end of our talk. "Are you going to start straight away?"

I stood up, too. "I thought I'd send Sergeant Fearon to York to nose around a bit. I want to spend some time with Sergeant Bell on his computer fraud." I paused, letting things settle a bit in my mind. "I'll make up my mind about the murders when I see the reports."

"Fine, Stewart. Just keep me informed."

"Depend on it, sir."

On the way back I stopped at Shelly Fearon's desk just long enough to give her my orders. She gave me a beautiful smile. *Reward enough,* I thought as I crossed over to Bell's desk.

"Morning, Sergeant Bell." I got a bit of joviality into the three words.

"Sir," came the curt reply, his eyes still glaring at the screen.

"You're going to ruin your eyesight like that, Sergeant." I pulled up a loose chair while he ignored my advice. I looked a little more carefully at the Scot. A thin faced, sandy haired man with worry lines etched permanently into his forehead. He had a sharp-pointed nose over thin pursed lips and a long oval chin with a seven o'clock shadow. He turned towards me and I noticed a purple birthmark an inch across on his left cheek. His eyebrows made a query.

"Fill me in on what you're working on. A quick outline."

Alec Bell grimaced, his jowls falling even further, an expression of distaste. For me, I wondered, or the case. He seemed to be a thoroughly dislikeable sort of man.

"Seven months ago a travel agency with seventeen offices ceased trading. It was a limited company, five directors, none of which could be contacted when Joe Public started to complain. We got called in when it was discovered there was a deficit of three million. I was responsible for searching their registered office—in Morley, out of the way little place away from the main business area." He pointed to a stack of twenty or so plastic storage crates full of papers and ledgers and computer discs. "That's what we got."

"Not serious enough for the Serious Fraud Squad." I made it a matter of fact rather than a question. He looked at me for a moment, wondering perhaps if I was making a joke.

"No," he said at last. "Not exactly. The local office was already investigating a false passport scam and the fraud was discovered almost by accident. We reckon there was an informer, one of the local lot, who tipped them off about our going in. As it happened, we went in a day early because of manpower on another case so we got some of the documents before they all were shifted."

"Things do get complicated, don't they?"

"Well, it's down to me to prove we were right before we hand it all over to the Fraud boys."

"And this has taken three months, so far?"

He nodded. "Me and two others, they've helped out occasionally—I've put in what time I can spare between other cases. Chris Smythe, one of them, has located the directors—a family affair—living in Northern Cyprus."

"Oh hell. No extradition treaty with the Turkish Cypriots. So what's the problem Sergeant? They tell me you're the computer whiz-kid here." Perhaps I shouldn't have said that, it had been a long time since Bell had been a kid of any sort.

He turned his pale blue eyes on me; they gave him a sort of fishy look. "Because, Inspector White, every one of those files is encrypted. I've broken seven so far and there seems to be no general key to the whole lot, each one is different." He gave me what I thought was a smile. "If you can do it, you're welcome to try." Maybe it wasn't a smile. "Or if you can get us some time on a Cray, we can break the files in hours."

Ouch. This was one touchy guy here, one very big chip on the shoulder. "I'm not here to teach you how to do your job, Sergeant Bell. You know what's best. What I am here for is to know exactly what each of my staff is doing, okay?"

He nodded.

"However, give me a list of the codes you've broken so far. Fresh eyes, different viewpoint. I might be able to make a helpful suggestion. Leave it on my desk anytime."

Alec stared at me for some seconds before he turned away. I don't think he knew just how to take what I'd said, suddenly he turned back, becoming brisk and business-like. "Certainly, sir." He clicked his mouse and a few seconds later his printer began to work. "There's the list. Anything you can do I'll appreciate."

"Thank you, Sergeant. Carry on the good work."

I took the list and walked across to my office looking at it—that is, my eyes pointed at it, but I didn't see a thing. I don't think I'd ever been so angry with myself. I disliked Bell, there was no two ways about it and I was equally certain he disliked me. I'd let him get to me; that was the reason for my anger.

I dropped his list into my in-tray and spent the rest of the morning going through the reports from Huddersfield CID. Soon after twelve, I leaned back in my chair and noticed Bell's list, which was seven lines long:

FAR HORIZONS ACCOUNTS FILES—BRANCH ORDER

HE60A4WHARFE

HE0012HODDER

HA003BCONWY

HA1016WITHAM

MA00CABLYTHE

CO0044VURNWY

CO011FWENSUM

Presumably he'd come up with something on those seven. Had Bell already decoded them? I stared at the combinations of letters and numbers. The same prefixes recurred throughout, in no reasonable order. The numbers didn't appear to possess any regular order and the words—apart from one or two which might have been local place names—were gibberish. Perhaps that was what they were, strings of gibberish to ensure that anyone reading them would be mystified. *No miracles today then*, I thought. I committed what I had gleaned to memory nevertheless, a useful trick of the mind if you can do it. Lets the brain put it on the back burner.

On my way out to lunch I stopped at Sergeant Bell's desk. "How did you get the words in the keys?" I asked him.

“There’re two files in each folder, one is a data file and the other’s an index to it. In each case, one of the index entries contained the key.”

“Were the keys hidden?”

“Hidden in plain view. The record which contains the key doesn’t appear to be in any particular position. I can’t say by looking at the index which record contains the key, I’ve had to try each one until it works, which means that an anagram of the indexed word decrypts the data file.”

“It’s a fiddly way of going on. How did you latch onto these particular words?”

“Actually it wasn’t me who found the first one, it was Micky Ryan. The one he was looking at had the key in the first index record, he noticed it was an anagram of the river Wharfe and just tried playing with it. The others are anagrams too, there’re towns—Conway, Blythe—well a village, Hamble, Orwell—an author, and Hodder, something to do with books, Wensum.” He shrugged. “Various things.”

“All six-letter names.”

“The encryption system uses a six letter key. Standard substitution method, nothing special there except we can ignore anything other than six-letter words.”

“The prefixes?”

“The two first letters are some sort of prefix, the other four—the data record reference. They’re in hexadecimal, that’s computer…”

“Yes. Thanks Sergeant, I know what hex code is. What was in the files that you’ve decoded?”

“Not a lot that’s helpful, I’m afraid. Customer’s names—genuine customers with addresses. Holiday details, carriers, costs and so on. Nothing to suggest false passports.”

“Then why code them, I wonder?” A question more to myself than to Alec Bell. “Anyway, keep at it Sergeant, looks like perspiration not inspiration on this one.” Bell seemed a little less unpleasant this time or perhaps it was me that was a little less on edge.

After I returned from lunch, I found a man installing the PC I’d ordered. He had assembled the workstation in front of a bookcase and was connecting the peripherals. It was a PC—not like the Mac I had at home which was still to unpack. However, it was the latest model and a lot faster than mine; the department would keep it up to date for me.

“Nearly done, Guv,” he said as I came to stand behind him. “Nice job, this one. You’ve got several packages pre-installed, manuals—such as they are these days—are on your desk. A few games in case you get bored.” He stopped the pointer on the Games entry and a list of half a dozen dropped down the screen.

I glanced at it, then away again. "Games and bored. Fat chance of either around here."

"Yeah, know how it goes. Know how to use it? Need instructions?"

"I'm okay, thanks. Pretty familiar."

"Fine." He pushed the power button and waited for it to boot up. He ran the mouse to and fro and tapped one or two keys. "Mouse okay, keyboard okay. Can you sign this chitty for me?"

I signed on the dotted line, and he gave me a mock salute as he left.

"Call me if you've got problems. See you."

I left it running and went back to the M62 murders case until late in the afternoon, about four thirty. There was a knock on the frosted glass door panel and Shelly Fearon came in without waiting for an invitation.

"Guess what."

"What?"

"Our redhead did a runner from the hospital before the York police saw him."

"Interesting. Anything from the pub he stayed at?"

"Several prints which may or may not be his. Harry took dabs from the landlord and his wife and the cleaner who was in at the time. He'll eliminate those and we'll see what we're left with. We may have the prints on record."

"And the suspect?"

"They all say he was American—from his accent, though I suppose it could have been faked. The landlady liked him, probably because he left a hefty tip." Shelly sat on the corner of my desk swinging her leg and eyeing my new computer. The screensaver had kicked in long ago and the machine was busy putting all its effort into making a little policeman with a very tall pointy hat wash the inside of the screen.

Shelly said nothing and turned back to me finally. "She—the landlady, that is—said he was wearing a green suit when he arrived, which doesn't tell us a lot. He also wore rose-tinted spectacles."

I looked up sharply, tapped the heap of paper on my desk. "The injured man from the service area said that, too."

"Exactly. Coincidence?"

"I don't think so. I think you're right, I think he's the same man. All you have to do now is find him."

"Me?"

"Okay, us then."

"Have you any ideas?"

I shook my head. "Not at the moment. We'll have to let it lie for the time being, see if our friends in blue come up with something."

"What if he does it again? Murder, I mean. Do you think he will?"

"I can't say, not enough to build up a profile yet. I hope not of course but it's out of our hands at the moment. Anyway, Shelly, you've done well on this one. I'm afraid it's back to the grind now until something happens."

"Well, thanks for the day out, Boss." She winked. "I did get a glimpse of York Minster in the distance. Catch you later."

At home that evening I cooked a stew and shared it with Pip. I unpacked another case of goods and chattels and fell asleep around midnight on top of the bed with the dog lying across my legs.

Just before six a.m. I had a dream. I was making love to Sandra, an athletic brunette I had known a year or so ago. She liked to take the dominant position and in the dream she was sitting astride me with her pelvis weaving patterns of pure magic. Suddenly, as these things happen in dreams, her white face was replaced by the dusky features of Shelly Fearon who seemed to have joined her and was looking over her shoulder.

Black surmounting white and both of them sitting on me, their combined weight pressing me into the mattress. I lunged out, trying to push the monstrous burden off me only to wake as Pip yelped and jumped off the bed.

I sat bolt upright, cold and clammy in the cool morning air, and stared at the whorls and knots in the natural wood of the bedroom door. Sandra had been another short and disastrous relationship, the story of my life. Was my subconscious warning me off Shelly or just warning me to be cautious?

I got out of bed and headed for the bathroom, stooping to stroke my reproachful dog on the way.

CHAPTER 11

Early morning mist hung across the river and obscured the weir at Tadcaster. The large, three-story house built from blackened York stone looked out across the river over a long, overgrown backyard from where Robert Cleghorn studied the three rows of windows.

The ground floor appeared to have been converted to a reasonably sized apartment, the upper two floors looked as though they were still in need of repair, the windows were grimy and the paint was peeling. He peered through a downstairs window, hands cupped around his eyes and saw that even here the work was only partly finished with trestles and cans of paint lined up along the rear wall. The place suited his needs, nobody would be calling to do the good neighbor act.

More to the point, the backyard contained a well-preserved World War II air raid shelter, partially buried in the ground. Concrete steps led him down to a rusty iron door which, opened easily. It smelled musty and damp and he didn't like the cramped feeling of the low roof—he'd been in too many bunkers in Iraq and they all felt like gloomy caverns. There was no light switch. He returned to his car and grabbed a flashlight from his luggage. The place could easily hold thirty persons, presumably big enough to shelter the occupants of the house in its heyday. More recently, it had been used as a garden store: terracotta planters and the rotted remains of fruit nets were heaped in one corner and a few garden tools were propped against the wall near the entrance.

He thought back about the two pool players. *Shiftless, maggoty looking skin. Kids, no not kids, young men. Old enough to be earning an honest living. Ha, probably never done a day's work more than likely, know the type, seen 'em before. Freaking animals,* he said to himself. *Not even animals.* He laughed out loud and turned to go.

On his way out, Robert looked up at the signboard: Barnard and Graham, Solicitors. The address was back in the main part of the town. He checked the time—it was coming up to nine and the offices and shops would be opening soon. He needed a clothes store. His head felt cold without the bandage, so he needed a hat and warmer clothes in general.

Kirkgate ran off the main street, where the solicitor's office was situated and here, he found a shop where he bought a sheepskin deer stalker and green three-quarter-length wax coat with a removable lining. He also got a thick sweater and put it on immediately, explaining to the shop assistant that he was used to much higher temperatures. Actually, he supposed that he would acclimatize eventually, but Robert did not plan to be in the UK long enough to adapt.

He left the shop intending to head for the lawyer's office, but saw two banks, one on either side of Kirkgate's junction with the main thoroughfare. Either of them would issue English money against Alan's gold cards. *Things were improving,* Robert thought, and time was moving on. Once he was through with real estate business, he'd drive back out to that diner and have some lunch.

By a little after 11 a.m. he had secured a three-month lease on the house—the agent had seemed pleased to be rid of it. He bought some bedding from a place close to where he'd parked the car and from a convenience store, a box of groceries. He also purchased a screwdriver and some typewriter correction fluid.

After lunch he went back to the house and carried his suitcases, groceries, and bedding into the apartment and locked the car in the garage. There were three bedrooms on the ground floor, the largest was furnished and ready to use. Robert laid out a couple of blankets with a duvet on top. He had a few hours' sleep to catch up on so he locked up, wrapped himself in the duvet and was dead to the world five minutes later; dreaming.

"You've been selected to join an elite company of men, Cleghorn. You've proved yourself to be a good soldier. However, we believe there are ways you can serve your country even better. Are you ready to serve?"

"Yes, sir."

Robert turned over in his sleep, pulling the warm quilting closer against the chill of the empty house.

"Yes, sir. Yes, sir. Yes, sir. Yes..."

Another voice spoke. "You have trained with knives and firearms. You have killed with these weapons; I shall teach you to kill with nothing more than your bare hands." The image of the sergeant who had taught him came back, the man was walking as he talked, first to the right, then to the left, Cleghorn stared straight ahead, standing to attention, listening. "There may well be a time when you have been disarmed. This is when you can be at your most dangerous; a disarmed man is not expected to attack. A man who can kill and maim with only what God has given him is at an advantage."

Robert Cleghorn began his training. It was grueling and painful. His arm was injured in a knife attack, but he was still expected to continue training.

"I promise you," he could hear Sergeant Moodie's voice in his ear, "I promise you, Cleghorn, that you will act without thought; react to any situation without having to stop and think about it."

Robert fought against his instructors. He had no weapons, they were armed with a variety of edged weapons and hand guns. Live ammunition was used and a round scarred him across the right shoulder. Robert disarmed one and broke his collar bone before bringing himself to a stop. He expected a court martial for injuring a superior and received a commendation instead.

"Autonomous actions," Sergeant Moodie told him. "Just like your heart pumping or your lungs breathing, your muscles work without you having to tell them to. You're becoming a natural born killer, Cleghorn. Like a wolf in the forest. Instinct. Your enemies will fear you."

Of the ten men who had started, four dropped out. Of the five who remained with him only Vinny Keoghan offered any kind of friendship—it lasted until action in the Gulf separated them.

"There is no flashy ceremony," Sergeant Moodie told them in his quiet penetrating voice. "Your uniform will change; a medal will be issued to each of you. That's it. You have all done exceptionally well and an exceptionally high success rate, too."

The man next to Robert slapped him on the shoulder in congratulations. Robert turned, in a split second his boot had crushed his colleague's instep and as he fell, was about to stamp on the other's throat before he heard his name being shouted.

"Cleghorn," Roared Moodie, his voice no longer soft. "Leave him be, you mother..." Only again, there was no disciplinary action taken. Such incidents were the price paid for honing men to such an edge.

Attached to Recce Platoon, 2nd Special Forces Group, Robert Cleghorn shipped out to Kuwait. The badge on his cap was a gray wolf against a darker gray background.

The nights were cold, freezing sometimes. The days had been mercilessly hot, rising to 140 degrees Fahrenheit. The huge camouflaged tent gave little protection.

He wound the duvet round him and muttered in his sleep. Sweat soaked the blankets and irritated his skin.

"Ah!" Robert woke shivering and rolled out of the bed clothes. He blinked at the wan daylight coming through the dirty window panes and looked around himself for several seconds before he realized where he was. "Goddamn nightmare. Look at the Goddamn state I'm in." He stumbled to the bathroom and turned the tap on. There was no water. Belatedly, he realized that the main was probably turned off. Might even need the water company to come and turn the damn thing on. He didn't know.

Sometime later he had located a shut-off valve under the kitchen sink and turned it on. He threw cold water over his face and chest and wiped himself down; discarded the sweat-soaked bed linen and found another clean blanket before attempting to go to sleep again.

They were sitting under the huge awning, still coming to terms with the ever-present heat when their orders came. They were urgent: in less than half an hour Robert and his comrades were airborne, getting ready to drop two hundred miles north of the Iraq-Saudi border. The twelve of them had forty-eight hours before extraction, forty-eight hours to locate Saddam Hussein's Imperial Guard and radio the coordinates back for airborne attack.

The Euphrates River was an easy reference for the helicopter pilot; it gleamed like quicksilver in the faint moonlight as they watched it pass by below them. Although there were a dozen in the party, Robert only remembered two: Vinny Keoghan, his large, laconic friend with the smile full of teeth and a deceptively lazy style, and Artie McIntyre, a fellow Floridian from Naples, a pocket Hercules with intelligence to match his muscles and a wicked sense of humor. Artie and Robert had continued their training in Kuwait together; they had come to know one another's strengths and weaknesses. Artie was stronger than himself though not as fast. They filled in each other's weak spots—in any kind of a brawl, the pair of them were sudden death.

Robert Cleghorn snored as he dropped off to sleep once again and his mind replayed the rest of the mission. He and Artie were paired off this time. They dropped into the night air some ten miles further along the designated course than the previous pair. They were the final team and they had a hundred-dollar bet on with Vinny Keoghan that he and Artie would win.

They hit the ground, Artie's feet thumping down three seconds after Robert's. They ran for the edge of the circle of sand blown up by the rotors then waited for the machine to move off before getting a fix on their position. Their intention was to move north until they hit the Euphrates and then westward. Their instructions had been precise, minimal: find the enemy position, report, avoid hostile action and return to the pickup point at the end of the forty eight hours.

They were wearing thermal suits to combat the freezing desert temperatures, their backpacks holding two days' rations. Radios, knives, handguns and night scopes completed their supplies, rifles were inappropriate for this mission.

The two of them worked like well-oiled machines. Two hours later they had reached the river bank and turned west and minutes later they spied the red glow of campfires that were visible only from behind the enemy lines. The scopes revealed tents, no sign of the tanks that had been expected. Almost certainly the fighting vehicles were there but camouflaged or hidden and, in order to discover the whereabouts, they would have to move in closer. Neither of them thought about it, they approached from the west and stopped at the top of the next low sand dune. A pontoon bridge had been put across the river; they could just make out the outline of a pair of sentries at its center, the red spark of a cigarette glowed fleetingly on a man's face—they were not asleep.

The camp covered a vast area. Long tents, prefabricated equipment huts, and numerous sand dunes prevented their obtaining a complete view. With unspoken agreement they began to work their way around the perimeter, scrutinizing every fresh piece of ground that came into view. About an hour later, their persistence was rewarded. What seemed, at first, to be another low dune turned out to be netting and under it was the unmistakable outline of a TK150, proof enough that they had discovered Saddam's Imperial Guard.

Instead of retracing their footsteps, they headed south to get far enough away to make radio contact as quickly as possible. McIntyre fell; he had stumbled over a trip wire and undoubtedly raised the alarm. Their instant reaction was to go to ground, Robert pointed to a dune some fifty yards away and here they huddled into the sand hoping that the desert camo combat uniforms would hide them from notice.

It was a slim chance, they knew, a vain hope which lasted little more than the ten minutes it took for the camp to come to life. No sooner had a powerful flashlight outlined them against the sand than they were hemmed in by a semicircle of excited men brandishing guns and knives and making the sort of din you expected in a children's playground. An officer of some sort shouted orders in Arabic and they were taken, disarmed and marched over to the nearest of the tanks. Each was tied upside down to the tank tracks and left that way with a pair of soldiers guarding them. A few minutes later, another officer arrived and this time spoke to them in English. He accused them of all sorts of impossible feats of espionage and questioned them—with the aid of a rifle butt—about their orders.

The first blow laid open the flesh over Robert's cheek bone. The second smashed into his temple where he could actually feel a lump growing. The third stroke landed somewhere behind his ear and was severe enough to save him from the rest of the interrogation.

When he came around again, it was dawn. What had woken him was the black silhouette of a figure coming between him and the brilliant sunlight. When his eyes were focusing properly, he saw that there were four men wearing khaki uniforms and black turbans. As they cut him loose and he tumbled numb and boneless to the ground, he saw Artie still tied up. His friend was dead; sightless eyes stared straight into the rising sun and the side of his skull was caved in.

They threw Robert carelessly into a jeep and propped him upright between two of them while the others climbed into the front. His senses became unnaturally sharp; Robert could smell their sweat, see grime ingrained into the hands and fingernails of the two who flanked him. The posture of all four spoke volumes—confidence, disdain, supremely aware that they were the cream of their country's elite forces, so arrogant that they had not even tied his hands or feet.

What affected Robert most of all was not the sickness from being left upside down for half the night nor the physical pain, he was anguished over the death of his friend. He was almost certain he had a concussion because his vision seemed to fade behind a red haze and his thoughts became ever more incoherent. Only one single urge sustained him—remain alert and bide his time.

The sand was bumpy with rocks and wheel ruts and the jeep lurched from one side to another throwing all of them about like so many sacks of potatoes. The Iraqis laughed as though it was a fairground ride and they were still laughing when their prisoner killed the man on his left as the vehicle's back wheels momentarily left the ground.

Robert's right palm swung round in an impossibly fast curve, impacting the man's nose and smashing the bones up into his brain. Death was instantaneous and almost in the same instant, he kicked the ankle of his right hand guard and clapped both hands over the man's ears as he involuntarily bent forward. The fellow's eardrums ruptured as a gun turned towards him from the front passenger seat.

Robert seized the barrel and pulled it past him with one hand and jabbed two fingers straight into the soldier's eyes. The driver joined in the melee, grabbing at the gun and at the same time trying to control the careering vehicle. The American pulled the gun free; he reversed it and shot the driver without bothering to consider the consequences of a driverless jeep. It slewed round in a tight circle, its inner two wheels off the ground. Soft sand caught hold and it stalled, righting itself with a bone-jarring thump.

A minute later he pulled the driver out and, with four-wheel drive engaged, managed to get it out of the loose surface and onto the barely discernible track. Robert killed the fourth guard and propped three of them upright in the vehicle before appropriating the driver's distinctive turban. He drove south as fast as the jeep would go.

Robert hated the dreams. He had long since lost the notion of fear. Nothing mattered except reaction and he hated the dreams with an intensity it was difficult to understand. Robert's memory of the time covered little more than three years, in reality while eight had passed since those days. Yet the dreams persisted with a clarity that might have come from yesterday.

Robert Cleghorn washed the memory away with a cold shower. It was the only kind he had available at the moment.

CHAPTER 12

On Saturday morning I went to the office hoping that I'd get off early enough to get down to some unpacking in earnest. I also wanted to call at a butcher's and get some meat scraps and bones for Pip. I'd moved the furniture around the previous evening, shifting the desk sideways and the computer station to its right, so that I could use one or the other just by swiveling the chair. There was a memo—a sticky note—stuck to the computer screen:

The bus you are interested in is making a trip next Wednesday.

Superintendent Flowers had left it there; his signature was at the bottom. Funny, I'd not noticed before but his writing sloped backwards. Was he left-handed? I couldn't remember. What I wanted now was a flip chart or maybe a whiteboard and I'd feel at home and something else too—a good big pad of paper. Some people doodle while they think, I write long lists with lots of arrows and circles and squares: it's my way of thinking, externalizing my thoughts so I can see what I'm mulling over.

Someone had seen me come in; an officer knocked and looked round the door. "Morning, sir." The someone had a big cheery grin. "Understand you're a bit of an angler?"

"True enough. Come in… Metcalf, isn't it?"

"That's me, sir, Andy Metcalf. Annual fishing contest for policemen. Fortnight from now, from today in fact, at Ulleskelf, River Wharfe. Likely to be interested?"

I laughed. "Thanks but no thanks. I don't know what you've heard, but my fishing is purely therapeutic. Non-competitive."

"Fine. Just thought I'd ask, sir."

"Thanks for the thought anyway. Anything else let me know,"

Metcalf went out, leaving the door open. I got up to close it and stopped halfway. I reran the conversation twice before I had it. *Wharfe,* he said. I went back to the computer and Googled R I V E R S and found an alphabetic list, a very long list. I tried again, specifying "United Kingdom" and was rewarded with something a bit more manageable. I referred back mentally to my memorized register of code words from Alec Bell's fraud case, and saw that there were several matches including *Wharfe,* of course. Then I checked the list of games and related files in my computer. Ah yes, there it was, "CrossPatch." I started it up—excellent, this should help

Sergeant Bell. I copied it off onto a CD and went into the outer office where Sergeant Bell was glued to his monitor. "Morning, Sergeant."

He gave me a quick eye blink. "Sir."

"That computer file problem of yours." I dropped the disc on his desk. "This is a crossword puzzle solver."

He looked at me owlishly while I explained. "This is a program that will work out all the sensible anagrams of a group of letters. Check the other index files for anagrams for the names of rivers—those seven words you gave me are all British rivers. So rivers—as well as places, people, whatever."

"Rivers?" His face was a picture of a mixture of surprise, chagrin, and male menopause. I turned away to make sure he didn't see the grin that I couldn't stop and crossed to Shelly Fearon, another of the three or four officers doing Saturday duty.

I don't know whether it was perfume, soap or just pheromones but she smelled good. "Morning Sergeant. I've got a small problem you might be able to help me with."

"Certainly, sir. If I can." She had a dark green sweater on; it complemented her skin—the color of wild honey yet smooth as a plum. "What's the problem?"

"I want at least eight officers in four cars next Wednesday—include yourself in that. Our immigrant friends are flushed with success, they're making another run."

The corners of her mouth which had been rising in the beginnings of a smile, turned down. "We're not going to try and follow them into the market again."

"Oh no, our friends in the *Nicies* can do that. If things work out right, we'll be following them to their final destination."

She lowered her voice to a murmur. "Permission to speak freely, sir."

"Of course Sergeant."

"The grapevine says that the *Nicies* are placing the blame for the last fiasco on us, are they going to do the same this time?"

"The squad's a bit unhappy about that?"

"Damn right, sir."

"This has nothing to do with the *Nicies*. Just tell them that if I'm right, we'll be showing the *Nicies* how it's done."

She grinned. "And if you're wrong?"

"Trust me."

I got away in time to get some serious unpacking done, though Pip had to share my meal again. He was getting a bit too fat on all this rich food so I took him down along the river. Next week, I'd catch the butcher before he closed.

CHAPTER 13

Robert Cleghorn had lost track of how many taverns and bars — no *pubs,* they were pubs here — he had been in and out of Friday evening. Tonight, Saturday, he visited eleven before he came across the boys he called Blondie and Tattoos. It was a small place away from the main streets. Through the right-hand window Robert could see a pool table and Blondie was bending forward, taking a shot. There was no need to go inside, by moving just a little closer he could see Tattoos as well, glass in hand watching his partner. He brought his car closer and waited at the side of the road.

The pair emerged from the pub a little after eleven and sauntered down into a busier part of the city. Robert checked the road signs; Piccadilly, it was called. He read it again because he thought that was in London. They went into a KFC takeout and came out carrying trays of chicken piled high with French fries which they took back to their own car in a side street. The car was one of those little Fords they had over here; it looked a dark green in the street lights. They sat in the car until Tattoos had finished eating; he started it up and drove off.

The American followed them for a mile or so until it stopped for Blondie to climb out. The boy tossed his empty food tray into the gutter and went into a house with three white steps to the door. All the houses were similar: steps, no front yard; Robert noted the number and the name of the street and continued to follow after the car when it moved off again.

Eventually it stopped outside an apartment building and Tattoos climbed out, searching his pocket for door keys. He was about to unlock the main entrance when Robert spoke up.

"So, my tattooed friend. No pool cue tonight eh? Just bare hands?"

Tattoos jumped six inches and—Robert gave him credit—recovered almost instantly, grasping the bunch of keys so that his fist was full of sharp protruding pieces of metal. "Hello again, Yank." There was no sign of stress in his tone, as though this sort of thing happened all the time. "Come back for another lesson?" Tattoos made to step forward.

Robert grinned. "This lesson's for you."

"I'm listening." Tattoos moved his foot again, actually taking a step this time.

Robert turned his head. He appeared to be looking away but his eyes remained fixed on Tattoos, alert for the first movement. When it came it was exactly what he had been expecting. The fist with its splayed forest of keys came up towards his face, ready to blind or gouge—at the very least, to disfigure the American.

When the fist arrived, Robert had already dropped below it and stepped to one side. He punched Tattoos once on the biceps—a classic blow: the arm went dead. His muscles spasmed, the lifeless arm dropped to his side, and the keys dropped, tinkling on the pavement.

Robert Cleghorn's movements were like poetry. There were no pauses. As the bicep punch went home, his right hand went up to twist his fingers into the man's hair, pulling him further off-balance until his legs ran to help him stay upright. He stumbled forward, accelerated, and was guided by Robert into the side of the Ford Fiesta. Tattoos's head hit the central door pillar and he collapsed in a heap at the edge of the sidewalk like a bag of bones. Robert retrieved the keys and found the one for the trunk. He picked up the unconscious form and bundled Tattoos inside and closed it; it was a tight fit, something gave as the lid came down.

He drove away, leaving the Insignia where it was, a few houses further down the street.

Blondie was sitting on the lavatory seat with the window open, smoking blow when the doorbell rang.

Robert could hear voices through the door.

"Open the door, Valerie," shouted a woman.

"Why me all the time?" This was a younger female. He heard the rattle as the safety chain came off and then the younger voice again.

"Bloody kids. Nobody here."

Robert Cleghorn had walked away before she opened the door and hid behind hedge as she spoke. He didn't want witnesses telling the police about him. Up to now, he was certain that he had done nothing to cause the police to come looking for him. That was the way he meant it to stay.

In any case, Blondie could wait. He already had something real nice to look forward to. *Why'd I never think of this before?*

He went back to the car, humming, *Whole lotta shakin' goin' on.*

Robert never really thought it out in words; it was just the way things were, the way things went.

Now was life after Stephanie, after that swine of a brother had filled her head with lies about him and married her. *Then* was before that, when she'd been sweet and they'd had a good time together.

Suddenly though, Stephanie was not so important anymore. When that pool cue had been smashed over his head, Tattoos had suddenly become the important one. Stephanie wasn't here, Tattoos was.

He'd been happy, he realized, over the past two days. He'd been absorbed in setting things up, chasing round all the drinking places he could find. Blondie had got away with it for the time being. Tattoos would occupy him for the moment and Blondie could be looked forward to.

Robert drove the car down past the house into the yard and swung it round in a great circle, cutting a swathe through dandelions and nettles and then backed it up to the bomb shelter's door. Tattoos was conscious when he opened the trunk but groggy. Robert hoisted him out, dragged him through the dirt and down the steps.

Inside the shelter, he picked up a flashlight and shone it on the bright chains dangling from a pair of old hooks in the roof. With a grin of real pleasure, Robert fastened the chains around his victim's ankles and hoisted him up, upside down, until he hung with his head a foot above the floor.

Now came the fun part.

CHAPTER 14

John Merrick was bemused. No, more than that, incredulous. There were two letters on the desk in front of him, one from the Governor's office and the second from James Strakes, a dentist from Fort Myers.

The letter from the Governor's office stated quite clearly that Alan Cleghorn was on holiday in England and therefore, the John Doe in the morgue was Merrick's responsibility and not the Governor's. The other letter identified without doubt the dental work in the John Doe's mouth was Alan Cleghorn's.

Merrick depressed the switch on the intercom connecting him with the outer office. "Murphy, you there?"

"I surely am, John."

"I want a run down on all Alan Cleghorn's relatives. Right?"

"Sure th…"

"You contact any of them you can and get one of them over here to identify this here body. And Murphy…"

"John?"

"I want it done sooner than soonest, okay?"

He flicked the toggle up savagely. *Play me for a fool, will they? Cleghorn in friggin' England, my ass.* He slapped the desk with the flat of his hand. *If the Governor thinks Alan Cleghorn's in England, there must be someone who's gone there. So who? The murderer? Someone should be warned.*

Merrick's chair creaked as he leaned back and tilted the front legs off the floor. It might not be his responsibility, however experience had taught him if you didn't cover your own ass, nobody else would do it for you. Trouble had a way of coming back and biting you in the ass even when you knew you'd done everything right.

Someone should be warned.

But who?

CHAPTER 15

Robert Cleghorn never allowed emotions to reach his face unless it suited his purpose; it was a habit of many years. However, when he heard the voice on the answering machine yet again where Stephanie was staying, he took a good hard kick at the wall in front of him. Four times he had gotten that same message about being away. Had Alan had another number to reach her? One that he had committed to memory or written down somewhere other than in his diary?

Robert had thought that his brother's visit to England was expected; now he was beginning to have doubts.

For the time being, he put the annoyance from his mind and fetched the five-liter plastic can and the loaf of bread in from the hallway. He filled the can with water and took them together with a flashlight out to the old bomb shelter, dropping them on the ground while he pushed his captive's car back away from the door. Inside, the wide-angle light beam revealed the man still hanging upside down from the chain. The figure was still.

It was the third time he had taken bread and water out to the boy, lowering him to the ground to eat and drink before hanging him up again. The first time Tattoos had remained silent; Cleghorn had not spoken either, merely watched him for any sign of an attempt at escape. On the second day, he found Tattoos bathed in sweat and shivering—the result of detoxing: needle tracks on the inside of his arms showed the extent of his habit. The shivering changed to violent shaking as soon as he had been released. He begged Robert to let him go. The shaking became pure anger, the begging turned to threats. A few well-aimed kicks in tender places put a quick stop to both.

Robert went further in, alert for trickery, breathing shallowly—the smell of urine and feces was stronger each day. He shone the flashlight at Tattoos, moving the beam up to his face. Whereas before, the boy had shut his eyes tightly against the glare, this time there was no movement and his eyes were open to mere slits. Again, he wondered if it was a trick and moved the torch nearer. Still no reaction. He reached out to check the pulse of the flaccid amr. The pulse, when he found it, was weak.

"Tired of cold turkey, eh?" he said aloud, knowing that he would be feeling the worst withdrawal symptoms by now. "Can't take it can you, tough guy? Like giving though, don't you?" Robert supported the other's weight and unsnapped the shackle. He was interrupted as the boy began coughing and drooling a stream of white mucus.

"Feeling a bit sick, eh?" He got Tattoos down on the floor and fastened the chain to his wrist back into the hook in the ceiling. He knelt down and poured water into the other's mouth. "Come on, bud, we want you to be feeling good by the time your friend Blondie joins us, don't we? We all want to enjoy the reunion, eh?"

Tattoos seemed to slowly come round; he opened one eye fully before closing them both and spitting out a bolus of phlegm. "Kill me, pig. Kill me, don't torture me."

"Ha!" Robert really appreciated the remark. "Torture you? It's not me that's been torturing you, son. That's you and you alone. If you're going to stick needles in yourself and pump poison into your veins, what do you expect? Been getting sweet dreams, eh? Spiders walking over your eyeballs? Rats nibbling your nuts?"

Tattoos lay silent and still. Robert realized there were only two ways to end this: either he left the stupid kid to die or he had to take the initiative and do something about his condition. He sat and thought about it for a while. With a sigh, he dragged the limp body out of the shelter and heaved it over his shoulder to take the unconscious boy into the apartment.

He dropped Tattoos into the bath fully clothed and turned on both faucets. He returned to the kitchen and heated a can of soup and made hot, strong instant coffee. Robert thought that he remembered reading that addicts trying to shake the habit needed sugar. He stirred six spoonfuls into the coffee and took them both back to the bathroom.

When he returned to the bathroom it took a few seconds for the situation to penetrate; it had seemed impossible that Tattoos was fit enough to escape but there was nothing in the bath except dirty water and a single shoe. A sudden icy draft from behind a billowing curtain brought Robert back to his senses. Cursing his stupidity, he dropped the two mugs into the tub and ran back through the kitchen and out the back door.

The bathroom window was at the rear of the place, overlooking the backyard with the river as its farther border. The only light came from the lighted windows of the apartment and, considerably farther away, a few street lamps. They cast a dim glow over the wiry grass and weeds and the heap of trash next to the garage. The riverbank was a dim line of bushes with the bare poles of leafless saplings reaching up into the darkness.

Should he go for the flashlight? He decided against it; it had been left in the bomb shelter and would take too much time to find. Scanning the backyard continuously, he moved away from the house, into the darkness as his night vision improved. First, he went to the gates which closed off the yard from the driveway, he shut them firmly and moved forward again. He still had on the coat he had worn when he went out to see to Tattoos; the night air cut through the lightweight pants he was wearing as though he were naked. He hoped this wouldn't take long, cold was something he disliked intensely. He ran lightly down toward the dark silver river where the best cover grew along its margin.

There was no sign of the escapee and he began to feel worried. Robert really did not know whether he had intended to kill the boy or just have some fun by frightening him. He gave a mental shrug. *If the punk died, what of it? One piece of useless human garbage less. They should give him a medal for it.*

He had been responsible for a lot of deaths during the course of his life; most of them had been casual affairs—too unimportant to remember. Some stood out in his memory, the result of a hard-won fight, the product of careful scheming, even someone whom he respected. Most though, were minor matters, gone beyond recall since he had been in the hospital.

There was that big steel worker though, he remember that one. He took a dive off some third floor scaffolding—with a little help. Was that before or after Ashton Sanatorium?

Robert snapped out of his sudden reverie by a half-glimpsed movement to his left. The dense bush suddenly sprouted a bar or a pole coming at him with vicious force. Learned instinct threw up his arm and he took the blow on his biceps; the pole glanced off his shoulder and smacked into his head. Without thinking he moved to the right to minimize the force of the stroke.

His left arm was temporarily useless. He bent and surged forward into the dimly seen attacker. His head struck something soft and yielding; there was an *oof* of expelled breath and a groan of pain. Cleghorn's head had butted Tattoos in the solar plexus; he fell backwards with the weight of the American on top of him.

Robert felt the tingling sensation come over him, warming him against the bitter cold, a white mist descended, obscuring his vision. His left hand was making ineffectual grabbing motions, opening and closing like a badly adjusted machine. But his right hand found Tattoos's neck and was efficiently squeezing until the windpipe collapsed and all resistance died away.

The jeep had run out of fuel after nearly three hours of driving and fifty miles of desert separated him from the Iraqi Imperial forces. It was still dark and abominably cold and there was no option other than to leave it where it stood and start walking south, orienting himself by the stars.

The other teams would have made rendezvous at the pick-up point by now, so it was footwork all the way—150 miles to the Saudi border, he reckoned. Kuwait lay to the east as did the bulk of Saddam's army. Westward were hundreds of miles of empty hostile desert between himself and Jordan.

He trotted to keep warm with his hands in his pockets and the four water bottles strung clumsily around his neck. His head ached abominably but the discomforts were all in the background. By concentrating, Robert could keep it that way, concentrating on just putting one foot in front of the other at a pace that he knew he could keep up for miles, for hours.

He continued, deliberately semiconscious, running on automatic and only when the night sounds changed did he come awake again. Oddly enough, it was a light which brought him to full alertness, as if someone had… there it was again, a spark, someone lighting a cigarette and in the darkness, like the flash of a lighthouse beacon. Robert turned west; away from whoever was smoking, then after a few minutes, south again. He had taken no more than ten paces when he heard voices this time, male voices, Arabic.

What he had run into was a new line of fortifications, dug in, fox-hole style. He dropped to the ground and began to crawl, avoiding dry grass that might rustle, twigs which might snap. He estimated he'd gone about thirty yards when he reached the next hole; there might be others further in between the ones he had found. Robert dared not pass between them, and it might take hours to get around them.

It was no use. Robert could not live with inaction and began to crawl carefully towards the foxhole he had just passed, intending to take a closer look. He took it slowly, carefully and when he was perhaps fifteen feet away, a soldier suddenly materialized out of the darkness and began to relieve himself. It was the sort of thing nobody would believe if he were to tell it as a story. Although the man was turned away from him, the American could feel odd drops of spray, smell the sharp acrid odor of the urine. Silently, he rose to his feet and just as the other was buttoning his fly, Robert's right arm went round the soldier's throat, the left palm against his head, applying the stranglehold with pressure to the man's carotid. The body went limp in his arms and he let it sink quietly to the sand before going onto the foxhole.

The other occupant was asleep with a blanket wrapped around him. Propped against the far side were two AK47s, Robert climbed down and used the butt of one of the automatic rifles to club the sleeping man to death. Apart from the heavy thud and a faint moan of escaping breath, the killing was silent. He looked around the trench; there were water bottles, rations. The dead man had a watch on his wrist, Iraqi issue. He took that and the blanket, water, food—as much as he could carry easily—and a rifle with ammunition. A careful scrutiny of the surrounding area and Robert climbed out and began to crawl, hoping that the fortification line was not too deep. After a hundred yards without seeing anything further, he got to his feet and began to run, carefully so that his new provisions did not rattle together and make noise.

No one had seen him. He was spotted twenty-five miles further south by a British pilot and picked up an hour after that by a special forces helicopter.

When he came to, the boy's body was under him; Tattoos was cold and dead: he had known that as soon as he touched the body. Robert was cold too, and felt as stiff as a plank of wood as he unclamped his hands from the kid's neck and got to his knees. It was still dark and he could bury the corpse without anyone seeing him. He wanted to be rid of it as soon as possible.

He dragged it through the bushes and tipped it into the swiftly flowing river and watched as the current took it away. It might even be swept all the way to the sea.

Robert Cleghorn was pleased to be unburdened of the boy's corpse. Somehow his thinking had altered over the course of the night, vengeance no longer seemed appropriate. He had got bogged down, he had forgotten what he had come here to do and that was *find Stephanie.* Maybe the bang on the head jarred his thinking loose again. Whatever, he felt a lot better.

CHAPTER 16

Tuesday was one of those uneventful days that come along occasionally. You need them so that you can catch up on those jobs you always put to one side; in this case, it was the super's books. I wanted to reorganize them so that I would have enough space to organize my own stuff; computer discs, CDs, books and papers. There was also a record of my work. I kept a database up to date on a more or less weekly basis, and everything I learned was available on demand.

Ten o'clock and I was just about done when Andy Metcalf knocked on the door and breezed in. The DC, organizer of all the many unofficial clubs and syndicates, was smiling as usual. While I was always pleased to see that my staff was happy, I did wonder how he kept it up. "Morning, sir. Wondered if you wanted to join the squad's lottery swindle."

"Tell me about it."

"Thirty-six places, you can buy as many lines as you like and any returns are pro-rata. If we put ninety lines in and you had four of them, you'd get four-ninetieths of whatever we won. That's one… um…"

"Yes, yes. One twenty-two and a half."

"Right, sir," he said with admiration for my math ability in his voice. "We used to do ninety when Shelly's old man was here, but he ran off with his secretary and I couldn't get her to chip in instead."

"Well no, I can see her point, even with you using your most tactful manner." I was being a bit sarcastic; he didn't seem to notice.

"That's right. I put it to her really tactful, but she still said 'No.'"

"That's women for you, Metcalf." I paused. "Did you say 'Shelly'?"

"Yes." My question puzzled him.

"Shelly Fearon?"

He nodded.

"Ah. I didn't know. I don't discuss staff behind their back."

"I know what you mean. It's not fair. Ralph Fearon was an inspector in the Traffic Division. Ran off with this cute little office type. Quit the force and took a small-holding in Somerset, according to gossip."

"Wanted to be a small farmer, get out of the city and all that?"

"Right. Suppose he's directing goats now or chickens." He laughed.

Hints were obviously lost on Metcalf, and in any case I wasn't sure just what the news meant to me, either. I changed the subject. "Put me down for four lines then, you pick the numbers."

When he left, I pondered Shelly. She had told me that she was married when I'd made that terribly clumsy invitation to take her out. Did she hope that her husband would return to the fold? I gave a mental shrug and got back to work, the lovely Shelly put firmly to the back of my mind.

In spite of the slow day, I still didn't get out to the butcher's. I cooked a steak pie and split it sixty-forty with Pip. Afterwards, I threw sticks and Pip enthusiastically retrieved them until my arm got tired.

Seven-thirty, Wednesday: I was in the office planning the disposition of cars for my expected swoop on illegal immigrants. I had to assume that the coach would follow the same route and time scale as before and I used a Leeds A-to-Z to check the street names and list them; I marked the positions on the map with a red marker pen. The coach would be in the city around ten or ten thirty, closely followed by the *Nicies*. I wanted the cars located by nine o'clock.

I could hear my DCs laughing and joking in the outer office as I worked, and at eight o'clock, I went outside and switched the overhead projector on. The buzz died away quickly.

"Morning ladies and gentlemen." They said *morning* back, a nice healthy racket which was a good sign of morale and—I considered—a good sign that they accepted me as boss. "Well now, the day has come for us to redeem ourselves and put a bit of egg on the faces of our colleagues in the NCIS. Does that meet with everybody's approval?"

"You'd better believe it," said someone. The "yes sirs" and the "ayes" and less repeatable language from the others was deafening.

"Let's get down to it then." I popped the map onto the projector's stage. "These are the positions where I want cars placed."

The briefing went on until everyone was clear about my requirements, at which point, someone brought me a paper cup of coffee. "Thanks," I said. My throat had become a trifle dry by then.

"Car one, that's me with DCs, Wright, and Asquith—we'll be in control. We shall have a cellular phone each and there'll be two in each of the other cars, backups, in case one of them breaks down. Now, if all goes as expected, one of us will call each of the support cars to say 'Go' and you'll do exactly what we've just discussed unless we call you again to tell you to stop. Okay?"

Ferrimore's arm went up. "What exactly are you expecting to happen, sir?"

"One of two things. If I'm right about this, you will see the fastest bunch of quick-change artists ever. They'll leave the designated bus, or maybe the bus itself will be changed—I don't know. If I'm wrong, you'll see me tarred and feathered and drummed out of the Ridings Regional Crime Squad, shortest career ever. Either way, there'll be a bit of a shindig at the nearest pub tonight. Oh, and by the way, we're using cellular phones instead of the police radios because I think our target may well use a scanner to catch our transmissions."

As they went off to pee and get ready for an hour's vigil, the phone rang in my office. "Eight forty-five, prompt, in the garage," I shouted and went to pick up the phone. It was Superintendent Flowers.

"Just thought I'd wish you luck, Stewart, and to say that the coach passed through junction forty-one on the M1 about ten minutes ago."

"Hell's bells. They're at least thirty minutes early."

"That's right, the Nicies did ring five minutes ago to inform me that they were coming onto our patch. Any problems?"

"No, sir. Thanks for the information. The bus will be here about nine thirty—we'll be in position by then. If all goes well, sir, the beers are on me tonight for the participating officers. You'll be very welcome if you can join us."

"I might just take you up on that, Stewart. The Old Man tends to frown on fraternization with the lower ranks. I think we could put this down to squad morale, don't you?"

The Old Man sounded like something out of the Edwardian era. "Squad morale it is, sir. We'll expect you if we see you."

At nine-oh-one, my car was in position on a patch of waste ground about a hundred yards from the dozen or more work units built into the arches beneath the railway viaduct. It was the same viaduct that we had followed the bus through last week but this time, we were on the other side of the bridge, the city side. A new steel warehouse on our right covered most of the car from observation by anyone in Blackwater Lane.

A surprising variety of businesses were working under an operational railway line with its accompanying noise and dust. There were carpet fitters, double glaziers, small builders and a car repair shop, and several had no sign boards at all—private premises I supposed.

It was Wright who spotted the cyclists and pointed them out. Ten or twelve riders were assembling on the pavement near the road bridge; one of them was speaking into a mobile phone. "The buggers," he said and fell silent.

"Twenty-three minutes past nine," I said as they began to straddle their machines while the phone man waved his arm. Moments later, the familiar green and cream bus came into sight and the cyclists pedaled off under the bridge.

I was watching the units opposite me as two adjacent pairs of doors were opened—the glazier and the garage—just as the bus swept round the bend. The bus braked hard and squeezed into the supposed glaziers. Simultaneously, an identical vehicle, down to its registration plates, drove out of the garage and on towards the city.

Thirty seconds later a carload of *Nicies* came through the bridge's arch, the driver looking just a little tense and then suddenly relieved as they caught sight of the coach.

"I don't bloody believe it." Wright breathed.

"As simple as that," said Asquith.

"Well, it had to be. It was the only logical answer." I kept a reasonably serious expression on my face, but inside I was laughing like a jackass. My night-work had been rewarded, even if I never did get to the butcher's for Pip. Several times I had sneaked round these units with a flashlight, looking for evidence and found very little: there was a very large something in the garage and absolutely nothing in the glazier's. There were also a couple of grazes on the door timbers with green paint embedded. Still, it had been a long shot, and I was mightily relieved that it had come off, so far.

"Keep watching the doors where the bus went in. If the passengers come out call our teams and say 'Go' otherwise… aha, here we go, thought their journey might not be over yet."

The bus had been in there about ten minutes, and we watched as the driver eased it out. The stripes down the sides were now red and the registration number was quite different. I would bet that both registrations were real and probably belonged to both of these buses—they just got shared. The passengers were all still aboard, even the three women in the back with the distinctive hair ribbons. It started forward, signaling left to pass once more under the viaduct. I turned round.

"Right lads, in you go, arrest anyone you find in either of those two units. Sergeant, call our other teams and give them the bus registration and the red stripes, tell them to follow it, staggered trailing, the full works, as we discussed."

Moments later and two officers lighter, we were following the bus and caught up with it on the way back out to the M62 motorway. We followed it for twelve miles, first us then car two and so on, until it passed through Bradford out onto the Thornton side. It turned down a narrow road alongside a gloomy waterway; it led to a huge former woolen mill.

We stayed back on the main road and observed through binoculars. It was heartbreaking really, all those people—fifty or sixty—in their bright and colorful Pakistani clothes being marched into a dark grim pile of sooty stone like that. You could almost see them look up and wonder what they'd got themselves into, what had all that money bought them? "Poor beggars," I said.

"Are we going in then?" Wright asked, his voice as somber as I felt.

"Not yet. Wait till they're all inside: then we have them like rats in a barrel. If we go in too soon, we'll risk losing the organizers, the ringleaders, if you will, and we'll have a lot of frightened people running around in a panic." I chewed my lip in anticipation.

We watched a little longer. "I think it would be a very good idea if you rang the superintendent and explained where we are and what the situation is. Ask him for some extra backup..."

I stopped and cleared the lump in my throat. "Extra backup. He can liaise with the Bradford police for us. Tell him that I'm guessing there will be a lot more than a single coach load of people in there."

I got out and walked back to where the other four cars were parked out of sight. I explained the situation and told them about the numbers I expected.

An hour later twelve squad cars from Bradford City Police joined us. We went in and only then did we realize the extent of the problems that confronted us. Two floors of the mill building were dormitories. Three quarters of the space housed females; the remaining quarter was for men, including a dozen Pakistanis who worked as security for the people who ran the place. The rest of the premises was filled with fabric, finished garments and sewing machines of all vintages.

Seven hundred illegal immigrants took turns to work and sleep, hot bedding it—three shifts using the same beds in turn. They made cheap copies of expensive sports gear; I recognized knock-offs of Puma, Adidas, Sergio Tachini, and Nike. There were stacks of garments everywhere; they probably went out for sale in flea markets all over the country.

I was outside, talking to an inspector from the Bradford City Force when Superintendent Flowers arrived. As he got out, so did the driver, who opened the rear door. Inspector Sowden from the *Nicies* climbed out of the Daimler. The expression on his face was one that would stay with me forever. It made up in a small way for all the misery I'd just seen.

Later we found out it was two Indian brothers, Sinjid and Ravi Patel, who were bringing the immigrants in. They kept them in place with a double blackmail threat. If the illegals didn't work or complained, not only would they be reported to the British authorities, they would be deported back to Pakistan. Not a lot of love lost between India and Pakistan.

The Patel brothers apparently thought they were invincible. The computers in their office were wide open, not even a password to protect their data. We had the names of the buyers, suppliers, lorry drivers, and all of the workers with their overseas home addresses.

The long bar at the Angel, the pub most favored by our people, was doing great business. Shelly had left her murder inquires behind. The whole squad was there, thirty men and ten women. A round of drinks for them all cost an arm and a leg, but I paid cheerfully. This was a morale boost for which I'd gladly pay a month's salary.

Well, a week's, anyway.

It took me a little while to realize that Shelly was no longer with us and when she still hadn't returned by the time I was ready to go, I wondered what the matter was. I found her outside, leaning back against the doorpost wearing a most peculiar expression. "What's the matter?"

"Someone's pinched my car." She looked at me, challenging me to say something flippant.

I grinned. After a moment or two, Shelly's lips twitched and she giggled. "What a bloody police force. Can't even keep our own cars safe."

"I'll give you a lift if mine's still here," I offered when we'd both quelled our hysterical laughter.

My car was still there, and on the way home, we rang for a Chinese takeaway—two Hung Wah specials and a large portion of spare ribs for Pip. Shelly lived in a small cul-de-sac of three-bedroom semi-detatched houses. To my surprise, when I'd worked out where we were, my own cottage was only a couple of miles away.

"Don't mind the mess," she warned me as she unlocked the door, but if there *was* a mess, her definition and mine were two different things. I went through to the lounge while she took the food into the kitchen. The room was predominantly blue: royal-blue carpet, eggshell wallpaper, and floral curtains and seat covers.

She brought the meals through and put them on a long teak-framed coffee table with a glass top. "There's a food warmer in that cupboard. You light it and put the stuff on. I'll be back in a minute."

I did as she asked and when she still hadn't come back, I went into the kitchen. Shelly was actually waiting for the coffee in a French press to steep before bringing it out. The aroma set my mouth salivating. It brought back memories of my father making *real* coffee, as he called it.

I smiled. I felt like giving her a hug and a prolonged kiss, but I didn't. Nothing had changed since the last time we'd been doing the domestic bit, and I prided myself that, having been taught a lesson, I didn't go and forget it.

After the meal, I made excuses about letting the dog out at home. However, thinking about it afterwards, I realized that Shelly probably knew about the cat flap in the back door. Anyway, when I got in, I took Pip out for a quick thrash round the orchard before turning in.

All things considered, it had not been a bad day.

I toyed with the idea of ringing Dad and talking to him about Shelly. In the end, I didn't; it would only get his hopes up. He didn't think I knew how much he wanted me married and giving him grandchildren and it wouldn't have been fair to him. To me either—there would be unsubtle hints and references. I'd never hear the end of it.

CHAPTER 17

He held the hand mirror and looked through the bathroom mirror, twisting his wrist until he could see where the injury to his head had been, just behind the left ear. Robert judged the damage to be minimal; he'd put up with far worse.

He put the hand mirror down and looked at the reflection of his face. His eyes looked sunken and Robert thought his face seemed pretty gaunt. His head still hurt like crazy and maybe that was what made him look ill. He took two ibuprofen, washing them down with a glass of water. He realized as he swallowed that he was quite hungry. *When the hell did I eat last*? He shook his head, which only made things worse. *Can't remember, but I guess it wasn't anything much.*

I'm a fool—a goddamn, stupid fool. Letting things give me the run-around like this. Should be me deciding what to do, not young punks like Tattoos. Robert ran his fingers through his red hair. *Well, no more. Gotta cover my tracks and decide what to do. Damn police, just because they're English, don't mean they're idiots.*

There was that altered license plate. He had almost forgotten about that, but it wouldn't hold them up for long and they'd eventually conclude that a red-haired American with the name of Alan Cleghorn had been acting in a suspicious manner. Well, he'd eluded the police in the past; there was no reason to think he couldn't do it again.

Stephanie was the priority for God's sake, that's why he'd come over here in the first place. Alan had certainly told her a pack of lies; once he was able to see her, everything would get cleared up. Tattoos didn't matter; the boy lived alone. Robert had found that out easily. With the slightest—*encouragement*—Tattoos had babbled incessantly. Tattoo's car had been payment on a gambling debt: it wasn't registered to him. Robert had decided to appropriate the tiny car to use in place of the rental car.

Robert suddenly felt better; he realized that his thinking was clearer. This whole business was going to be straightened out. Change his appearance a bit, use the punk's car, forget Alan's credit cards, and he was anonymous again.

Melt into the background. He grinned as he went through to the living room and emptied the contents of his pockets onto the table. There were several credit cards in his brother's name, almost six hundred pounds cash—that was about a thousand dollars, give or take—and the huge sum in traveler's checks. He had two passports, two driving licenses, keys, small change and tissues. The credit cards went to one side, and he looked carefully at the traveler's checks before deciding that the "A" could be changed to an "R" and his own passport used to cash them.

Robert sat down and tipped the dining chair back on its back legs. Alan's credit cards could be used to trace his whereabouts. He wondered if the police had actually started in on that yet.

Memory of the murders surfaced like something he had read in a newspaper. If the police had traced the credit cards, they could have placed him—or at least, placed Alan—at the gas station on the M62 and in York as well at about the time of the murders. If they hadn't, then all they had on him was the falsified license plates on the rental car—hardly a capital crime, and he could always say it had been stolen if they got that far. Why hadn't he called the agency, then? Easy. He'd been ill, too ill to report it! *Got a helluva beating, knocked me out cold, had to go to the hospital in fact.* No, that was going too far. The ambulance—he seemed to recall an ambulance; the driver would know where they'd picked him up.

No, keep the police out of things. Hell! Maybe he could leave a false trail, use Alan's credit cards...

Robert drove the cramped little car into Leeds, twenty-odd miles from York, and enjoyed a four-hour shopping spree with Alan's credit cards. Not once did anyone try to take any of the cards out of sight, reach for a phone, call a manager. He bought several changes of clothing, a new pair of large, darkish, sunglasses. There was also a portable color TV because his apartment only had a radio, a cell phone, new bedding and groceries. Finally, using the gold card, he visited two travel agents and purchased airline tickets to two different destinations.

Back at the apartment, he burned Alan's passport, the credit cards and the clothes he had worn the day before. He dropped the old rose-tinted sunglasses in the trash.

He was humming when he went into the bathroom to apply hair bleach and color. He'd been careful to buy a woman's brand, as if he were buying something for a girlfriend. His hair changed from red to a ruddy gold—it was still near enough his own passport photograph, yet different enough to change his appearance.

Goodbye, Alan! Long live Robert.

He was in excellent humor as he plugged in the TV and experimented with the Teletex facility. The sales lady at Curry's had explained it to him and once he'd got the hang of it, it was quite simple to use, if a trifle slow. Neither the national nor the local news carried anything remotely connected with him; he took a shower and dressed in some of his new clothes.

He was ravenous, and set to cooking a large steak pie in the microwave oven. Robert picked up the remote control and clicked the TV on again and watched the same news items flash onto the screen as before.

The microwave pinged, and he took the pie out, cutting the crust to let the steam out and allowing it to cool down a little. He made some instant coffee and sat down to eat and watch the TV. He was almost ready to turn the screen back to a non-news program again when something new caught his eye.

DEAD BODY FOUND IN RIVER OUSE AT SELBY TODAY

The dead body of a white male was found floating in the river Ouse at Selby this afternoon. Local boatmen unloading timber at Ousebank saw the body which had become trapped by an anchor chain. They removed it from the water before calling the police and ambulance services. The police refused to speculate on how long it had been in the water or on the cause of death.

Robert got out the area maps and found the town of Selby. About ten miles from Tadcaster, ten miles of river bank. He smiled knowingly. *No way are they going to be able to trace the body here.* He switched the TV back to some mindless game show, and went on with his meal.

At seven o'clock, he called Stephanie.

This time the phone was answered on the third ring; he planned to put the phone down once he knew she was there. She wouldn't want to speak with him after all the lies Alan had fed her. He would have to put her straight on those before anything else and that meant going to see her.

"York 5897714," said a voice, the tone, bright, cheerful. It was Stephanie's; there was no mistaking it and so unexpected that his response was automatic, like his defensive reactions.

"Is Stephanie there? Stephanie Cleghorn?"

"This *is* Stephanie Cleghorn," she said. "Who is this?"

Damn, damn, damn. He couldn't stop himself and blurted out, "It's Robert, Stephanie. I just wondered if we could meet, talk about old times, stuff like that?"

The phone stayed silent for long seconds although he could hear her breathing on the other end. There was a click on the line and he thought Stephanie had hung up, but she'd switched on the recorder. When she spoke again, her voice was changed, lower, serious. "What are you calling me here for, Robert? Has Alan let you call long distance? Has he put you up to this?" Her voice was rising now, harder, angry.

"If he has, Robert, you can tell him it's not going to work. I am not coming back to him. Never. Understand?"

What? She doesn't want to talk to me, she... no, she said she wasn't ever going back to Alan, she's not mad at me, she...

Robert made his voice softer, comforting. "This doesn't have anything to do with Alan, Stephanie. Believe me."

Stephanie sounded wary. "Okay, then why are you calling me?"

"I'm calling to talk about things between... us."

"What things, Robert? What are you talking about?"

"Look, let's get together, get something to eat. We can talk about what happened three years ago—before you married Alan, before I had to go off to the Gulf. I know you loved me then and I don't know what Alan said to you to change that."

"But..."

"No, hear me out, Stephanie. We had a good thing going and I want a chance to straighten out the lies he must have told you."

Stephanie's voice was filled with incredulity—if not downright disbelief. "What *are* you talking about? I didn't meet you until after Alan and I got married, after you were released from the mental hospital. You were a bloody pill-popper then and it sounds like you still are, worse than that sadistic brother of yours. Now go and pop a few more pills and bugger off."

The phone went dead.

How could she say things like that? What about the dances at the senior prom, those weekends at Bonita Beach, the parties, motorbike rides? Was her memory as shot as his own, did hers fade in and out? *Freakin' Alan's done this to her, must have done. He's beaten her up, brainwashed her, made her live a lie.* He looked out of the window. *What the hell did 'bugger off' mean*? He could make a guess.

Robert slowly put the phone down, it rattled against the cradle. Alan had never let on that she had left him. His vision narrowed. All he could see were those three whole weeks he had worked his guts out in his brother's backyard and all he had said was "put your back into it, it's all got to be ready for when Stephanie comes home."

The man must have been deranged, imagining things...

He leaned back and looked at the pictures on the silenced television. A hospital or something, like the one at York, like...

They'd held him down while a nurse injected him in the arm. He'd got back from the desert not sure whether he had been walking or crawling when the helicopter had picked him up. They had taken him back to base and listened to what he had to tell them before putting him to bed. There was a memory of injections to make him sleep; that wasn't a hospital, though. It was a military place—he was certain. He remembered the pills, though. When had it been? The pills had been to make him sleep, like the injections had: sleep and dream, a time of dreams.

"Come on, Cleghorn. I've been standing here for five minutes waiting for you to reply." He was a tall man, white-coated like all of them. A tall man with a sneer. *"You wanna eat or not? Yes or no? If you don't answer I'm going to pour it in the slop bucket."*

God, that was a bad time. Must've been ill with something. Robert smiled fleetingly; he hadn't answered the pig and the meal hadn't gone in the trash can either.

Where had she got the idea he had been in a mental hospital? Pills? Yes, he always took pills—unless he forgot to. He didn't need pills now, though. Nothing stronger than ibuprofen.

He got to his feet, went to the sideboard, and looked inside. He needed a drink to help him think, but there was nothing there. Robert was sure he had brought some bottles home with the groceries. He tried the kitchen cupboards, looked in the hall. Nothing.

Stephanie had things wrong—that was all there was to it. He had to get her alone somewhere and make her remember the truth. She would remember eventually. It was just a matter of time.

Man, I need a drink! He could put a bottle away quite easily. He grabbed up his jacket and went out.

The interior of the Green Bottle was all low, old world ceilings with vast black beams and rough plastered walls. Horse-brasses and hunting horns were tacked onto the timbers with brass foot rails along the front of the bar counter. Wednesday nights were always a bit slack and the barman was already reconciled to a poor night. When the American showed up it was a pleasant surprise, one that went from merely keeping the barman company with war stories to quite a rise in the usual takings. He had to fetch another bottle of Southern Comfort before his customer was satisfied and that was between the Jack Daniels and before sampling some of the single malt scotches.

God bless Americans, he thought as Robert dropped him a ten pound tip and disappeared into the night. *Send me more of them.*

Bridge Street looked a little hazy and a little unsteady to Robert as he retraced his footsteps. A few late drinkers hung about, stepping aside for him, standing in doorways and watching him curiously. They thinned out after he turned into Kirkgate and headed for the far end.

"Hello, love," said a voice from the shadows. "Need some company?"

"Stephanie?" He peered into the gloom, nonplussed.

The voice chuckled. "That's right, love. Stephanie." She smiled at him and dropped her voice. "Whoever you like. Your place or mine?"

An arm came round his back and supported him. "My, but you've had a skin-full, dear. Just along here, and don't make any noise."

Later, Robert had no real recollections of where he had been taken or even of walking there. He remembered climbing into a bed of willing arms and soft breasts—huge breasts pressed against him. He couldn't remember touching them or of having intercourse with the woman. He held her tightly and whispered to her, "It'll all work out now, sweetheart, you'll see; now we're together again." She had kissed him, and he had fallen asleep, dreamless and content for the first time in his adult memory.

Then it was morning—early morning—and he was being shaken.

"Come on, come on you lazy bugger! And don't say a thing. You've got to be going before the kids wake up."

Robert looked up, first at the too-bright electric light with its too-pink lamp shade and then, somewhat unwillingly, at the woman in panties and a truly vast bra. She was the other side of forty, her hair was bleached and frizzed and the kindest thing he could think of about her face was that it needed make-up.

He sat up, clasping the side of his head as a shaft of pain seemed to split his skull apart. Once on his feet, it was a little better. He got his pants on and then his shirt. A jacket hung on the corner of the bed; that was his, but where were his shoes? Down there, peeking out from under the bed. He bent to retrieve them and was rewarded with another spear of pain. He pressed his feet into them and stood up, turning around and around.

What in God's name was he doing here?

"Fifty pounds, that'll be." The woman held her hand out, tried a smile on and then gave up. "Fifty pounds for my services."

"What in hell are you talking about?"

She put a hand on her hip and struck a vaguely coquettish pose. "You were happy enough last night when you were trying to get that limp thing in." She pointed at his groin.

Slowly Robert gathered what this was about. "You must be joking. Sex? I've never paid for sex in my life and I ain't starting now."

"Pigs. That's what all of you are." She struck out at his face, but he caught her wrist. He wasn't ready when her left hand came up and scratched viciously at his neck. "Pig."

"Look, I never did a thing to you last night. Now you stop all this or your kids are going to hear and then what? Hey, they'll know their momma's on the game."

"What about Stephanie, then? What's she going to think when you come back with scratch marks all over your face?" Her hands shot out again, fingers crooked to gouge; Robert caught hold of her wrists before she reached him.

"Stephanie? Who told you about Stephanie?"

"You did," she hissed. "Thought *I* was your precious Stephanie." She spoke in a coy, little girl voice. "It'll all work out sweetheart, we're together again now."

Robert was angry but controlled himself, freed her wrists with a pushing motion. "Don't you dare use Stephanie's name against me, you old bitch. I'm going, and there's not a thing you can do about it."

"*Sod you,* Yank." A knife appeared in her hand as if by magic, an old kitchen knife with a very sharp edge—a knife that she must have kept for her own protection.

This time, it had just the opposite effect, provoking an unthinking reaction from Robert. He caught hold of her wrist again and knocked it against the edge of a dressing chest so that the weapon went clattering across the room. He flung her on the bed and took hold of her throat with one hand, his vision misted over leaving just her face and neck in focus. He squeezed, watching surprise and then horror cross the woman's contorted features. Robert increased the pressure as she squirmed and fought against his grip with ever more desperate strength. He had to use both hands to crush her throat, until her tongue protruded and the last rasping rush of breath had been expelled.

Filthy slut, he thought. *Using Stephanie's name like that, pretending to be her so she could take me for a lousy fifty pounds.* "You don't know what she's like," he told the dead woman, then shouting: "You're not Steph! You're not fit to speak her name."

He let himself out of the room and descended the stairs quickly. The door at the bottom had a slam lock, he pulled it open and found himself on the street and actually recognized where he was.

Robert turned right and began to walk briskly. He thought back and realized that he had really enjoyed the killing. It was the first time he could remember feeling anything other than indifference—he actually felt exultant. Anyone who made things difficult for him from now on had better be careful; he could end up doing this to anyone who opposed him for the sheer pleasure of it. He began whistling as he turned in at the gate to his apartment and made a couple of dance steps to an imaginary beat.

Bopping at the High School Hop was the song going through his mind.

CHAPTER 18

A mountain of new paperwork awaited me on Thursday morning. I wanted to rest on my laurels, but I was pleased that I had come in early enough to deal with some of it before the other officers arrived. The requisition notes that needed signing went into one pile, general information went into another and advertising and junk mail went into the waste basket. I'd worked through a third of the stuff before I turned up anything interesting, a note from Superintendent Flowers informing me of an appointment with the Chief Super that morning at promptly nine-thirty. *Probably wanted to meet the new guy now I'd been here for over a week.* Then a second memo popped up, from Harry Venables telling me he had recovered several sets of prints from the abandoned Insignia in York but with no matches on the computer. The hair type that had been lifted was definitely Caucasian and the fibers were natural wool dyed red and brown.

The third one was the one that brought me joy. A yellow sticky note read: *Thought you might like to have this. Keep up the good work.* It was signed by Flowers. The letter it was attached to was from the American Embassy in London noting our interest in Alan Cleghorn, a United States citizen. It gave a contact number in Sebring, Florida with a name: Sheriff John Merrick. Now that certainly raised my interest, a sheriff. Had Alan Cleghorn been a bad lad over there, too?

I almost dialed the Florida phone number before I remembered the time difference between there and here; I rang our telephone center instead and asked what the local time in Florida was.

"Three in the morning, sir."

Five hours behind us. The sheriff would be tucked up in bed unless his duties had kept him up. I'd try this afternoon.

I resumed my mail inspection and found a note from Sergeant Bell. The decrypted files held international telephone numbers, and some of them were already logged into the computer system for known drug dealers. He reported that he'd passed an encrypted resume of all his findings to the British police agencies and to Interpol; he had gone about as far as he could and was available for other duties.

That presented me with a small problem. Could he be brought onto the murder squad? I preferred not to do so. He may have the virtue of dogged persistence, but he also seemed to get up most people's noses. I would have to find something more fitted to his talents, something he could work on his own. He seemed to like it that way.

And further down the day's pile was something that would interest Alec Bell. A large building firm with contracts throughout Yorkshire had been receiving threatening letters. There were lightly veiled threats to personnel. Though nothing lethal was mentioned, I considered it important enough to follow it up immediately. One couldn't be too careful in these trying times. Bell should find that right up his street and plug the gap in his timetable.

Nine o'clock. A knock on the door.

"Come in, Sergeant Fearon."

She came in. "How did you know it was me, Sherlock?"

"The door wasn't closed. I could smell you, Sergeant. Take a seat for a moment, nearly finished here." Several moments later, I looked up.

"Actually, I didn't know you were in," she said. "I came in the front door."

"The front way?" The penny dropped. Of course, the *front door*—not by way of the car park, so she would not have seen my car there. "Any news about your car?"

She shook her head. "Not so far. The boys in blue are keeping an extra-special eye open for me. However, I came to see you about our abduction."

"Really? What about?"

"The abduction has now become a murder."

"Murder? We aren't getting after this man fast enough, you know."

"Mmm, that I do know. Our man Varley has turned up in Selby, in the river to be exact."

"Not drowned I guess from what you've said so far."

Shelly shook her head. "The pathologist has seen the body. He says it was death by strangulation and that's not all: the victim's ankles show marks that Fenwick—the pathologist—suspects are the imprint of chain links."

"This Fenwick is quick off the mark, isn't he? It'd take me twenty-four hours to get as much as that from our own man."

"Selby. Little town, nothing much happens there except for drunks and wife beatings. Doesn't have anything else to do."

"When do we get the official version, on paper?"

"Between five and six today. Post-mortem is in progress now."

"Suppose we go over there, get a word with him, and look at the body?"

"He may be prompt, but Doctor Fenwick is a stickler for channels. The harder you push, the longer you wait."

"Damn. Call the murder squad together for ten, will you? I've to see C.S. Grimes at half past nine; I should be out from under by then."

"Right, Boss."

I did like the way she said that.

"Er, Boss?"

"Yes?"

"You could smell me? Am I using the wrong soap?"

"If that's your natural smell my lady, don't ever use soap. Smells like flower blossoms to me." I grinned and left her for my meeting with Grimes. I was steered into a sumptuous office at oh-nine-three-oh on the dot by a very prim and proper secretary. She would have made an excellent prison warden—not necessarily in a women's prison, either. She was stiff enough to use for a coat rack.

Chief Superintendent Grimes looked up at me from under bushy eyebrows, a startling black beneath his snow-white hair. The smell of pipe tobacco filled the room and behind that was the smell of the leather-covered furniture he favored.

He stood up and the smell of tobacco smoke increased. He was a very large man, taller than my six feet by three inches or so, and, at a guess, fifty pounds heavier. He extended a hand like a ham and took my own in a sure grip; he shook it once and released me.

"DI White, I presume?"

I nodded. "Correct, sir."

"Sit down, Inspector. Make yourself comfortable." It wasn't easy on the hard leather upright chair reserved for visitors. He took up a pipe, an old yellowing meerschaum thing, and lit it with two long puffs. "I normally meet all the new men, welcome them to the squad, sooner rather than later. However, your case is a little different, my time was heavily committed and while I was attending meetings and conferences you became a celebrity. What do you think of that?"

"Well, perks of the job, sir. The er, meetings and conferences I mean."

Grimes sat back and laughed, a deep guttural sound which was unsettling. His speaking voice was a distinctive tenor. "Good one, Inspector. However, don't assume I like the merry-go-round." He puffed at his pipe and blew a huge blue plume towards the ceiling. "I've just grown used to it, I suppose." He fell silent for a moment.

"I was speaking to the Chief Constable of Bradford last night. Been filling my ear with accolades to your cleverness, Inspector. Superlative on superlative. Can't get over you allowing his men the credit for arresting the Pakistani illegals."

I said nothing, I sensed dangerous ground here.

"Why did you do that, I wonder?"

"Because the men who mattered weren't there, sir. The Patel brothers live in Leeds and we arrested them very soon after the Bradford bust, as soon as we knew about them, using the documentation we'd had ready for the coach organizers. In fact, we have completed their questioning. Perhaps you would advise me. Do we hand them over to the *Nicies*? By this afternoon I expect to be able to provide you with a full list of names of everyone involved on both sides of the channel."

"The Patels will tell you all that?"

"Not exactly, sir, but we also took the coach drivers into custody and two men from India supposedly visiting relatives. I suspect they were here to receive payment and prefer to go to prison in England rather than having their hands chopped off by their bosses."

Grimes nodded in a leisurely fashion, a look of respect on his face. "I expect they do, Inspector, I expect they do. Anyway, you've started well, keep it up. What are you tackling next?"

"The M62 murders, sir. Except that it's the M62 and York murders now."

"You can handle it?"

I nodded. "I'm quite confident on that point, sir."

"Mmm. Well, I'll let you get back to your duties. Oh, and by the way, send the Patels to Bradford when you're through with them. I'll let the *Nicies* know where they are then."

"Very good, sir." *Wily old bugger.*

"And one more thing, Inspector. I didn't vote for your appointment."

Nonplussed, I was not sure what to say. "I see, sir." Seemed the best response under the circumstances.

"Don't prove me right, Inspector."

I smiled most of the way back. Things had gone my way since I had arrived here, and there was no denying the luck involved. However, I grew a bit more solemn over the last few steps. Luck could be good or bad; luck was a coin with two sides. Being a copper meant watching your back as well as getting the job done. A sobering thought and not an altogether pleasant one.

I was perfectly self-assured when I got back, though a lot less cocky than when I'd left Grimes's office.

The incident room had all the modern conveniences: bulletin boards, white-boards with multi-color pens, a digital video recorder, a projector and even several tables and chairs. It goes without saying there were two computers, one of them on line to the Police National Computer, the other running a database of facts and supposition about the current murders. We had all the photographs from the M62 murders spread out over a couple of tables. Several people were looking at them when I came in.

It was the first time I had met many, if not most of them and similarly, those people had still to get to know me. Everyone looked up as I entered and conversation dwindled. People stood back and folded their arms or stuck hands in pockets. The sort of thing you do when no one knows exactly what to do. I picked up a handful of colored pens as I passed the seat Shelly had placed for me and went to stand near a wall board.

"Morning, sir." Someone broke the silence; I think his name was Boyle and there was the quite distinct sound of a group of people relaxing. "Thanks for the drinks last night." So he'd been round at the Angel, that's where I'd met him.

"My pleasure." I nodded. "By now, you'll know we're looking for a murderer. You'll already have your own opinions and that's good because they will all be different, just bear one thing in mind: this is one complex character."

I scanned the faces and pointed to the nearer pictures on the table. "At first glance it looks like retaliation, what the Yanks call payback. Action followed by reaction. The one young man, Smith, who is still alive, is on crutches with a smashed kneecap, not an ordinary injury from an impulse attack.

"Forget his statement, I'm sure he and the two dead men tried to mug our friend Cleghorn who retaliated by incapacitating him and killing his partner. Okay, retaliation—very efficient, very fast, very effective, but retaliation. What happened next was not; Cleghorn removed the bayonet and chased after the third youth. Maybe he'd been standing watch, to make sure the mugging was not observed, but he had a good lead on Cleghorn who didn't catch up with him until he was in the middle of the bridge across the motorway. That's where he killed him."

I looked around again, noticing some to whom this was news, and others who had already got this far.

"That was murder, pure and simple. The other could be argued as overreaction in self-defense. I think this means the American was anxious to avoid identification."

Someone, Shelly by the looks of the handwriting, had put up the three names on the wallboard. Smith on the left; Chosely and Beardsley, the two murder victims, on the right, further down was Varley.

"The following night, Cleghorn was in York where he was attacked by two men in a pub. Either he's a thoroughly dislikeable chap or he's got *victim* written all over him. I don't think it's the latter unless he's a victim of circumstance. Anyway, he suffered a head injury there and got carted off to a hospital where he walked out sooner than be interviewed by the police."

"Now we come to conjecture. He seems to have caught up with one of his two attackers and abducted—or persuaded—the man to accompany him, probably from outside his flat in York. This man," I tapped the board under Varley's name, "was fished out of the river at Selby yesterday, thirteen miles from York. Um, strangled."

There was a brief buzz of conversation which quickly died away again. I carried on. "We have to find this vigilante before he falls foul of any more undesirables. I want no stone left unturned, research the background of the latest victim; find his partner because logically, he's next on the list. I want maps of the area with Cleghorn's known movements shown, also where Varley was found and where the body might have been dumped into the water. That place needs searching for clues, any clue we get is one more than we have so far. And," I paused for emphasis, "I want it done yesterday. Okay? Any points need airing?"

"Yes, sir." The young man had a red face, self-conscious or natural, I didn't know.

"And you are…?"

"DC Scaines, sir. Just back off leave this morning."

"Welcome aboard, Scaines. What have you got?"

"The river, sir. That's going to be a lot more difficult than you might think."

"How's that?"

"It's not just the Ouse, sir. Three miles north of Selby the Wharfe joins the Ouse, so it could be two rivers. As a matter of fact, two more join the Ouse in York and there are several boat marinas. The body could have been dropped off the side of a boat or even from a bridge. Could have come thirty miles before it got snagged."

"I see. Hmm. Know a bit about rivers, Scaines?"

He made with the modest bit then. "Do a fair bit of fishing. It's in the family; I was brought up around these rivers. Yes, know them pretty well."

"Excellent. You're in charge of the river search then." Scaines's face fell. I bent towards him. "I'm a bit of a fisherman myself, actually, so I know about rivers, too. I know a lot more about coroners though. I'm prepared to bet a tidy sum that by tea-time we'll know when he died, how long ago, how long he'd been in the water and what brand of cigarettes he smoked. That should give you a good start on how far to backtrack up the river or rivers. Okay?"

"Yes, sir." A lot less bumptious than when he started.

"Check with the boatyard people and find out what else they might know, question the river pilots—they know the sand banks and the speed of the currents and undertows. They'll probably hazard a good guess as to where your body hit the water."

"Right, sir." He grinned a bit sheepishly.

"Right Scaines. Selby's tidal isn't it?" He nodded. "Makes it even more interesting."

I looked at the rest of them; most were smirking. "Any time a member of this squad has something to say, say it. I'm here to listen to anything so long as it's constructive. Sergeant?" I turned to Shelly.

"Will you organize them into teams? I think DC Scaines will need a bit of help, too. I'll be in my office when you're finished."

I strode through to my desk, dealt with some paperwork and was noting my actions on my own computer database when she came in a little later.

"Be right with you, sergeant." She stood with one hip leaning against my desk while I finished up. I looked at the door; she had closed it. Good, I could keep this informal. "Now then, Shelly. I don't want anyone getting complacent with this job—or thinking I'm going to pull a rabbit out of a hat. I had a feeling about our Coach Trippers which paid off. I've got a feeling about this one, too. It's going to be a toughie. What do you think?"

She was dressed in an expensive-looking cream-colored suit; I wondered how much of her salary went on clothes. Her perfume was different too, more musky than flowery. Anyone looking less like a police officer was hard to imagine.

"Well, you said it yourself, sir. He looks like some sort of idiot, leaving a trail plain enough for anyone to follow. Somehow it makes me uncertain, puts us on the wrong foot. Suppose he isn't bothered if we know?"

"What, like diplomatic immunity?"

"It's a thought. I was thinking more like drugs. Maybe he just doesn't care. Whatever." She shrugged. "We've lost him for the moment. He's dumped the hire car and his physical description may be out of date by now. We don't know enough about him to predict his movements. You're right; it's going to be a tough one."

"Have the York police come up with anything on Varley's partner, from the cue-bashing incident?"

She shook her head. "Not so far. Varley was involved with drugs—as a user, not as a pusher. Made his money, over and above his Giro-dole money, by hustling at pool. Several people have mentioned a friend, a blond kid, though no one can put a name to him."

"It's a pity. Like I said, if logic has anything to do with it, he is next on Cleghorn's list." I sighed and sat back. "I'm at a loss here. I don't know what to make of the man. He doesn't fit any of the standard psychological patterns. Kills in retaliation, to cover his back, and then for revenge. Like one of those martial arts characters, you know…"

"Bruce Lee?"

"That's the one. Maybe he's been watching too many movies."

"Perhaps we should check what was showing on the trans-Atlantic flights last week."

I grinned. "We'll notify every force in the area, send out the description we got from the publican and his wife and make sure that all violent death reports are on my desk as soon as we get them."

I paused and looked at Shelly with a new thought coming to the front of my mind.

"I've a feeling this man, Cleghorn, is starting to enjoy—or enjoys—what he's doing. We have to catch him sooner rather than later."

At one o'clock—eight a.m. Florida time—I rang the telephone number provided by the American Embassy and spoke to a Deputy Schwarz. "May I speak to Sheriff Merrick, please?"

"You surely could, sir, if he were here," came the measured reply. "I reckon he'll be taking breakfast down at the Golden Corral right about this time. He'll be in here around nine or so. Is there something I can help you with?"

The privileges of rank I thought, disappointed though not showing it. I had to preserve the spirit of international co-operation here. "Well, I really need to speak to Sheriff Merrick so could you ask him to call Detective Inspector White in England when he gets in? I'll give you the number."

"Is that right?" said Schwarz. "You're English? Oh my, my wife'll be tickled pink when I tell her I've been on the phone with someone from England. Her folks came from there, y'know, from—let me see, from Norfolk. Her great Grandma was a Pattinson, maybe you've heard of the family?"

"I'm sorry, I don't know anyone of that name. Will you let the sheriff know?"

"Don't you worry yourself, sir. I'll call John now, on the radio. Detective Inspector White, that'll be the English Police Department?"

"That's right." I winced at his calling us a department but didn't feel like correcting this very polite transatlantic colleague.

"Well 'bye now, have a nice day."

Sheriff Merrick must have gulped his breakfast down and got back to his office post-haste because he rang me back in less than ten minutes.

He introduced himself. "John Merrick here, Highlands County Sheriff. Guess this has to do with Alan Cleghorn?"

The man's voice was two octaves lower than my own baritone. It was a voice I liked immediately.

"You're on the ball, Sheriff. My name's Stewart White and yes, I'm interested in what you can tell me about Alan Cleghorn."

"Hope my deputy didn't run up too much of a bill with your phone company?"

"Sorry, Sheriff. Not sure I understand."

"Got a kinda slow delivery has Mr. Bob Schwarz, comes from Minnesota. Folks up there got a lotta time to fill, take things pretty easy, talk slow. Anyhow, call me John. You wanna hear about Alan Cleghorn?"

"Thanks, John, you must call me Stewart."

"Fine. Well, Stewart, you maybe think you're looking for Alan Cleghorn, but I have to tell you, you ain't."

That caught me off guard. "Then…"

"I've got Alan Cleghorn laying here dead in the county morgue. Been identified by his dentist and his uncle so I'm fairly sure of my facts. Reckon whoever it was that killed him has assumed his identity."

That hit me just as hard as John Merrick's first assertion. It also answered a lot of questions like why wasn't the killer bothered about our identifying him. The reason was that he wasn't who we thought he was. "Sorry, John. That's a bit staggering."

"Know how you feel. I found it just as staggering 'cuz the Governor of Florida himself told me my corpse was alive and kicking and visiting in England, place called Yorkshire? Took it on myself to inform the US Embassy in London, left them my name and number in case of… well, I don't know in case of what—but that's why you called, I guess."

"You said whoever killed him probably assumed Cleghorn's identity. How was he killed, John?"

"Some sort of martial arts blow, karate, judo, kung fu, according to our medical examiner. Delivered right to the throat."

I nodded, realizing John Merrick wasn't going to notice the kind of blow. "It's the same man all right. Fractured one man's kneecap with a kick and killed two others with a bayonet, strangled another."

Merrick whistled down the phone line. "Sure has been a busy boy. Unfortunately, nobody here saw a thing. Cleghorn's got this new place out between a lake and a golf course, nearest neighbor's a quarter mile off. We've questioned the regular club members, local tradespeople and the like, no one's seen anyone 'cept for this red-headed male."

"That's him. A redhead, about five ten."

"That's Cleghorn, although he's more like six one, a bit on the heavy side. Whoever's impersonating him must look much the same"

"Hmm. The description I have says he's well-built yet not overweight."

"I've read the forensic reports and quite honestly, they say diddly-squat. We've got some fingerprints, but they could be anybody's—the tradesman, his wife..."

"What does his wife have to say?"

"She's nearer you than me. She's English—and according to Cleghorn, she's visiting with relatives over there, and he's been planning a vacation with her for some time. If it wasn't for the fact that I've got Alan Cleghorn dead in my morgue I'd believe it all."

Thoughts chased each other around my head. "Do you have an address for Mrs. Cleghorn? Got a maiden name?"

"No to the first question, and the second one poses a few problems. First name's Stephanie... hang on, let me find my notes... formerly Stephanie Yates, but that was when she was married to a Major Yates, an American officer serving at a place called Menwith Hill in Yorkshire. You know where that's at?"

"I do, that's the RAF station near Harrogate. It's supposed to be the biggest electronic monitoring station in the world."

"That so? Thought the Russkies would'a had a lock on that. Anyway, our Major Yates died of leukemia, but her marriage qualified her for US citizenship. Yates is what appears on her papers."

"I have to explore every avenue that comes up, John. This man's a walking disaster area, and he's got to be stopped. Can you help me in any other way?"

"Anything at all. Give me a f'rinstance, Stewart."

"Credit card details, a recent photograph—anything else you might think useful. I'd be grateful for anything. Whoever our killer is, he's got to bear quite a resemblance to Alan Cleghorn because he's used the man's passport. He's maybe using everything else belonging to Cleghorn."

"That's about right, Stewart, I'll get right on it. You gotta fax number there?"

I gave it to him and thanked him.

"Been a pleasure, Stewart. Let me know how things work out."

"Depend on it." I broke the connection.

CHAPTER 19

Amanda looked at her cousin and shook her head. Until yesterday, Stephanie had been bright, bubbly, and happy; now she sat in the bay window looking absently out at the rock garden at the side of the house. Stephanie was a brunette; the shining cascade which usually rippled over her shoulders was disheveled and dull. Her face still bore traces of last night's makeup and clear signs of tear stains on her cheeks. Stephanie's thoughts were miles away, back in America with her bully of a husband, Alan. "Come on, Steph," she started brusquely. "Tell me what's up. The sooner you share whatever it is the sooner we can forget all about it."

Stephanie turned her brilliant green gaze on Amanda, eyes that Amanda would have given her right arm to possess. "It's Robert."

"Robert?" she asked blankly, all her preconceived notions fleeing.

"Alan's brother. He's found out where I am. He phoned me last night."

"Alan's brother?" Amanda only seemed able to repeat the other woman's words. "Alan's… God, he's the one who's," she searched for a suitable word, "a bit tapped?"

"A bit? More than a bit, over the edge and beyond, I think. He called me up and made out we'd been in love! Can you imagine? He went on and on. Talking about how we'd been going to get married before Alan came along."

"Is that why he actually rang you?"

"Wanted us to meet and talk, straighten things out, as though we'd just had a bit of a tiff. All we needed was to throw ourselves into each other's arms and everything would be all right again."

"Weird."

"Weird is right. And I've just remembered, he thought it was only a couple of years ago."

Amanda raised her eyebrows. "Should be in an asylum."

"How long is it since he was involved in that war?" Stephanie wondered aloud.

Amanda shrugged. "Five years at least?"

"Said that if he hadn't had to go off to Iraq, we'd have been married two... no, three years ago. I remember when he came back, he was on medication."

Amanda chuckled. "I remember you saying something about that. Hope you told him where to get off."

"I certainly did. Told him that he was mad as a hatter and slammed the phone down."

"Well, at least he's three thousand miles away. Forget him, hon. Neither he nor Alan can hurt you here."

"That's just the point Amanda. He *isn't*. I dialed 1471 and got the number he used afterwards. It was a cell phone and I checked with the operator, made out it was a life or death matter and wheedled some information out of her. It was a UK phone. He's here, in England."

"Well, so what, Steph? You know our security system here, top of the range. We're connected to a security company. They'd be here in less than five minutes if there was a break-in or we pressed the panic button."

Stephanie did not reply, turning back to the window again, chewing her bottom lip. "You don't know him, Amanda," she said at last. "You know the SAS?"

"What? Here in England?"

Stephanie nodded. "He was something like that in the States. That's why he went out to Iraq. He spent years in mental hospitals when he returned to the States; takes some pretty heavy meds to keep him calm. Alan said he was like the Hulk if he didn't take them, he got angry so easily. It would take ten men to stop him doing anything."

"Sounds to me like Alan was putting you on. Those sorts of things don't happen in real life."

"They do, Amanda, they do. I can remember him hammering his fist against a truck's windshield because the driver cut him off at an intersection. He smashed it to smithereens in one go."

"A what?" Amanda asked.

"A windscreen, he shattered a windscreen with his bare hands."

"Okay." Amanda lifted her hands, palms outward. "Let's just calm ourselves down, all right? Look at things sensibly. Why does this bozo think you're in love with him?"

Stephanie shook her head. "Alan said that he's always lived a lie, like some sort of fantasy world, even when he was a kid. Maybe he's got me mixed up with someone else."

"How about calling the police then? Warn them that he's on the prowl and in need of medication, restraint even. Maybe he's already done something crazy and they're out looking for him, maybe they'd jump at the chance."

"What can we tell them? I left my husband because I got fed up with him hitting me? His brother's a mental case and he's out to get me? I think they'd probably cart *me* off to a padded cell. Anyhow, I'm pretty sure that they wouldn't be able to do anything on the strength of one phone call."

Tears ran down Stephanie's face again and she turned to cling to the other woman. "Oh God, Amanda, I'm scared out of my skin. I've rejected him. He might try to kill me!"

Amanda held her tightly and frowned to herself over Stephanie's shoulder. "I'm sorry, Steph, I'd no idea you were this frightened, really." She paused for a few moments, patting her cousin's shoulder. "There's a simple solution to all this, you know?"

Stephanie leaned back and looked at Amanda. Amanda was five years her senior and built to a much less slim and delicate pattern. Unkind friends swore that there was horse in her ancestry and it *was* true to say that she got on with horses rather well. Still, she had been known to quicken the hearts of certain local males. They appreciated her fuller figure in a tweed jacket, her generous buttocks held in check by riding breeches. Even her no-nonsense manner had its appreciative following.

"What solution?"

"Did I ever mention Scar House, the lake?" Stephanie shook her head. "No. Well, probably not. I hated the place in a way. Paul bought it six months or so before he died, it's a cottage north of Pateley Bridge, in the Dales. The damned man bought it without even telling me until it was all settled. The most beautiful place on Earth, he said, he could paint to his heart's content without ever being disturbed—which was all true. It *is* the most beautiful place and no one is going to disturb you up there. It's just that Paul's idea of heaven wasn't mine. You could hear a pin drop a mile away. No conversation, no radio or TV, no phone. The loudest thing up there was the sound of Paul's brush strokes. I never went near the place after the first visit. He put one *mod con* in, electricity, so that he could see to paint. I wouldn't go back."

"But if you hate it…"

"With you and me, it would be different. We'll throw everything in the estate car and zoom up there. We can stay as long as we want, do what we want. It'll be great."

Stephanie smiled again, like the sun coming out. "Really? It sounds fantastic; no one would know where we were. Let's go now." She shivered involuntarily. "Honestly, the sooner we're away from this place, the happier I'll be."

"Well not this moment. I've got to leave money for the milkman and cancel delivery. Oh, and the papers, too. Look, take a shower Steph—you look awful. Get your face on and I'll organize everything. We'll be away by teatime."

By teatime, I had received copies of Cleghorn's bank and credit card statements, his passport numbers and a color photograph of a smiling redhead in sunglasses with a golf club over his shoulder. The passport photograph had also been sent to me so that I could compare the two.

The passport photo showed a considerably younger man than the other, suggesting that the former was a much older picture. The face was less jowled, maybe a little less forehead beneath the hairline and it was serious—no smile, as required on passports. All in all, though, there was not that much difference, and I knew I could recognize him from either picture—but to what end if our man was a different person all together?

I passed it all onto Shelly with instructions to get the pictures duplicated and to contact the various credit card agencies. "Don't have them stopped, though." I told her. "They'll get us a fix on his whereabouts. Oh, and the photos—get someone out to visit Smith at the hospital in… " I waved my hand, unable to remember the familiar name.

"Bradford General?"

"That's it. I want to know what differences there are before we send a picture out; we can doctor the copy to target our man."

At five p.m. on the dot, I contacted the pathologist to ask for information on Varley and was given the findings. Fenwick had an educated voice and enunciated everything clearly and precisely, a bit of a pain.

"Just a minute while I get the file." I waited two minutes and Fenwick was back on the line. "The man died from reflex cardiac arrest—someone put their hands around his neck and squeezed tightly. There is a large bruise to the right side of the larynx, presumably where the killer's thumb pressed and several smaller and lighter bruises on the other side which I would assume to be the imprints of fingers. Several fingernail impressions in the skin too." The doctor paused. I could imagine him pursing his lips. "A number of abrasions which I would describe as the results of defensive actions on the part of, er, Varley." It was the first and in fact, the only hesitation in his speech caused, I suspect, by Fenwick seeing something he usually did not see.

"Defensive actions?"

"Varley had obviously attempted to pry the fingers away from his throat."

"Ah. Any other marks, Doctor?"

"Scores, Inspector. Virtually all of them caused by collisions with things in the river and sustained after death, except for the chain marks on the man's ankles."

"I see. What do those marks suggest to you?"

"That he had been hung upside down for some time. The pressure was applied against the ankle bones; the skin was torn from above down to the ankles where the metal had penetrated, so there is no doubt as to that."

"Any skin or blood samples underneath the nails?"

"There were. Whether his own or someone else's is not known as yet. That analysis has yet to be done. I'll let you know when it's completed."

"Thank you, Doctor. Time of death and time spent in the water, is there anything you can say about that?"

The doctor's tone altered. He was on less certain ground here. His first words confirmed my feeling. "Not so easy, Inspector. You see, we gauge the time of death from stomach contents or core body temperature. The water will have cooled the body faster than usual—much faster—and the man seems to have hardly eaten anything for some time, some days, I would guess. If you want another guess, then I would say twenty to twenty-four hours since he died; the same for the time of immersion."

"Well, that's fine, Doctor. Thank you very much. What about a written report?"

"Tomorrow if the analysis work is finished. The day after, otherwise."

It had been a long day. There was a supermarket in the shopping center across from the offices and I went in and bulldozed my way through wall-to-wall students. Shelly had mentioned there were thirty or forty thousand students in residence during term time. It felt like at least half of them were in Morrison's.

I got out with a chicken tikka masala—microwave in five minutes. Pip wouldn't care for curry, and he needed some doggy vitamins, anyhow. I ended up with six tins of dog food, as well. Ugh!

Snow was falling by the time I'd got up to the parking space the force rented for our cars and I wondered, as I joined the homeward line of traffic, how it would affect the search along the river banks. Altogether, though, I was satisfied with the day. We had acquired more information: factual stuff, not just surmise and guesswork. I felt reasonably confident that something would turn up soon; there was that sort of expectancy you can sometimes feel when something definite is going to happen.

Pip didn't meet me at the front door like he usually did. I wondered if I'd shut the kitchen or lounge door by mistake. My little friend would take a rather dim view if I had. I switched the lights on and went through; the kitchen door was wide open but no Pip. *Rabbits*, I guessed and headed for the back door, picking a flashlight out of the basket under the work top.

I could do with a light out here, I thought, flashing the beam around and shouting Pip's name.

The yard was hemmed in chiefly by brick walls and a short run of chestnut paling with a stout wooden gate out to the orchard. It was covered with snow, but there were no paw prints. He must have gone out some time before. I thought there was no way out of the yard and that's where I was wrong. In softer earth under the wooden fencing I found a heap of soil now covered in snow and a dark hole beyond. No problem for Pip; he had found a way out.

I went through into the orchard shouting at the top of my voice. "Pip!" Nothing. I was getting a little rattled by this time as I threaded my way through the apple and pear trees. "Pip, you little devil. Where are you?" There was a small sound to my right. "Pip?" A muted bark answered me from over by the border and feeling an immense relief I went that way, fanning the light from side to side.

"Pip?" There was a hedge just here and shining the light along the ground I could see a dog's rump and a rather limp tail. "You got yourself caught in there?" The tail raised and lowered itself and a faint whimper answered me. "Come on then, you silly little bugger."

I got my hands around him, trying to find what he'd got stuck in. There seemed to be nothing, but when I took my hand away, it was sticky—sticky with blood. The flashlight showed a wide patch of pink-tinged snow.

"Cut yourself, you poor little fellow. Take it easy now, we'll..." I eased Pip out from between two hawthorn trunks and used the torch to see where he had injured himself and saw exactly what was wrong.

Someone had shot my dog. His front quarter had been peppered with shotgun pellets.

Cursing steadily, I wrapped my jacket round him and cradled him against my chest. I walked as fast as I dared back to the house and laid Pip down on the kitchen table, covering him up before going to fetch an electric fan heater to warm him up. When it was going, I opened up the Yellow Pages and looked for "veterinary surgeon" entries.

The third one who answered agreed to come out to the house when I explained how Pip had been shot. I was trying to spoonfeed him while I had the phone, although Pip wasn't interested. It was as though the vet could see me. "And don't feed him until I've seen him," she said.

Well, Pip licked my hand a bit, feebly, that was all. The side of his neck was bleeding. His ear, his left flank, and foreleg had also taken the blast. I filled a bowl with some warm water and started to bathe him, get some of the clotted blood off his fur.

I think it took about half an hour for the vet to reach me. When she saw the state my Pip was in, she moved pretty briskly. "A shotgun wound."

I nodded. "It's a mess, isn't it?"

"I'm afraid it is. I think he's maybe lost quite a lot of blood. How long since he was shot?"

"I don't know. I got home and I couldn't find him. Before the snow started, anyway."

"Oh, I see. I thought maybe you'd had an accident."

"No, no." I caught on slowly. "No, I found him out in the orchard at the back, under the hedge. I think it's a farm next door."

"I see. Well look, I'll give him a couple of injections, one to help with the blood loss, another to help with the pain, and then I can start taking the shot out. Are you squeamish?"

I shook my head. "I'm a police officer," I told her and almost visibly fainted away when she took the bloody folds of my jacket away.

"It's different with strangers, isn't it? Nearest and dearest is another matter. If you'd like to help, make a pot of tea for us both." She smiled, and the kind words brushed aside my concern long enough to notice it was a lady vet, too. A rather lovely lady vet, around thirty... with bloody fingers.

I turned away and filled the kettle.

By the time the tea was brewed, and I had poured out two large mugs, Shirley Kelly, the vet, had removed most of the shot and was dusting the wounds with powder. "Sulphanilamide. Not quite as bad as it looked though bad enough. Thank you." She took the mug in one latex gloved hand, leaving smears of blood on the handle. "I haven't the time to shave the poor little blighter, but I've got the worst of the shot out and hope it will do the trick for the time being. I don't suppose you know who did this?"

"No." I shook my head and downed half of the tea in one gulp. It tasted awful.

"Well, Mr. White. Time will tell if we've saved his life. If you're a religious man I suggest you pray." I shook my head. "Then hope very hard. Either way, he's never going to be the same again. For starters, he's going to be blind in the one eye."

A police officer becomes desensitized to the many ways people die or are injured or mutilated; it's the only way to handle things like that. But hearing that about Pip, well, those words hit me very hard.

I froze up and heard my voice far away saying in some pretty foul language what I was going to do if they ever found out who had shot Pip. I must have been staggering around because I bumped my backside on the sink and the shock brought me out of it.

"I'm sorry." I said slowly. "Really, I'm very sorry, I don't usually run off at the mouth like that or in such colorful language." I must have been waving my tea mug around, too. It was empty and there was lot of tea-ish looking liquid on the floor.

Shirley shook her head as though she was accustomed to ranting pet owners. She said, "I want to take Pip back to the surgery, it adjoins my home and we can keep a proper eye on him—if that's all right, Mr. White. Let me have your home and office numbers, and I'll keep you abreast of events."

"Of course," I said. "I'm very grateful for your help." She was ready to leave soon afterwards. I carried Pip out swathed in towels in his basket and put it on the back seat of her Peugeot.

"Goodbye," she said.

"Goodbye—and thanks."

What a literally bloody evening! She left with Pip close to ten o'clock, and it was twenty minutes after that when I realized just how damned hungry I was. I put the chicken meal in the microwave, and it seemed inevitable that the phone would ring at that precise moment.

"Inspector." She didn't have to say who it was, but she did anyway. "This is Shelly Fearon."

"Yes, Shelly, what is it?" I might have sounded a little brusque, but there was no help for it.

"We have another strangling. Tadcaster, that's between Leeds and York, remember? It's a woman."

Almost gratefully I pushed—shoved—everything else to the back of my mind. "Give me the address, Shelly. I'll pick you up at your place."

"I'm already here boss, at the scene. Just arrived, two minutes ago." She gave the address.

"I'll be right there."

Her lips were blue; there was froth and blood around the mouth and nose. Her tongue protruded. I felt nauseous and if Shelly hadn't been there I'd have probably run to the bathroom and vomited, not that I had much in my stomach. Still, I could taste the bile at the back of my mouth.

"The pathologist?"

"On his way, Boss. The doctor's just left and our scene of crime officers should be with us any time."

"Anything been touched or moved?"

"You should know me better than that by now. None of us has touched anything. The boy, the woman's son, found her. He's a teenager, said he phoned the doctor as soon as he saw her color so I don't think he touched her either. Oh, he found that knife on the floor; it's his mother's and he just picked it up."

I moved carefully around the room, noting the position of the body, the clothes lying on the floor and stopped when I came to the knife resting on the bedside table.

"Has he been able to tell us anything? The son?"

Shelly shrugged. "Found her this afternoon when he came in from his newspaper round, after school. Apparently he comes in here about teatime, makes sure she's awake. Says she spends a lot of time in bed."

I grunted and bent down to look at the knife more closely. It was a kitchen knife, one of those that come in sets, pointed and damned sharp. There were prints all over it, smudged and bloody.

"Actually, Boss, I'm pretty sure he knows about his mum's—er—activities, though obviously he doesn't want to acknowledge them. When he says he makes sure she's awake, I assume it's to make sure she's all right. It's often a rough business."

"You can say that again, Shelly."

"The only other thing he told us was that her visitor was maybe Russian. He was shouting at her when he went out first thing. Nosteff. Know any Russian? Eastern European maybe. He went off to school when the bloke had gone. Do you think it's a name?"

I smiled a bit grimly and shook my head. "It's all I can do to remember how to speak English sometimes. No. I can't say I've heard the word, maybe we can try some dictionaries in the morning."

Footsteps sounded on the stairs. I looked up as a uniformed Sergeant knocked on the door.

"Stay outside would you, Sergeant? It's a small room and pretty crowded. I'm DI White, by the way, and this is DS Fearon."

"Sir. Sergeant Philips, Tadcaster Police. The doctor, er, Billings, called the desk about the, er…" He nodded to the corpse. "It was me on duty so I called your lot in because of the advisory."

"Advisory?" I was a bit vague, I'd just noticed the marks on the woman's throat, they were partly hidden by her chin. However, I could see there had been an unusual amount of pressure applied. "Sorry Sergeant. Something caught my eye. Advisory?"

"You wanted immediate notice on any violent deaths. Is this what you wanted?"

"Hardly wanted, Sergeant, though I know what you mean. And yes, I've a feeling this could be another one."

I wished I had had a laptop with me, with all the photos that had been scanned into the main database. Having them at my fingertips would have been useful. "I'll know better when I've checked the bruising against our records; from memory, I'd have said that the impressions were very like those we got off Varley, the Selby victim."

"That sounds like wishful thinking, sir."

I aimed the camera and took half a dozen Polaroid shots of the victim's head and shoulders. "I don't think so, Sergeant." I turned to Shelly. "Contact DC Scaines and tell him to prepare to bring his team here. I'm certain this is the work of the same person. If I'm wrong about the pattern of bruising I'll countermand the order but Tadcaster's on the river, the Wharfe, and it runs into the Ouse, doesn't it?" I turned back to Philips again. "How far's Selby from here, Sergeant?"

"Sixteen miles or so, by road that is. No idea how far by river, though."

"Hmm. Well we'll cover that shortly. Do you know this woman, Sergeant?"

"Maggy Ashton? Me and every other male in the town above sixteen and I think she showed some younger than that how it went too. Called herself a working mother, but you'd better be careful how you describe her if the papers want to know."

"How's that?"

"Tadcaster, families. Kick anyone tonight and the whole place is limping tomorrow."

"Hmm. I've known places like that. Can we get any more light in here? No?" Shelly silently offered me a small flashlight. "Thanks." I looked at Maggy's fingernails and received quite a surprise. I guess I had a few preconceived notions about cheap prostitutes. Her nails were beautifully manicured and painted with a pink pearly sort of polish; there were also generous scrapings of skin and blood. "Children?" I prompted.

Philips nodded. "Yes. Four. Chris who's the eldest, the one who called the doctor. Then there are two girls and the youngest who's a boy. I got one of the WPCs to take the three of them round to one of Maggy's sisters."

I saw Shelly's mouth tighten when she heard "WPC"—Woman Police Constable. Technically, we were all just police constables now, but some of the older folks couldn't or wouldn't give up the term.

I gave her what I hoped was a sympathetic grin and handed her the flashlight. "Thank you, Sergeant."

I straightened up. "Thanks for your efforts, Sergeant Philips. Our own scene of crime officers will be here shortly so we'd best move out of the way." We went out onto the landing, and I shut the door on the tragedy.

Outside, we said goodbye to Sergeant Philips and walked towards our cars.

"Things are heating up, Shelly. This time we're on the scene before the local police and I'm positive those prints match; I'm going back to the office now to check them. Don't forget to call Scaines, and we're going to need co-operation from Philips and his boys."

"See you tomorrow, Boss."

"See you. And thanks for the hustle. I'm pleased we were onto this so soon." I started to walk off and stopped, I had just had one of those thoughts. "Shelly."

"Sir?"

"*Nosteff.* Try *not Steph.* I talked with Sheriff Merrick in Florida this morning. Alan Cleghorn's wife is English and on holiday here in Yorkshire. Guess what her name was. No prizes."

"Steff?" She frowned. "Stephen… Stephanie?"

"Exactly. Think our murderer is after Cleghorn's wife as well?"

"Maybe though it doesn't make a lot of sense. *Not Stephanie.* That's a bit of a stretch or an inspired guess, Boss," she said doubtfully. "What could it mean?"

"No idea. I'll work on it." I turned away again. "See you in the morning."

The office was a better idea than going home, anyhow.

John Merrick was not known as an aggressive man, quite the reverse in fact, so when he slammed the receiver down with a bang, Bob Schwarz looked up in surprise. His boss was visibly shaking with anger.

"Nerve of the guy." John fumed. "Thinks I'm just some Florida cracker." He swung round to face Bob. "Said he'd see I'd lose my job if I didn't do like I was told. I'm a friggin' elected official, not some Washington toady."

"Who? The Brit?" Bob asked.

"No! Stewart White was all business, polite… No, that was some high mucky-muck ass—" Swearing, too, was not characteristic of the usually soft-spoken sheriff and Bob made sympathetic noises while John's fingers beat a staccato tattoo on his scarred desktop.

Who had made the call, he suddenly wondered. There'd been no name, no agency mentioned. *Couldn't have been the FBI,* he said to himself. John had had dealings with the Feds before, and they were never shy about saying who they were. Besides, this guy's voice was arrogance itself, arrogance mixed with contempt. He re-ran the terse conversation in his mind.

"Merrick?"

"Sheriff Merrick."

"Why in the hell are you asking about Robert Cleghorn?"

"Because it's my job."

"You keep your nose out of things that don't concern you, boy. And this don't concern you. Understand me?"

"Who is this?"

"That don't matter a lick . Just do as you're told or you'll be out of that Hicksville office of yours 'fore y'can say 'knife.'"

His caller hung up. Merrick immediately ran a search on the phone number: *"no information available"* flashed on his computer screen. *National Security?* he wondered and shook his head. He'd not dealt with them, but he doubted they were that different from the Feds. *So who would know I'd been running a computer search?*

At six-foot-six and three hundred pounds, Sheriff John Merrick was an imposing figure, and although he would be the last to realize it, that fact colored his thinking. Now the Sheriff was a real nice guy, no one would say otherwise, but people he met would automatically side step, look up at him, and tend to agree with him. It immunized him against threats. Threats only strengthened his resolve.

So maybe you've got some powerful friends. Well, so do I, shithead, so do I, and there's more than one way to skin a rabbit. He looked at the phone, picked it up. "Martha, can you get me... No, forget it, thanks." If you couldn't go in the front door, there was always another round the back.

I looked at the phone. Three days since I'd rung Dad, and with things heating up the way they were, it might be a lot longer if I didn't take this opportunity. Besides, Cleghorn was going to bring quite a bit of publicity down on us. I called.

"Sutton Coldfield 583..."

"It's me, Dad. Thought I'd better let you know that I'm investigating a murder, and you might see me in the media." There was a longish pause whilst the implications sank in.

"Can you handle it?" he asked.

Well, that was succinct, I thought. "Yes, I just didn't want you worrying if I get so tied up that I can't phone you for a few days, a week or so." I kept Pip's state of health to myself; no need for the both of us to worry about that.

"Fine, Son. I'm not going to worry now you've warned me. How're you getting on? People friendly, are they?"

I gave him a chuckle. "No knives, no arrows sticking out of my back yet. Yes, I'm fine thanks."

"You feeding yourself properly?" I could feel him frowning. "You used to forget to eat when you were busy."

No need to make conversation, I cut it short. "Sure I'm eating. Now I'm phoning from work so I've got to go. Say one for me next time you're kneeling down, will you?"

"Course I will, and don't let the sods grind you down."

"Not a chance, Dad. Bye."

Chapter 20

Robert Cleghorn pulled up a little ways down the road from Stephanie's place and examined the windows through a pair of binoculars. Dusk was fast approaching, and he waited to see behind which windows lights would come on. As he waited, he considered the day's events.

He had slept well the previous night and had not awakened until around ten o'clock. After breakfast, he had cleaned the apartment room by room until it gleamed like a new pin. Outside, he swept the dirt floor in the bomb shelter, cleared away the plastic bottles and the wrapping paper from the bread, and threw the old fruit nets over the bare floor. He considered going to check along the river bank but realized that a line of footsteps in the snow along the edge would draw attention. If the police came, they would find nothing.

Finally, he packed all of his new belongings into Tattoos's car and headed towards York. There was a McDonald's on the way. He stopped for fifteen minutes and ate a Quarter Pounder with Cheese washed down with hot coffee.

He went around York on the bypass and then north to the little village of Brideswell, where he had come that first day. He coasted to a stop at the point where he was standing.

He stiffened. Someone moved in the large room with the bay windows. Robert adjusted the glasses and steadied one elbow on the passenger seat. No, this wasn't Steph, this woman was taller, bigger. Not Stephanie's delicate figure and her hair was… mousy, he decided—and short. Stephanie's hair was long and dark.

How many people are there? Any men? A family? The house was big enough for a family. *Dogs? Were there any dogs?*

Robert had no idea why he was here. He ought to have called her first, he thought.

He had completely forgotten his abortive call the previous day.

Robert's memory was oddly disjointed. Some memories stayed, others went. Some might return days, months or even years later, others disappeared beyond recall. Some memories were present only as vague feelings: apprehension, ecstasy, compulsions, and others as vague, fragmented pictures. Sometimes he wondered why this was so; other times he assumed everyone lost a few memories as they got older.

All he had at the moment was a diffuse feeling that everything would be all right if only he could get to Stephanie and talk to her.

What could he do? Knock at the door and ask for her? He saw the cell phone poking out of his jacket pocket on the passenger seat. Call her, now? She'd come and talk to him, wouldn't she?

What if Stephanie wouldn't come out? Break in and confront her, perhaps. Robert knew he could do that even if it meant setting off an alarm. So what? He could carry her out of there and be off down the road in three minutes.

Surely she would come out of the place sometime.

Inside the house, Amanda had everything organized as her cousin came down the stairs, the ends of her hair a little damp. "Okay?" Amanda asked.

"Fine." Stephanie leaned over and planted a kiss on Amanda's cheek. "Thanks. Have you got a gun?"

"A gun? A shotgun. Paul used to blast away at the pigeons now and then."

"Can we take it? I'd feel a lot happier if it came with us."

"Hmm. Right. I think I know where it is."

Several bags sat next to the garage door along with two cardboard boxes of groceries. "These are the last. If you can chuck them in the car, I'll get the dogs. And the gun."

There were two dogs, a five-year-old Rhodesian Ridgeback and a German Shepherd with a floppy ear, three years old. She came back with them and Stephanie held the vehicle's rear door open to let them spring up and settle down in the back.

"There's the gun and a box of cartridges and that's it. What are you putting on? It's going to be chilly tonight."

Stephanie went back into the hallway and took a heavy topcoat with a hood off the pegs. "Think this'll do?"

"Just the job." Amanda already had on a puffer jacket and thick ski pants. She put out the main lights, leaving on the randomly switched lights which were controlled by the security system. "Let's go."

Stephanie climbed into the Discovery's passenger seat, and Amanda closed and locked the door through into the house. A radio control on the dash started the main garage door opening. She started up the big diesel and backed out.

Robert watched the garage door cantilever upward and the big silver-colored station wagon reverse out. The vehicle was filled with boxes and bags. *Off they go again,* he thought. *Why the hell can't they stay put?* The woman he had glimpsed earlier was driving and next to her was another figure. *Stephanie!* He grinned although it dropped a little when he saw the dogs peering out of the rear window.

He felt like jumping out and running across. He could have the door open and a stunned Stephanie out of there before the dogs could react, close the door and bring her back here! But it was too late. The car continued out into the road and started forward before his thought was finished.

Damn! He knew better. Act, don't think.

Robert started the engine of the Ford and followed the Discovery, keeping some distance behind.

The journey turned out to be interminable and boring. Miles and miles of narrow country road leading off into the gathering darkness. He could not risk letting them know they were being followed, and that meant driving with only the parking lights on and just close enough to keep the red tail lights in view. It was hazardous driving, and several times he had to wrench the little Ford back onto the highway when he felt the wheels hit the soft shoulder of the road.

Finally, hours later, the lights of a town appeared. He passed a road sign, *Pateley Bridge*, and then drove downhill towards the center.

Great! It was late; they'd have to stop here. He'd grab Stephanie the minute the car stopped. He jerked the wheel to the right. The roads were narrow and dangerous for someone used to driving on the other side of the road.

But the station wagon did not stop; it went through the town and over a river gleaming slick and black beneath the bridge.

Open country again and even narrower roads, something he would have thought impossible. *Passing place* he saw on a sign and then again. Not even room for two cars to pass each other except at special places. Robert shook his head and continued to drive. He had to turn on the headlights—there was no alternative—and he had to fall further back with just the odd glimpse of red lights to tell him they were still ahead.

Suddenly Robert realized the taillights had been gone for some minutes. He had lost them and it annoyed him. They must have turned off, but where? He backed the car along the faint ribbon of lighter black. A road: he turned up it and drove for a mile or so. Nothing ahead but blackness. He had lost her! Should he turn back here or go on a bit further?

"Damn it!"

Amanda pulled up at the barrier at the foot of Scar House reservoir. She opened the window and slotted a plastic card into the scanner at the side of the road. The barrier lifted and dropped again after they had gone through. "We'll be there soon, Steph. You're going to love this place, I just know it. Just wait until morning when you can see the view."

"Are there many houses up here?"

"A dozen or more in the next four, five miles, probably you won't see them. They're dotted about on the hillsides, and then there's the village though they're early sleepers up here, I'll tell you."

"What was the barrier for?"

"Keep out the undesirables." Amanda grinned and gunned the engine to take them up a steeper part of the road. "Public has to pay to come up here; it's a National Park. Owners—like us—have the cards to get through after five o'clock when the barriers lock. Discourages the vandals—and the courting couples, they have to go somewhere else to do whatever they do nowadays."

"Can't you remember? It's not that long ago."

Amanda chuckled, deep in her throat. "No, I suppose not. I don't suppose they've thought of anything new to do yet.

"Aha. Here we are. We'll have to remember to phone in a grocery order tomorrow. They deliver twice a week so it's not as uncivilized as you might think. There's a radio in the back and a portable TV, and we've got the cell phone. Pretty decadent, really."

They had turned into a fenced road, the lights illuminating the front of a large stone built house which seemed to back into the hillside behind it. The driveway was quite steep and led up to a double garage door just like the one back at Brideswell. Amanda pressed a button on the dashboard and the door opened. An interior light came on and the door rumbled closed. Stephanie realized she had been holding her breath and let it out in a long sigh. Now, she felt safe at last.

He must have driven twenty miles in three different directions before he gave up completely. Robert found what he thought to be a parking area and drove into it only to find it was the wide entrance to a farm.

"The hell with it," he muttered and pushed the shift into the top left corner. He drove slowly up onto the virgin snow to the right-hand side of the road and switched off the engine.

Despite his being a natural-born night person, he had no inclination to go tramping about the wintry landscape. He had no way of familiarizing himself with the territory. The dark would be his enemy rather than his friend in these circumstances.

He left the dash lights on so he could check the fuel gauge. Fresh snow began to fall and the needle showed less than a quarter of a tank full. The gauge was hardly a reliable guide, but he could not afford to take the chance that there was enough gas to run the engine throughout the night for warmth. He got out and went around the back and rummaged through the stuff in the trunk. He came back with the duvet—that and the parka he wore would keep out the worst. Besides, he could run the engine for short periods.

By adjusting the driver's seat to its rearward limit Robert managed a tolerably comfortable position. He got the duvet wrapped around him and turned off the lights, sleep claiming him within minutes.

He was in a white room with roller blinds at each of the windows. A large ceiling-mounted fan hung above him, motionless just now, white, like the walls and the ceiling and most of the cabinets around the side of his bed.

He occupied the bed. It was something he had only just become aware of and the enigmatic green traces on the screens of the bulky white equipment moved as he moved. When he breathed, a green line rose and fell, if he held his breath, it flat lined; on another, a green dot went bouncing mad, dancing in time to his raised heartbeat.

Robert dropped his head back to the pillow, willed himself to quiescence, concentrating on that green spot until it lay down and bumped rhythmically along the base line. He closed his eyes when the alarm sounded and grinned to himself as attendants, anonymous in glaringly white uniforms, came in to check the electrical connections and run diagnostic tests on the monitor.

His heartbeat rose a little but did not exceed thirty five beats a minute. They looked at him oddly and pulled up his left sleeve where a needle, strapped to his wrist, entered one of the veins in his arm. They changed the medication and injected some colorless liquid into the long flexible tube that fed him.

Robert's eyes closed, though he was conscious enough to hear what went on. The grin, welded to his lips, slackened a little.

"Evil-looking guy, isn't he? Lucky as hell, though. Look at this X-ray." Robert opened his eyes a sliver, though his eyelids looked shut tight; a useful trick. He saw latex-covered fingers tracing a branching pattern of fractures, like the dendritic structure of a river system. "You couldn't guess he walked a hundred miles in this condition and lived to tell the tale."

The voice, though high and light in tone, was male. The voice which replied was lower, richer though quite definitely female, East Coast. Not Boston. New York maybe.

"We have to operate though, and soon."

"Well," there was a note of uncertainty, "I'd rather not go in. If I drill here, look, and here it will relieve the pressure on the brain tissue. We have to wait; we can't do it until the swelling reduces."

"He could die before then."

"He could die on the operating table, especially if I open him up. Either way, I'd rather he died than ended up a vegetable."

"You'd better keep that sort of thinking to yourself, Berwick."

"You going to turn me in?"

"Who to? Colonel Rogers wants a hero. He'll be just as happy with a dead one as with a live one."

"That sounds awful."

"You getting all moral on me, sugarplum?"

"It's your grammar that's awful. 'To whom', not 'who to.'"

"Now she's an expert on grammar. Keep the drip going and inject morphine every hour on the hour. Don't loosen the restraints. I'll look in again this afternoon."

"You're the doctor."

Robert heard every word. His ears were working fine, it was just his mouth that wouldn't obey him when he attempted to speak, nor would his hands when he tried to wave. Tears eased out from under his eyelids for the next twenty-five minutes, he fell asleep again when they injected the morphine.

CHAPTER 21

I knew it was going to be one of those days as I headed for the office, but I didn't know why until the first telephone call.

"Inspector White?" It sounded like Flowers' voice, albeit bit formal.

"Yes."

"Superintendent Flowers here. Please come through to my office right away."

I quickly sorted through the papers on my desk and went. If the call wasn't sufficient warning, Joe Flowers's face was. Gone were the usual niceties, the buddy-buddy attitude.

"Shut the door, Inspector." There was no doubt who was the boss and who was the bossed—or that my honeymoon period had just come to an end.

I stood straight up, hands down my side and watched him, waiting to learn the reason for the abrupt change in attitude. There were several newspapers on his desk, and I guessed whatever had gone wrong was there in banner headlines.

"Seen the news, Inspector?"

I shook my head. "No, sir, I've not had time as yet."

Flowers snorted. "Serial killer on the loose in Yorks." He read the headline and pushed the *Sun* to one side. "Strangler claims second victim. Rather restrained for the *Mirror* don't you think?" He carried on, "Police have no answer to Yorkshire murders. He paused, then added "I think that was the local *Post*."

Flowers was looking up again. "My phone hasn't stopped ringing since I came in. Every hack in the UK wants to know what we're doing. I've had local councilors calling, two public safety groups wanting to know if there's a gender connection. Christ, White, why wasn't I briefed?"

Ah. There was the crux. All this sounding off because Flowers thought he'd been kept in the dark. I had come prepared of course; I opened the file and laid it in front of him. "The second strangulation was discovered last night. I don't even have any information from the labs yet. I have nothing except for these few Polaroid shots which I took myself." I spread the photos apart. "I've spoken to no one about it except to my sergeant and the forensic team. I borrowed some of the print records and did a computer check myself; that was two o'clock this morning, downstairs."

Flowers was a bit mollified. "Hmm. And what was the result?"

I pointed to a paragraph on the page long summary. "Positive. Subject to official confirmation, we're looking for the same man. However, the man we've been assuming was Cleghorn turns out to be someone else, someone who's assumed Cleghorn's identity. He's got to look like Cleghorn because he came into the country using Cleghorn's passport."

I rushed on while I had the floor. "I've no idea who went to the press, sir, but since the man on the passport is dead…"

"Dead?" Flowers checked the summary I'd given him.

"Well, we could get the press off our backs by letting them print the snap we have of Cleghorn. He isn't going to object."

"Fine, except the snap isn't the murderer. How do we explain that?"

"I don't know, sir. We can get the picture doctored, so it looks more like the description, but I wanted to ask your advice before we sent it out. Incidentally, the murderer is also being sought by the Florida police, quite a popular guy."

Joe Flowers let his breath out in a noisy rush and shook his head. "Quite," he said. "I already have the Old Man asking me why didn't I put a more experienced officer on the case. Suggested I should have taken personal charge of the investigation."

"Well, if that's what you want, sir…" Being fairly sure he didn't.

"Good God, no. Me? With two CDIs and four DIs to mollycoddle?"

"Well, I've got four DS's and thirty-odd DC's, sir." I smiled a little, sensing that the crisis was over. "And they're all working flat out. Look, suppose we ask the press to put these shots on the front page with a caption saying the police are seeking information regarding the man who has an American accent. It'll maybe jog someone's memory and without our actually saying he's the murderer."

"Well something along those lines." The Super frowned. "I'll get the legal department onto it first. Can't leave ourselves open to claims from his relatives."

"I'm sure you're right, sir. Anyway, I'm rather in the thick of it. Do you mind if I carry on?"

Flowers had already moved on. "What? Oh yes, get on and for God's sake, keep me informed."

Back at my desk, the mound of paperwork had grown. Most of it had to do with the murder case: reports from scene of crime, the fingerprints, forensics and the pathologist's report on the Selby corpse. There were also a couple of memos from Shelly and Alec Bell.

I started wading through them; it was tough going. Flowers was calmed down and the heat off for the moment, and my mind kept switching to Pip's condition. Eventually, I phoned the vet and her assistant told me he was still in the recovery room and would be there for at least another forty-eight hours.

At least he was still alive. Well I couldn't do anything more for him right now, back to work. I managed to get down to some solid work. Forensics had sorted out the fingerprints on the Avis hire car and had two unidentified prints on a piece of luggage. There were two blood types on the Selby body: Varley's, and one which didn't match the body. I sent off for DNA analysis and for what it was worth, I faxed copies of the two unknown prints to Sheriff Merrick.

The search crew who had been covering the riverbanks had so far come up with nothing and snow was now hampering their efforts while Varley's next-door neighbor had rung us to say he had not returned—we now knew why, of course. His car hadn't returned either, she remembered it as being a green Ford Fiesta.

Bits and bobs. Pieces of the puzzle that would eventually come together. I put my head in my hands and rested my elbows on the desk. I was rubbing my eyes when there was a cough from the direction of the office door. I looked up. Shelly Fearon stood there in a fur-trimmed brown coat which came to her ankles.

I smiled at her. "Hello, Sergeant. What's new?"

"I think we may have found where he's been staying, sir. In Tadcaster."

"Cleghorn—his double, I mean. Brilliant. Is he still there?"

She shook her head; a small smile came and went. "I don't think so, sir. One of the search team officers took a careful look through the windows, but we can't get in without doing some damage. We're maintaining a discreet watch."

"Well, it's better than nothing. How did we find it?"

"Tadcaster Police. They've been asking about strangers since the woman was discovered. Somebody had said the house had been let recently. One thing led to another and they found a local agent had let the place to an American with a three month lease. We're chasing up some keys."

"A red-headed American?"

"The very same. Also, sir, DC Cotes visited the man in hospital, the one with the fractured knee cap, um, Smith?"

I nodded.

"Said the picture was definitely the man who attacked him and the York landlady and her husband agree. His face was maybe a little thinner, had more hair."

"Time elapsed between when the photo was taken and now. Maybe hasn't had a haircut recently."

"But, sir, we know it cannot be the same man." Shelly was being firm with me.

"Right Shelly, so who is most like the suspect, other than the suspect himself?"

"I don't know. Maybe a twin?"

"Maybe so. Merrick didn't say anything about a twin and he didn't say anything about a brother, but either is a possibility, right?"

"Right."

"I want you to go out to Tadcaster, Shelly. Take charge of the teams out there and drive them a bit, see what you can come up with, eh? I think I'll speak to Flowers about handguns, if our redheaded friend returns; I don't want him getting near enough to try martial arts tactics on my officers. Oh, and by the way, remember Varley's car, it's a green Ford Fiesta, Cleghorn—or whoever—may be driving it."

When Shelly had gone, I sent another fax off to Merrick in Florida with the query about siblings and then went down to the incident room. I wrote "Sibling?" next to Cleghorn's photograph, and I was still updating the information on the wall boards when Alec Bell tracked me down.

"Guv, got a minute?"

"Certainly, Sergeant. Do we need to go back to the office?"

"I don't think so, sir. It's this troublemaker at the builder's premises."

"Troublemaker?" I had no idea what he was talking about.

"Yes, sir. Letters? Threatening letters? Thought you might like to see this. Usual sort of thing you see on the telly."

It was. Bell had put it into a clear plastic folder. The words had been made up from letters clipped from an assortment of magazines. It was short and to the point; perhaps the writer had got tired of cutting letters out.

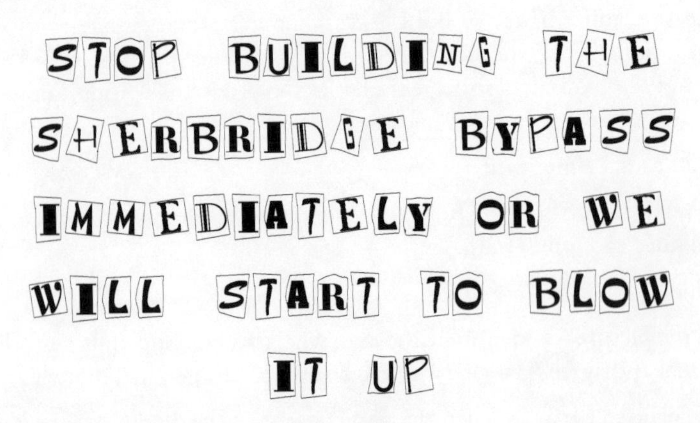
STOP BUILDING THE
SHERBRIDGE BYPASS
IMMEDIATELY OR WE
WILL START TO BLOW
IT UP

Ah, now I remembered the job I'd given Bell. "So now they're going start blowing things up? This was delivered to the contractors?"

He nodded. "Philibuild. The offices are in Wakefield. It came in the regular mail, a plain brown envelope which they unfortunately threw away before anyone realized what it said."

"What did they think it was? Junk mail?"

Bell shrugged. "Don't know, sir. The thing's been handled by several secretaries and the directors so finding prints is pretty remote."

"Try all the same. Get it down to forensics and if they do find anything, you'll need to take prints from everyone at this Phil… this place."

The look on Bell's face suggested I was telling Granny about sucking eggs. It might have deterred some but not me.

"Who were you talking to at Phil whatever it is?"

"Philibuild, sir. The managing director, Mark Adams. I told him he needed to take the letters seriously, and I asked him about his security arrangements. They have a contract with a small firm called Securix. A man patrols right through the night. I suggested he ought to start daytime patrols, too."

"Good. What did he say to that?"

"Not a lot. Talked about fixed price contracts and how the government should see to this sort of thing."

"Par for the course. Whereabouts is this bypass?"

"Sherbridge, sir."

"Yes, but I'm not a local lad. Where's that?"

"Between Selby and Goole. 'Bout forty miles."

I scratched my head and perched my bum on a table. "That note said *we*, I don't know whether it was in capitals or not but it did say we. At face value, it suggests an organization, a green one perhaps? Eco warriors and so on? Could just as well be a single weirdo, though, someone with a grudge."

I stood up again. "What's the time?"

"Two forty-five, sir."

"Not had any lunch yet. Thanks for the update Sergeant, keep on top of it, and if there's any direct contact, let me know immediately. We have to play for time of course and make sure they don't open any large brown envelopes until you or someone equally qualified is there."

The telephone rang; the switchboard had tracked me down too. It was the credit card people. I gave Bell the thumbs up and he went off about his business while I listened to the woman on the far end of the line telling me about Cleghorn's credit card usage.

"… several times throughout Leeds," she was saying. "That was…" she gave me times and dates. I thumped the table with frustration. He'd been here committing all sorts of felonies and we never knew. "Quite a small fortune," she finished off.

I got a sandwich and a mug of truly awful coffee while I sat in a corner and reviewed the day so far. I wasn't too happy. Flowers had shown me a side of himself I'd have preferred not to know about, and I resolved to make certain I did not see it too often.

Who had leaked the information to the press? As I returned to my office I had started to make a mental list of everyone who had known all the particulars. Actually, I needed copies of the papers involved.

"Oh sod it!"

There had been a pile of coins on the corner of my desk—five one pound coins. The desk sergeant had changed a fiver for me yesterday evening for the lottery fund, now there were only two.

CHAPTER 22

Robert Cleghorn's dream involved incessant pounding. There were baseball bats and bare knuckles and not quite understandable questions he was trying to answer. He was very relieved to wake and find someone knocking on the car window.

He was cold despite the fur-lined anorak and the duvet wrapped around him. The windows were covered in the delicate lacework of frosted breath. The beam of a flashlight played across the driver's door window as he looked for a button to lower it. Even when his numbed brain realized that the window had to be wound down by hand, it took some effort to break the seal of ice around the edge. He opened an inch wide slit at the top and the flashlight glared in, a pair of eyes appeared in the gap.

"What's the problem?" he asked. "Am I parked in someone's driveway?"

"Evening, sir," said the visitor. "Spot of bother?"

Spot of what? Robert wondered who he was speaking to and got the glass to move downward a little further. He could see now that it was a policeman.

"Ran out of gas, Officer."

"Gas? I'd have thought this car was a little old for that, sir."

Robert's mind was working better now; he tried to translate from American to British English. "Gas, Officer. Fuel? I'm waiting for a fuel station to open."

"Aha, petrol. You'll be waiting all night then. It's only a little after eleven o'clock. Nearest is back in the village, down there, but he won't open until nine in the morning. Not from round here then?"

"No, Officer. American. I'm a tourist." He remembered a sign he had seen as they went through Pateley Bridge. "Supposed to be going to Harrogate, guess I took a wrong turn back there somewhere. Stopped to look at a water wheel and maybe got turned around."

"Ah yes. That'll be that restaurant back in Pateley Bridge. What you should have done is turn right just there."

Robert sighed and gave his best befuddled tourist impression. "Well I realize that now. I thought I'd pick up another sign to put me right but the road seemed to get smaller and smaller."

"True enough, sir, and it doesn't go anywhere you want to go." He stood back and swept the flashlight along the side of the car. "Fiesta. Bit of an old car to go touring in, isn't it, sir?"

Robert answered smoothly, no hint of a pause. "Well, I'm not touring in it, officer. Belongs to a friend of mine, back in York. I borrowed it for the day while my rental car is in the shop."

"Pardon?"

Robert thought. "While my hire car is having a service."

"Right, sir. Got a name, this friend?"

He did pause a moment this time, trying to think of a British sounding name. "Brian Lewis."

"And an address?"

"1120 St. Mary's Drive." It was a street name near the pub he had bedded in but not breakfasted at.

There was a short silence. "No objection to me checking on that, sir?" asked the police officer.

"Of course not."

"I'll only be a minute or two, sir, and then I'll see if I can get some petrol for you." The policeman walked back behind the car and by craning his head out of the window, Robert saw the police car was backed up behind his own, effectively preventing him moving the Ford. He saw the interior light flick on as the driver's door was opened and go off as it closed. A second or two later it switched on again.

The American pushed the duvet aside and opened his door quietly. He slipped around the front of his car and down the left-hand side to where he could see the police officer talking into a radio handset.

He opened the door and reached in. The policeman put his hand out to pull the door shut again. Robert seized the extended wrist, pulled and slammed the door shut.

The policeman screamed as his arm broke. Robert pulled the door open once more and grabbed hold of the man's throat, the mists of anger turning from white to red in front of him as he squeezed. His victim's one good hand was futilely plucking at his fingers; Cleghorn ignored the feeble attempt. He could the feel the blood coursing through his veins; he felt cartilage collapse, felt the shuddering breaths that his fingers were slowly closing off. Cleghorn breathed deeply and evenly, his heart pulsed steadily at forty beats to the minute even when he lifted the body clear of the car and flung it to the ground.

As the policeman died, Robert Cleghorn had never felt so alive, so bursting with energy.

Later, when he came off his high, he dragged the corpse around to the back of the police car and bundled it into the trunk before starting it up, turning the headlights on and running it slowly down the hill, looking for access to the dense woodlands along the roadside. A minute or two later he saw a clearing leading into the trees and turned the car into it. The apparent lane between the trees narrowed and Robert eased carefully between the bushes.

"X159 this is Control. Over."

He looked at the dashboard, at a radio speaker from where the voice had come, just as the car struck a tree. It skewed round and came to a stop. The vehicle had been traveling very slowly and Robert suffered nothing more than surprise. The engine stalled and he could not get it started again so he switched off the lights and got out. It was not as far into the trees as he would have liked it to be, but even in daylight, he did not think it was visible from the road.

He walked back up to the Fiesta thinking of Stephanie and humming *C'mon over, baby* to himself.

It would probably never happen anywhere except in England. One to two inches of snow had fallen, followed by a hard frost which froze every molecule of water out of the air, coating every twig and blade of grass, every fence post and telephone wire with an icy mantle. Everybody's picturesque ideal of a winter's day—except Mother Nature's. *She* went about her business with silent disregard of picture postcard niceties. Within an hour a high pressure area had swept in from the Atlantic and raised the temperature by four or five degrees. Frost and snow melted within hours; only mud and slush remained.

Shelly Fearon was supervising the two crews at Hallgarth Apartments in Tadcaster. She inspected the bomb shelter in the garden with the aid of a small yet powerful halogen flashlight. The floor had obviously been swept beneath its covering of old nets; above, the corrugated metal of the roof gleamed dully in the light. The flashlight's beam swept from side to side, moved on and repeated the movement, after the central area had been covered. She brought the light back again—four metal hooks stood out in stark relief.

The roof material was galvanized and apart from an odd streak of corrosion was in good condition. The hooks, in contrast, were a reddish brown with rust except for two of them which showed the bright shiny metal of recent use.

Shelly nodded to herself when DC Scaines called to her from outside. She turned and went out, her colleague's face was grinning with excitement. "What's up?"

"There's a length of two by four here with blood on it and on the top of the bank, just beyond it, there are marks where something was dragged through the bushes. Some of the grass at the edge of the water has been broken away, too."

"Sounds pretty conclusive."

"Yeah. If the thaw hadn't come along this morning we might never have seen it; I guess this is where Varley got thrown in the river."

Shelly walked across the tussocky grass and looked at the bloodied piece of timber where it lay beside a low shrub with twigs broken along one side. "Let's hope its Varley and not someone else, too." She stooped and reached forward to pluck a few strands of fabric from the thin frost-blackened branches and dropped them into a plastic evidence bag.

She ordered photographs of the putative weapon, the scuff marks, and the bush with broken twigs before pulling her cell phone out of a pocket.

"Inspector White? DS Fearon. This is almost certainly where Cleghorn was staying, the estate agent recognized his picture, well, *our* reconstruction, but the place has been cleaned with meticulous care. There's an old air-raid shelter in the garden with hooks in the ceiling which have been used recently, and I've collected some fibers from a bush outside in the garden, in case they got blown away. I'll notify the scene of crime team to go over the place with a fine-tooth comb. What do you want me to do now?"

"Leave two officers there once the searches are over for covert surveillance. He might return there. Organize round the clock shifts although I think our bird has flown the coop. I guess you'd better come back here then."

"Right." She nodded to herself, agreeing with her boss about Cleghorn's departure. "Judging from the state he's left it in I think you're right."

"Well done, Shelly, you handled things well. Care to break the seal on a bottle tonight—over, um, a mousaka perhaps? With Pip being away, the place is a bit empty."

Shelly knew nothing about the dog's absence, though suggesting her company would be a good substitute did not do too much for her ego. Still, Stewart was probably trying to reassure her that no ulterior motives loomed, not that she believed him. He was a man, wasn't he? Though he did have a cheeky grin and now she came to think of it, a nice tight butt.

"So long as it's just a drink and a meal, Stewart, I'd love to share a mousaka. Don't forget I'm married."

Her boss ignored the cautioning note. "About eight? No need to dress for dinner." He broke the connection.

Shelly shook her head. "Pity," she said aloud, her features working with deeper emotion.

Chapter 23

In a small office somewhere in the CIA complex at Langley, Arthur McLeod watched several computer screens at once. It was not really necessary; any critical activity on them would be repeated on the large monitor directly in front of him. *Who will watch the watchers?* McLeod was one of those who did just that. Thousands of entries on the screens ranged in front of him were changed every day. The identity and location of every person making an amendment was logged along with the time of amendment, the same information was logged for inquiries.

It was rare for any one of those myriad accesses to cause an entry on the big screen in front of McLeod, though it did happen occasionally. It happened that afternoon just four minutes before he was due off-duty and the note displayed in the *action* column said to inform Hedges. McLeod did that.

"Mr. Hedges?" he said to the Deputy Director when he answered. "Arthur McLeod, Security Monitoring. We've got one of those alerts. Yes, sir."

Jack Hedges was in a meeting with Mason Kline, head of Section H. They had been discussing the on-going situation between North and South Korea when the telephone rang. Hedges picked it up.

"A four-two-niner?" He frowned, wrote down several points on his notepad, and put the receiver down. Then he cursed.

That was when Kline looked up. Hedges was biting his pen; it took a lot to surprise Hedges, now his eyebrows were all the way up his forehead. "Problem, Jack?" He kept his voice casual as though a curse from the coldest fish in Langley did not mean a whole pile of trouble.

Hedges murmured something and stared at Kline, his gray eyes looking right through Kline's to the back of his skull. "Recall Bob Cleghorn?"

"Cleghorn?" Kline chewed on his lip for a moment and poked the air with his pen. "The guy we recruited in Germany? After they sent him back from Saudi?"

"That's the one. Did some work in Czechoslovakia for us, went quite well until we had him go into Prague, to meet up with a courier and damn, did the shit hit the fan. *Jesus.*"

Kline shook his head. "And?"

"The courier turned out to be KGB. We think Cleghorn killed him," Hedges snapped his fingers, "just like that and two others before he got back to his pickup. No problem."

"So? What *was* the problem?"

"He was slightly injured. Our best guess was that he aggravated an earlier injury." Hedges rubbed the side of his head. "Brain damage perhaps. Went cuckoo. He had to be sedated and restrained, brought back Stateside and put into a secure facility. We kept him there, kept him under surveillance for a year or more in the hope that we could get him functioning and tell us what had happened."

"He didn't improve?"

"He became functional again, with the help of drugs to curb his violence, and a memory re-build to keep him stable, but he never got over the amnesia. He had to have constant medication once he was invalided back here and that was it."

"Until now?"

"Not exactly. The story goes on. I sent Eddie Kovaks out to see him. They'd worked together several times. Biggest mistake that *I've* ever made."

"Kovaks. Died of a brain tumor?"

"That's what it says in his file. He triggered something in Cleghorn, not what I'd hoped for however. Cleghorn snapped his neck and walked out of the facility as though it was a shopping mall."

Hedges stood up and went to a sideboard, poured himself a large single malt whiskey from a cut-glass decanter. "Been trying to find the guy ever since." He threw the drink back in one swallow and poured himself another. "Goddamn, that's better." He held the decanter up. "Mason?"

Kline shook his head. "So… what has happened now?"

"Someone has been asking questions about Cleghorn. That means he's surfaced again. The last time we had a lead on him was in Georgia, on a peach farm. We sent a team in to try and get him back into hospital; if he'd remembered anything, we didn't want him telling it to the world. Cleghorn sent two of *them* to hospital."

"Do we know who's been asking the questions?"

Hedges shook his head. "No."

The phone rang again. "This may tell—yes?" He put the receiver to his ear and moments later replaced it. "Yes, now we *do* know. Some two-bit sheriff in Florida." Hedges gestured with his drink at the paperwork spread out on the desk between them. "We'd better forget this for a while, Mason. I've got this persnickety old law enforcement officer who really needs wising up to the ways of the world."

CHAPTER 24

I reached home from the office about six-thirty, my earliest finish since taking on my new job. Cleghorn had been on my mind for days now. I had done everything I could and could only wait on the turn of events. Everybody who might need to contact me had my phone number and I could forget the business for an hour or two—provided I did something to fill the space in my brain.

Often, what I did at such times was cook. If I was pushed for time or too tired, I was perfectly happy with something from a shop freezer, but I did enjoy cooking, when I could devote the proper time to it. Tonight was going to be moussaka; I had gone out to get the ingredients I needed at four o'clock that afternoon, feeling like a naughty schoolboy playing hooky. The secret of this particular dish was quality minced lamb, freshly sliced eggplant and genuine feta cheese.

The centerpiece of my new kitchen was an Aga gas-fired boiler with its own oven. It heated the house and cooked food in its spare time, ideal. While it worked, I went for a soak in the bath with some aromatic oil.

Afterwards, I dressed in cavalry twill trousers and suede slip-ons. I pulled a green and gray striped shirt on as I went down the stairs. It felt a million times better than the blue suits with gray pinstripes that I mostly wore for work. It looked a lot better too, at least to my eyes it did.

A tantalizing aroma spread up the stairs from the kitchen as I went in from the hallway. *All I need*, I thought as I checked the bottles in the refrigerator door, *is the girl of my dreams and life would be great.*

I chose an Australian Chardonnay. Okay so white wasn't fashionable and Australian would probably make a purist weep, but I knew what I liked and I didn't think Shelly was likely to be a wine snob.

She arrived on the dot, another plus for this unattainable woman. I opened the door and gave her a big grin and a bow. "Welcome once more to my humble cottage."

Shelly smiled back and came in. "You're just showing off," she said as she slipped her sheepskin coat off. Underneath, she had on a smart trouser suit in damson plum with silver buttons at the throat and tailored pleats.

I guess I looked at her a bit too long. "Cat got your tongue?" she asked and I nodded as she went in to the kitchen. I hung her coat in the hall and followed after to find her looking at the dinner preparations.

"Is this a seduction attempt?" She gestured at the glittering cutlery and the napkins in silver rings, the ice bucket and the single candlestick.

"What? No, just for friends. The moussaka's got another ten minutes yet. Let's go through into the lounge and wait in comfort." I really did wish it was a seduction attempt, though. It had been years since I'd met anyone half as desirable as Shelly.

We sat either side of the coffee table, our armchairs more or less facing each other. There was one of those little pauses where no one wants to be the first to speak; I started the conversational ball rolling. "I know that working together isn't conducive to good relationships, and I'm sure you know I find you an attractive woman."

She angled her head to one side, acknowledging the fact. "You also know I'm married."

"I do. I've heard though—and believe me, I haven't been fishing for information—I've heard that you're separated from your husband."

"There are a lot of big mouths about."

"I have to agree," I shrugged, "I just wondered if you wanted to say anything about it. I'm a good listener unless this is a bad time."

"No. It's not a bad time." She looked me straight in the eyes, chewed her bottom lip for a moment or two. "My husband's a Catholic. Now, that's not important to me, although if he were to get to know what I'm going to tell you, he might think it is. What is important, really important, is that I'm four months pregnant. His child."

I was knocked sideways by the news for a few seconds, it was so unexpected. "And he doesn't know?"

There was a slow shaking of the head. "No, I don't really want him to—not for the reasons you might think, though. You see, Ian was the kind of man who would cause an argument to get his own way." She saw that she had lost me here. "Suppose he wanted new clothes, for example, and we couldn't really afford it; he'd deliberately start a row about it and end up storming out of the house and getting them, somehow it seemed to justify things for him."

"Hmm." Shelly was fond of clothes.

"I remember he wanted a set of golf clubs. Actually he'd already bought them when he started the argument although I didn't know it; he bought them instead of paying the council tax.

Shelly continued, "When he left to live in his new girlfriend's apartment, which he did after another row—it made it easier than just walking out—I didn't know I was pregnant. If I had told him when I did find out, it would've seemed as though I was trying to hold onto him. Do you know what I mean?"

I nodded. I could see how it could look that way.

"I'm not sure I want him back. I've enjoyed being my own master—mistress—for these last few months." She chuckled. "I kept the house and I had the mortgage rescheduled so I got a little money out of it. Really enjoyed spending it, too." She leaned forward, across the table. "Gave me some self-esteem back."

I grinned. She had got through the business remarkably well. I said something along those lines.

"Thanks, Stewart. Though you can see I'm not looking for a new relationship right now, can't you?"

"I guess."

"And I certainly wouldn't want to saddle someone with my problems."

I did understand and her news had made me re-examine my own feelings towards her. Even without the thought of the baby, did they run deep enough for something serious, or was I just looking for a pleasant diversion? I had no answer to that. Perhaps, being truthful with myself, I just wanted to get her into bed.

"Let's just say that you're a valued friend, then. And if you do need help later on, don't be afraid to ask." I changed the subject, afraid I had ruined the evening. "Glass of wine before we eat? I'm sure one small one will be fine."

Shelly nodded. When I brought the bottle and a pair of glasses in from the kitchen, I caught her dabbing the corners of her eyes. I pretended not to notice. By the time we started the main course, she was coming around again. I propped my chin up with my elbow, not very good table manners. "Seven years ago I was engaged to a girl."

"Engaged. I had you down as the keen but shallow type." She grinned to show that it was a joke. I hoped.

"From Stratford-upon-Avon. I loved her and thought she loved me." I made a face. "I think she spent more time with my mother than *I* did. We'd got a house picked out, deposit on it, all that sort of thing and then she went on holiday." I put a finger up when I saw Shelly about to interrupt. "I was studying, first round of police exams which would lead to promotion, couldn't spare the time."

"Aha. I can see what's coming."

"Yes, well she did seem a bit different when she got back, I thought it was just my imagination. A fortnight away, first time we'd been apart for such a long time. She broke the engagement off six or seven weeks later. Went to Canada, already had a new boyfriend. It was quite some time after that when I heard from her parents—well, her mother told mine—she was pregnant."

Shelly showed both concern and puzzlement.

"You see, Shelly, her leaving was a big enough blow but I never knew, won't ever know, if it was my baby she was carrying."

"It could just as easily have been her new lover's."

"Could well be but think what it would be like to bump into a junior carbon copy of yourself sometime in the future. Would I blame me for not trying to find out or her for not telling me?"

She turned her head and looked at me sideways. "One, you're assuming that your children will be carbon copies of yourself. And two, you're telling me that I ought to let him know anyway."

She was right about the first thing and I winced. "Okay, but just another point of view. If you did tell him and he has no intention of coming back to you then at least, he can't say that he never knew. He can't throw that at you, can he?"

"I'll think about it, Stewart. Thanks for telling me."

We might have talked more about our lives if the telephone hadn't rung at that moment. I got a tingle in my hand as I reached out to lift it off the cradle. "I think this is important."

"Hello, Stewart White here."

"Hi, Stewart. John Merrick. Had to call about those fingerprints you sent me. Boy, did *they* open up a can of worms over here."

There was an expectant pause. "How's that, John?"

"I could get myself into a heap of trouble by telling you, but I'm damned if I do and damned if I don't. And hell, we're policemen, not civil servants. Seems you were right when you said maybe there was a sibling. Robert Cleghorn, brother of our corpse over here. He's the one that owns those prints and he's one helluva bad boy. From what I can make out, he served with our Green Berets, you know—Special Forces guys? They want him worse than you and me."

I snorted into the phone. "Well—" I thought fast. "Well, John. It seems to me he's on my patch, so he's mine to take. Can you send me a photograph and, er… are you in a position to send me his service history?"

"Not a chance. They gave me the basics, verbally, that's it. Let me warn you, those guys are going to be banging on a lot of doors in the next few days. They'll want to come after Bad Bob themselves. I've got a trick or two up my sleeve, but don't hold your breath, I'll let you know what I find out.

I wasn't certain they would be able to bang on any doors in the UK—not legally, anyway. "Well thanks for taking the time to let me know, John. I appreciate it: I'll keep you up to date on developments. Oh, and by the way, you ever come over here, look me up. I owe you a few beers."

John laughed and said, "Sure thing," and hung up.

"Sheriff Merrick." I said, looking across at Shelly.

"As if I couldn't guess."

"Our killer is Robert Cleghorn, brother of Alan, who we've been chasing."

"Bad Bob. I could hear your Sheriff Merrick from here."

"The very one."

"A twin?"

"No, but the family resemblance must be a strong one. I don't know how much you could overhear..." I gave her a digest of what John Merrick had said.

"So what do we do now?"

"Back to basics, Shelly. We've got a name, a good enough picture and maybe the color and make of the car he's driving. If he uses one of his brother's credit cards again we shall be on his tail, we know what he was up to yesterday morning. What we don't know is why he's here. I've got one or two ideas to do with that. Need to do some thinking."

Shelly chose to interpret that as an invitation to go. I looked horrified and made her stay for coffee. At the offer of a second cup, she looked at her watch. "No, thanks anyway. It's been a lovely meal and a nice firm shoulder to cry on."

"Hell, Shelly, you're my friend. Don't forget it."

I got her coat and put it around her shoulders. "Cold out there, watch out in case there's ice."

"My place next time, okay? I'll think up something really different. Hey by the way, where's Pip?"

"He's been shot, shotgun, and he's been rather poorly. The vet's still looking after him at the moment."

Shelly must have read something of my pain in my expression. She squeezed my hand and brushed her lips across my cheek. "Just good friends, don't forget."

I went to bed; the dishes could wait until tomorrow. I didn't get to sleep all that soon either, thinking about both of my friends.

CHAPTER 25

Robert spent the night ten miles from the hidden police car with its gruesome cargo. Here, high up on the moors, it was still freezing, the snow three to four inches deep with a thin hard crust on the surface. He had risked running out of gas by running the engine off and on through the remainder of the night to combat the cold. Even so and in spite of being wrapped in the duvet and several layers of clothing, he was cold and slept only fitfully.

At seven o'clock he was feeling hunger pangs. He shoved his bedding into the back seat, made a careful three-point turn, and headed back to Pateley Bridge.

He found a small parking lot next to the river which tumbled along its course looking dark and cold. It was empty. He pulled in and walked along to the start of the main street looking for a café. He passed a newspaper stand, where a rack of papers hung in the doorway. The *Sun*, its headlines big and black, shouted at him: MURDERER!

A picture of his brother looked out at him. Robert pulled the hood of his anorak up. Was the new hair color enough to disguise him? He felt for change in his pocket. Damn, he had to go inside the shop to buy the paper.

The woman who served him wasn't interested in what he looked like; she had one hand wrapped around a big cup of coffee—no, it was tea—and was sorting papers into piles. He purchased some candy bars and a paper, leaving the shop as quickly as he could.

Outside, after the bright light over the shop's counter, it seemed barely light enough to read. He nibbled at a candy bar and considered his options for breakfast. He would find a café or a convenience store, eat fast, and get away as quickly as possible.

He turned around, looking up and down the street. It was virtually deserted, but the lights of a butcher's window caught his attention. The display was full of unfamiliar cuts of meat, though there was a sign advertising fresh pork or beef sandwiches. Robert entered the place and ordered one of each; they were made from big flat cakes of bread sliced in two. He bought a game pie too because he liked the look of it; it was quite substantial, and the butcher explained that is was made of various seasonal meats.

Back in the car, he switched on the tiny interior light and sank his teeth into the mouth-watering pie as he read the newspaper. He tried not to look at Alan's picture, which disturbed him.

> At a press conference called late last night by Inspector Stewart White of the Ridings Regional Crime Squad, reports of a dual murder in Yorkshire were confirmed. The man allegedly responsible is an American tourist named by the police as Robert Cleghorn.
>
> The body of the first victim was found strangled and floating in the river near Ousebank at Selby in North Yorkshire. The body was identified as that of James Varley, a local laborer. The second victim was Margaret Ashton, a woman of thirty-nine and mother of four children. She was found strangled in her bed at William Street, Tadcaster in North Yorkshire.
>
> Police believe Cleghorn is driving a green Ford Fiesta. Cleghorn is in his thirties, has red hair, and was a member of an American Special Services unit. He is powerful, possibly armed, and unpredictable. If recognized, the public is advised *not to have a go.*

Robert chuckled at the last sentence. Was "not have a go" a terribly polite British way of saying "armed and dangerous"? However, there was no mention of the policeman who had obstructed him the previous night, so at least *that* remained hidden. How had he been identified, though? Were British police more clever than their American counterparts? It hardly seemed likely, but the fact remained that they knew a lot about him, even to the type of car he was using. Robert knew he had to do something about it; but he had to consider his options carefully.

In the meantime, he filled the tank with gas at a station on the edge of the town and retraced his journey back up to the area where he had lost Stephanie the day before. With the benefit of daylight, Robert expected to pick up something—a crossroads or a driveway, perhaps—that he had missed the night before.

The turn up to the moors that he had taken the previous evening (which had led to the scene of the policeman's killing) passed by on his right hand. The next turn onwards was barred by a white drop-down barrier. A sign at its center point read: *Scar House Reservoir, National Park Land.*

Underneath, in smaller letter it said, *admission—50 pence.* Robert recalled the barrier although the sign had been invisible in the dark. Fifty pence—that was one of those fancy large, seven-sided coins. He fed the meter on the right-hand side of the gate, it rose and he gunned the little car through.

It was a dirt road. Ruts from previous traffic were frozen into its surface and threatened to take over the steering unless he took it slow and careful. Speed didn't matter this morning. He took the time to study the few properties on either side of him. Several appeared to almost merge with the stony hillsides and, judging by the tractors and agricultural machinery dotted about, nearly all were farms.

Four miles further on and right at the head of the valley, he reached the reservoir and the dam which held the waters back. He had seen only one house that didn't look like part of a farm.

He locked the car and left it on the car park near the dam. Walking up towards the water, he found a spot which commanded a view over the entire valley. He took out the binoculars and scanned the bleak landscape slowly, examining every inch of the hillsides from timberline on one side to timberline on the other. A week before, the freezing temperatures would have left him feeling nauseous, but he was more acclimated now and ignored the discomfort. He spent twenty minutes steadily checking each habitation and rejecting each one until finally, he recognized something.

A big-boned woman shoveled snow off a steeply inclined driveway, her movements vigorous and her breath showed as great clouds of white mist. The last time he had seen her, she had been driving the big Discovery wagon and he guessed the vehicle was behind the garage doors at the top of the drive.

The woman straightened up and began sprinkling powder from a big square box; salt, guessed Robert. He wondered how to get there because he could clearly see the stream from the dam leaping down the valley between himself and the house.

Never mind, there would be some way across it. He sang the words to *C'mon Over, Baby* all the way back to the car.

Tonight he was going to see Stephanie. Hell, everything was going to be great.

An overnight frost had turned last night's wet side roads into skid pads. Driving required an extra bit of attention, and I was late getting to the vet.

Nonetheless, it was obvious that I was too early for normal visiting hours. I persisted with the bell and, on the third ring, Shirley Kelly opened the door. I raised my hands in mock fend-off. "Look, I do apologize for such an early call. I've been horribly busy, but I just had to hear how Pip was before I went in today."

Shirley beckoned me in with the slice of toast. "Come on in—Detective White—isn't it? Let me put the wood back in the doorway, we're letting all the heat out." She accompanied the words with a nice smile which had me hooked like a pike on a lure.

"I've just been reading about the murders your office has been working on in the *Guardian*. Dreadful business, isn't it?"

"Horrid. The papers pounced on it—I didn't send the press release out until almost midnight—and it seems to be in all the papers this morning."

The door opened into a large hall with a staircase off to the right. A second woman came down the steps as Shirley closed the door. "Who was it?" she asked of Shirley. "Oh, sorry, didn't realize you were still here." She was slim and dark haired, wearing a dressing gown over pajamas.

I gave her a grin for good measure. "Stewart White, sorry for the timing. I just wanted to know about my dog."

"It's okay, dear. You remember the policeman I mentioned? I'll take him through to the surgery."

"Of course. That poor little dog. I'll get on with the breakfast. Oh, you've started without me."

"Only a piece of toast. This way, Inspector." I intercepted a glance between them which spoke volumes. *Hell's bells*, I thought as I looked away, *these two women are an item. I sure can pick 'em.*

Shirley led me along a passage and through a door beyond into a clinically white surgery. There was an operating table just off-center with overhead lights; I saw an X-ray machine and various other pieces of equipment. We went through the surgery to a second room where there were cubicles—obviously for pets recovering from treatment.

And there was Pip. I forgot women and murderers immediately. He was lying on his side, dressings around his chest and something was not quite right with his leg.

Shirley was there before me, peeling back the lid of an eye and examining the pupil, feeling his pulse before she turned to me. "Let me give you the good news first, Mr. White. Pip has had a blood transfusion to make up what he lost and he is responding well. The bad news..." she looked at me intently, "is that he's lost the sight of one eye and I had to amputate his left foreleg."

"Christ!" Nothing else came out, I can usually keep all my worst swearing inside my skull, this time I only just managed it.

Shirley went on. "He'll adjust to things very quickly, far faster than we humans. Don't worry, he'll get used to running on three legs and by tomorrow or the day after, you can take him home."

"Fu... Bloody Richards," I muttered.

"Sorry?"

I shook my head. "It's me who should be sorry. *Richards.* Someone I put away a few years ago. He swore he'd give me nightmares every night: get his revenge. I suspect he just got out of jail."

"My God." Shirley's hand trembled on the metal surface. "And he's used a poor little animal to get back at you?" She pulled a stool round and sat down heavily. "I've seen pets abused before but it's still difficult..."

I nodded. "Pets and people. Even in *my* job, you never really get used to it."

"Let's be thankful Pip's still alive then."

I nodded, too many emotions to speak for a moment. "Thanks anyway," I said gruffly, at last. "I'm very grateful for what you've done for him, for us." I turned to go; I just had to get outside.

"My pleasure," she said.

Out on the road, I sat in the BMW for a few minutes. Was having Pip alive like this better than having him dead? Was that just me being selfish? I'd just have to live with it for a while, see if the little fellow could really enjoy his life again.

I thrust Pip from my mind as far as I could and started the engine. I thought of how I'd almost propositioned Shirley Kelly, blushed, then got myself smirking.

Another note was stuck to my blotter when I arrived at the office. It was from Joe Flowers: *Report to my office, Nine a.m.* and signed with his initials. That brought me back to reality, accompanied by a strong feeling of *déjà vu*.

I had twenty minutes. I filled in with some paperwork until at eight forty-five, Shelly put her head around the door.

"Got my car back again and none the worse for wear. Uniform boys found it parked in the Cottage Road car park, by the old cinema."

"Well that's the best bit of news I've had today." I gave her a genuine grin. "See you later." I made a face. "Chief wants to see me at nine and I've a nasty feeling about it. Can you make sure all the reports are in from the team? Check for anything startling?"

"Can do." And she vanished.

Joe Flowers called me in when I knocked; he didn't invite me to sit. Instead, he stood up himself and, turning his back on me, looked out of the window. I could see concern in the stoop of his shoulders before he spoke. "What stage are you at with this Cleghorn matter?" He still didn't turn.

What sort of question is that? He had my reports; I could see last night's on his desk. "We have him down for four murders, sir. We know who he is; what sort of car he's driving." That was pushing it a little but I was past caring. "The only thing we don't know is *where* he is."

"And what are you doing about that?" His tone was pretty terse, and I was more than a little pegged off at his attitude.

"Every police force in the county has the details. You gave me permission to release the information to the press, which I've done. There's nothing else to do other than wait for leads." I suppose it did sound a little weak.

"Wait? Wait for leads? Another murder, I suppose you mean. The switchboard's still snowed under with calls and I got two calls at home from the Old Man wanting to know what I'm doing about it and now... what's all this in the papers this morning?"

Flowers fell silent and breathed deeply. At length, he continued. "He wants me to give the investigation to a senior officer, Stewart. How would that make me look? Huh? He's questioning my judgment in letting you continue with the case. *Too far, too fast were his words*—meaning you. What do you say to that?"

I sat down without being asked and tried to collect my thoughts. Pip. The Old M... Chief Superintendent Grimes, Flowers. What was real? What was important?

I retorted, "Too far too fast? What I say to that, sir, is this: the man obviously opposed my appointment and was outvoted. Now he's being over-critical about my efforts. There was nothing wrong with the way I handled the immigrant-smuggling case, was there? Because that was a success, but now, suddenly, I can't do the job."

I sighed deeply. "Let's say that you hand this inquiry over to someone else. What happens? They get a lucky break and the Old Man is vindicated, I'm rubbish and your judgment is poor. Or, they're as stuck with events as I am—more so because I've still got some ideas to look at. I'm still rubbish, your judgment hasn't improved and... we're damned if we do and damned if we don't."

"What's that?"

"Doesn't matter what we do, we're wrong and the Chief Superintendent will continue to blow smoke and fire."

I was out of breath and more than a little worried about shooting my mouth off like that. I sat staring at the carpet.

Flowers said nothing for almost a minute. "What will you do next, Stewart?"

I took the cue and replied as though I hadn't just shot my mouth off. "The man's a nut case, Joe. He doesn't fill any known pattern as far as I can see and therefore, he's unpredictable. I thought his violence was retaliation at first but Maggy Ashton doesn't fit. He killed her; his blood was there but there was no semen, no sign of attempted intercourse with or without consent. Now that's odd, considering she was a known prostitute." I was warming up now, not telling him what we were going to do next because I didn't know then. I was working up to it.

"Originally I didn't consider doing a psychological profile on Cleghorn even though I'd done quite a lot of that sort of thing at Birmingham. Well, it was an oversight, I admit it; we did think we knew who the man was, just seemed a matter of time before we picked him up. Now although we know who he is, we don't know what sort of person he is—the Florida police don't either. We don't know how he thinks or what he thinks. Ever had a rabbit in your headlights at night?"

Flowers nodded ever so slightly. "Can't tell which way he'll jump." Then he paused before continuing. "Next, Stewart. What do we do next?" He was back with the *we*, at least. "You see, there's something else that's got the Old Man wound up. Budgets."

I scratched my head. "Budgets? We're spending too much?"

"Let's just say he's not happy. He's also facing demands from Max Chesterman that the county should be guarding building sites against bomb attacks."

"Max Chesterman?"

"M.P. for the Sherbridge area."

"Ah. I'd heard the Philibuild director had said something like that."

"Well apparently he also said it to Chesterman who said it to Grimes who then asked who was dealing with it."

"Yes?"

"I had to tell him you'd put Sergeant Bell in charge."

I felt deflated. I'd got him looking reasonably at the Cleghorn affair and now he had brought this up. "I don't think that's fair," I said. Actually, I probably raised my voice a bit. "I said we had to take a softly, softly approach to this one and it *is* the only safe way. Bell quite rightly suggested that Adams—he's the MD at Philibuild—get some extra security in and he grumbled at the cost. Now Sergeant Bell is not one to leap to conclusions, he's steady and he's painstaking and…"

"And you thought he would stay out of your hair if you gave him this case."

That stung because it came close to the truth. "And he's the best for the job," I insisted.

"Okay." Flowers turned around, walked to his desk and sat down. He crossed his arms, a sign of tension although he seemed to have it under control. "Look. I stood in our corner and, as a matter of fact, I did refuse to hand the Cleghorn thing to someone else without talking to you about it. I don't care about the builder's thing—blowing up the new road. Bell *is* good at that sort of thing, I'm glad you've seen that even if you don't like him."

"I never said…"

"Oh, c'mon! *Nobody* likes him. Carry on with the murders, but for God's sake, Stewart, give me something I can throw to the Old Man, some tasty morsel."

And I did have something. The knowledge had been growing all the time I had been going over things with him earlier. "What's he here for?"

"Sorry?"

"What is Robert Cleghorn over here for? He murders his brother back in Florida, his brother was planning to come over here to holiday with his wife. The Florida police told us all that. Why did Robert kill him and assume his identity? Maybe because he'd been having an affair with his sister-in-law, this Stephanie. He kills the husband and joins her in his place."

"And the murders over here?"

"Circumstances to start with. The muggers picked the wrong man for a victim. Later on, something went wrong. He wouldn't have leased the apartment in Tadcaster if he'd been planning on killing off all and sundry. Maybe..." I paused, this was pure guess work, so what, it was only for Grimes's ear, I wasn't going to present it as a usable theory. "Maybe he's already seen Stephanie and they had a row, she blew him out, sent him a little crazy. He's got a volatile personality, there's no denying that. We've got to find this Stephanie."

"So? Do it."

"She married an American and we don't have a maiden name for her. I've had Sheriff Merrick look into it, though for reasons known only to the American bureaucracy, they can't or won't let us have any information."

"I thought she was called Yates from an earlier marriage. Didn't I see that in your reports?"

Bless him, the old bugger read them properly after all.

"That's right. Married to an American Major stationed near Harrogate."

Flowers nodded. "Menwith Hill. Practically my back garden. There's no church there. Not on the installation."

I considered what he had said for several long seconds before it clicked. I clapped my hand to my forehead. "So they married in a nearby local church or at a registry office."

"That's right."

"There'll be a record of the marriage with her maiden name. We can trace her family, former addresses and so on." I stood up. "Will that get the Old Man off our backs?"

Flowers grinned. "Go, catch, and skin him, Stewart."

Round one to me, round two to Flowers, I thought on my way back. I had given cause for concern, and there had been a couple of loose ends which I had not seen tied up.

I was trotting along the corridor making mental checklists when on impulse, I turned the other way and went down to the next floor, to the switchboard.

"Julie, who was on duty overnight?"

"Christine was here until six. I've been here since then."

"Do you know if she had a lot of calls about our murder case? Have you?"

Julie pouted her lips and scrolled the log down the screen. She pointed. "Midnight, there was one just before one o'clock. That was Chief Inpector Superintendant Grimes calling to see if Flowers was still here."

"Oh dear. I was here at the time, not that it would have altered anything."

"That's all until three though. Just routine calls to the desk sergeant. A few more between four and six. Quiet night."

"What about you? Taken anything to do with the Cleghorn case?"

"Had a *Yorkshire Post* reporter on at eight o'clock this morning, wanted to know if there was anything new come up. That's all."

"Thanks, Julie."

Flowers had just worked himself up over nothing or, more likely, it had been an act to get me worked up, to get me to concentrate. Crafty bugger. Crafty dangerous bugger to have as a boss.

CHAPTER 26

Robert knew his memory played tricks on him. He knew, too, that many of his dreams were memories he couldn't grab any other way. He was fully awake now and there had never before been a time when he had had a dream-memory while he was awake. A few seconds lapse maybe but not like this; this one had been a whole new experience for him. He had been sitting in the Fiesta, looking out over the wide expanse of water and waiting for darkness to fall. Reeds and small bushes were reflected with mirror like clarity in the still surface, a flight of water fowl arrowed down, their feet reaching for the water...

The picture was a restful one, on the wall facing him. Reeds, a broken fence, a small rowboat reflected in the calm waters of the lake. Three Canada geese were caught in the act of alighting, their wings spread to cup the air, legs extended.

It was a vision from an earlier time, probably ten years since, but it was so vivid he felt he could touch it.

It was his room at the facility, His room was neatly furnished: a bed, a night stand, a reclining chair with a TV and on a low stand, a VCR. The television was switched on and Robert was watching *Great Balls of Fire*, his favorite film—Jerry Lee Lewis's life story. It had reached the part where Dennis Quaid, as Jerry, had married his thirteen-year-old cousin. The action had slowed, the sound was low and Robert heard the door behind him being unlocked. He turned in time to watch the white coated male nurse enter; he was followed by Vinny "Crispy-both-sides" Keoghan.

"Got some company for you, Bob," said the nurse.

"Vinny?"

Vinny, a tall, well-muscled figure with a deeply cleft chin and eyes that never stayed still, came forward, his hand extended. "Robert. Hey, how're the bugs bitin'?"

Robert came to his feet and grasped the other's hand and said anyplace they wanted to because it was great to see his old army buddy. They stood for a moment, hands locked tight, looking each other up and down. Vinny and Robert had trained together, fought together, whored together; they had been inseparable up to the time the Army split them up into active teams.

They didn't notice that the nurse had left. Robert sat down again and Vinny sprawled on the bed. "Heck, still watching that old has-been?"

Robert nodded. "Picked up the habit from my Pa. Never get sick of old Jerry Lee. If I'd been born a bit earlier, I'd have gone to all his live shows, been there to see him at his best."

Vinny nodded, his gaze dancing around the room. "How's the old brain cage, Rob?"

Robert put a hand to the dressing over the shaven part of his skull. "Uh, don't call me *Rob*, okay?"

"Heck, Robert," Vinny said, quick on the uptake. "I didn't mean nothin'. Slip of the tongue, okay?"

"It's okay. You know what these doctors are like. One says one thing, another says something else."

Vinny remembered Robert's quick temper and carefully chose his words. "Sure do, got the same run around myself when I took some shrapnel in the chest." He thumped his ribcage. "They couldn't make up their minds about anything. You know when you're gettin' out?"

Robert shrugged. "Not yet. Why? Got a project?"

Vinny grinned, revealing teeth like a set of white tombstones, a toothpaste commercial ideal. "Sure do, feller. I'm here to make you an offer. How'ja feel about swatting flies down on a dirt farm?"

"Doesn't sound like much."

"Oh, I don't know. If y' look at it right, it's got its good points. Pay's good, locations vary and y'get the chance to rub out some prize scumballs."

"Sounds better than when you started. You signed on with the Mafia?"

Vinny shook his head and grinned. "Nah. Better than that. Our employer's kinda bigger than that and a helluva lot more powerful."

"The Army then? I just got out of that outfit."

"Come on, think. I resigned my commission to join up with the CIA, my friend."

Robert was surprised though not shocked. He had not thought too much about the future, the organization's low-key recruiting tended to go over his head. But now the idea was planted, well, it seemed logical. Both Vinny and he were the best at what they'd been trained to do—it made sense.

"I still don't know how long before I get out of this place. Are they likely to wait?"

"Damn right. You agree to sign on, they'll send their own specialists in to examine you. Run rings around this pussyfooting lot." Vinny hooked a thumb in the direction of the door. "Get you outa this bug palace and into somewhere a lot smoother and cooler. What you say?"

Robert nodded. "Yeah."

The birds hit the water, ruining the mirror effect and the sound of the multiple splash-down brought him out of the reverie. *The CIA. Forgotten that till now. Did I work for them?* Robert shook his head. *Can't remember.* He may have speculated about it before. If so, that memory too had gone. He did wonder why there were so many gaps in his memory, and knew enough about his profession to know that memories could be erased. It was harder to erase the memory of the memory.

Snow was beginning to fall again, obscuring the lake. It was heavier than before, the flakes bigger than quarters and sticking to the windshield. Robert decided to move now rather than later. Even though there was still light, he could have trouble in getting down the hill. He had been there for several hours without seeing anyone; Scar House Reservoir obviously attracted very few visitors in winter.

He followed the ruts back down the valley, keeping the speed down, staying in low gear. The turn-off came up, the one he had reconnoitered, the one which led up to the place where Stephanie was staying.

A police helicopter churned across the moors, its passenger looking for signs of the missing policeman, P.C. Harrison, or his car. Below, the snow covered everything in a uniform white blanket. It had drifted into long hillocks, shaped by the wind into weird and wonderful configurations which hid the roads and farm tracks; details were hard to make out. Passenger and pilot scanned the ground.

"Helluva place for a breakdown, Jack."

"Or worse. Been over twenty-four hours since he last contacted Control. I reckon he's had a crash, and I don't give good odds on us finding him."

Harrison's control at Harrogate had waited several hours before raising the alarm. Radio and cell phone reception was spotty on the moors and he frequently had to wait until he was in town to call in. When he didn't report in, they sent out two cars to follow his route. By then, much of the outlying roads were impassable. Later, when they sent a four by four, the conditions had deteriorated enough to make even this foolhardy. A helicopter was ordered as soon as the weather cleared and the light was strong enough to make the search worthwhile.

"The light will be going in another hour; it's almost three now."

"The fuel will be going sooner," said Jack Skunlow, the pilot. "Reckon I can stay up here another thirty minutes and then it's back to base."

They passed over several farms. "Plenty of vehicles down there, Barry. Suppose he's found shelter at a farm and the line's down? He'd be stuck there till this lot thaws."

"It's the best we can hope for at the moment; don't see any police cars though."

"Well they're white, aren't they?"

"With a great big number painted on the roof."

"Under cover then. Christ, there's more of this stuff coming down. Much thicker and we'll have to go, Barry."

"Yeah. What's that? Get down lower, so we can see under those fir trees. Look. That a car?"

Jack brought the 'copter down and branches thrashed, dumping clouds of snow into the dark recesses of the woodland. "Could be. Wait for the snow to settle."

"It is," shouted Barry, thumping the edge of his seat. "Looks as though it's crashed to me."

"Sure?"

"Certain. Coat of arms on the door, it's all tilted over, slipped into a ditch or something. Can you get down?"

"Can do. Rotor's blown the snow off and I can see a road alongside the wood."

Jack dropped the helicopter onto the roadway and as the blades started to slow, Barry was out of the cabin and wading through the knee-deep drifts with Jack not far behind him.

The car was a police car, the one they were searching for, but it was empty.

"Crashed the car and walked out of here. The ignition's off, lights are off. He must have got out okay. Down at one of the farms is my guess."

Barry shook his head. "This car's been here a long time, Jack. Snow's deep out there on the road." He tried the door and found it unlocked, he leaned in, the keys were still in the steering lock and he turned on the ignition. The radio lit up in fluorescent green and when he pressed the transmission switch, Harrogate answered immediately.

"... say again please."

Barry lifted the hand mike, thumbed the button again. "X35L here. Just testing, will call back shortly." He turned to his companion. "What do you reckon?"

"Something fishy. Pull the boot release; I'll see if anything's been nicked."

The boot lid swung up as Jack reached the rear of the car. "Jesus." He crossed himself and continued to look at P.C. Harrison's blue face.

Barry looked over his shoulder.

CHAPTER 27

Stephanie Cressington had married Major John Yates at St Mary's on the Mount Church in York. It had taken me an hour to unearth that fact and that her address then had been Piedmont, Beckdale Road, Huntington.

The telephone exchange gave me the phone number for the address and I spoke to a Mrs. Smythe, owner of the house for the past eight years.

"It was Stephanie's mother who owned it, of course," she said. "Evelyn Cressington. Dead now."

I asked some more questions.

"No. I've never kept in touch so I can't tell you about relatives. Try the Reverend Stokes here in the village. Michael Stokes has been vicar forever, since he was the curate here."

I thanked her and put the phone down, obtained Stokes's number from Directory Enquiries and spoke again. I came off the phone with three addresses of Cressington relatives living in the area. Trying Mrs. Amanda Holtby who was Stephanie's cousin—the only reply came from an answering machine, one of those chalet school and gymkhana sort of voices. Philip Cressington, he was an uncle and knew his niece was over from America and gave me her present address and phone number—it turned out to be the one I had just called, Amanda Holtby.

"Bloody Nora. Round and round in ever decreasing circles." I opened the door a little. "Sergeant Fearon."

Shelly Fearon came in, in a black suit with the barest hint of perfume about her. She wore a serious expression this morning too, and I wondered if her pregnancy was giving her problems. "Inspector?"

I didn't want to ask her about her health in the office so I stuck to business. "What are you busy with at the moment?"

She sighed. "The super gave me a list of callers who have supposedly seen Cleghorn. I've spent the morning discarding the cranks and re-listing the ones we ought to call."

I grinned quickly. "The public can be a policeman's best friend or his worst enemy. Goes with the territory."

"Fine, I've got that many calls from London and Edinburgh and from everywhere in between." She held up her hands. "I could do with a dozen pairs."

"Delegate it, Sergeant. Get Venables, Scaines, and Metcalf ready to leave in ten minutes—and Wright and Asquith. Two cars. I want you and Venables with me, we're going to York."

She frowned. "Whereabouts, sir, and why?"

"Call it a gut feeling. I've just been following up some addresses for Alan Cleghorn's wife; the best bet seems to be a village called Brideswell."

Forty minutes to Brideswell. Venables and Metcalf, the drivers, enjoyed themselves on the bypasses at Tadcaster and York, one hundred miles an hour and blue lights flashing. Amanda Holtby's house wasn't difficult to find, either. We piled out with collars pulled up against the cold and walked up the drive.

"What is this place?" asked Metcalf. "Fort Knox? Look at all the security."

I was pleased to see it. I knocked on the door expecting no response and got exactly that. "Well," I said, turning to my colleagues. "This is the house where Stephanie Cleghorn has been staying."

"Stephanie Cleghorn as in Alan Cleghorn's wife?" Scaines muttered the question as he craned his neck around to take in all the cameras and security lighting.

"The same and I've good reason to suspect foul play so we're going in. I'd prefer not to do any damage so spread out and see if you can spot a way in."

Scaines was as negative as usual. "Extremely well alarmed, sir. I can see pressure sensors on the ground floor windows from here; there'll be motion detectors inside, infrared…"

I nodded and stemmed his words by putting my hand in front of his face. "Yes, yes. Try not to forget we're the good guys here, okay?"

"Yes, sir."

"And time wasted always helps the bad guys, right? What do we do?"

"Get inside?"

And Metcalf came back with news of a partially open catch on the larder window. We followed him round and he used a penknife to pry it the rest of the way. We had entry albeit with alarm bells accompanying. It took Securicop five minutes to get there and we welcomed them at the front door with warrant cards and explained who we were. They switched off the alarm and we started to inspect the house as they left. "A quick once-over first, then report back." I said.

Ten minutes later, we reassembled in the main lounge. "What have we got?"

DC Wright answered first with a frown. "Nothing untoward, sir. Two bedrooms with wardrobes, doors open and obvious gaps in the clothes hangers."

"Like someone's been packing, sir," added Scaines.

"There're dog bowls in the kitchen, sir, and no dogs." That was Asquith.

"Small car in the garage, sir. Engine's cold, but there's obviously been another one, judging by the oil stains and mud off the wheels. Still soft." That one was Shelly Fearon.

I scowled. "So they've up and left, taken the dogs, clothing and so on. Someone go and check the news agents, the dairy if there is one, butchers, grocers… whatever there is in the village. Asquith and Scaines? Find out if a forwarding address has been left. The rest of you—look for papers, official stuff, holiday receipts—you know the sort of thing. I'll check the telephone book and answering machine."

I went into the hallway—an oak-panelled space almost as big as my living room. There were turned newel posts and balustrades along a wide staircase which curved up round the corner of the house to the next floor. Right by the foot of the stairs was a telephone table with a blue velvet seat. I sat on it and leafed through a notepad of phone numbers without drawing any obvious conclusions. I pressed the message button on the answer phone and waited for it to rewind. There were several names or numbers waiting for call backs with various terse messages:

It's Jane, dear. Call me about Charlie Boy. Will you? Dad's really interested in buying him…

Hey it's Mick, call me when you're back…"

It clicked off, and I noticed an attached recording machine. I pressed the replay button.

What are you calling me here for, Robert? Has Alan let you call long distance? Has he put you up to this?

I stopped the tape, rewound it a little and called the others. "Listen to this! Robert Cleghorn and his sister-in-law." I pressed the replay button again.

What are you calling me here for, Robert? Has Alan let you call long distance? Has he put you up to this?

Her voice rose a bit.

If he has, Robert, you can tell him it's not going to work. I am not coming back. Never. Understand?

There was a pause and then Cleghorn replied; I could almost see him frown.

This doesn't have anything to do with Alan, Stephanie. Believe me. I'm calling to talk about things between us. Not my brother.

What things? What are you talking about?

The recording continued with a conversation that seemed to be equal parts disbelief and misunderstandings. It finished off with Stephanie losing her cool.

You were a bloody pill-popping loony, and it sounds like you still are—worse than that sadistic brother of yours. Now go and pop a few more pills and bugger off.

The voice changed. *This is Detective Inspector White with the Ridings...* My call earlier that day. I stopped the tape. "Any thoughts?"

"Sounds like Cleghorn's a real screw-up. What was that about Iraq? Did he say three years or something?"

"That's what it sounded like," said Shelly, "but it doesn't matter whether he's screwed up or not, he thinks he's in love with her."

"Too true, both of you. Any other points?" There were none. "Let me sum up then. Robert Cleghorn is living in cloud cuckoo land, thinks the Iraqi War ended three years ago, thinks he's in love with a lady who definitely isn't in love with him, thinks they had a relationship, which his sister-in-law rejects. I'm inclined to believe her; she sounded too surprised to have made it up on the spur of the moment—even for our benefit."

"She did record the conversation, sir." Our careful Doubting Thomas.

"That's true, Scaines. We—I shouldn't leap to conclusions. However, she refers to her husband as sadistic. Was she on holiday or was she running away, planning a divorce? If she was expecting a call from her husband, she was perhaps prepared to record it as evidence?"

I pulled my thoughts together. "It appears that she rejected Robert and—leaping to conclusions again—the rejection could have led directly to the death of Maggy Ashton."

Shelly nodded, "Yes, Ashton's son thought 'Nostef' was a name, you thought it was 'no Stephanie,' an inspired guess."

I looked around. Everyone was hanging on my words although Scaines had the faintest of smug grins on his face. "I also leaped to a couple more—conclusions, I mean. This possible belief in nonexistent events may be the cause or the result of his mental problems. The fixation on Stephanie Cleghorn has brought him to Yorkshire. Now we've got to find the woman and, when we do, the murderer won't be far away. We just have to try to be there first."

I took the recorder from the answering machine and put it in my pocket. I'd get it transcribed later and maybe—I didn't know, maybe I could use it in conjunction with the press.

Shelly shook her head, spoke in a hoarse whisper. "These inspired guesses of yours, Boss. Don't they ever get you into trouble?"

"Too often," I whispered back, then, louder: "Carry on with the search. Call me if you find anything."

Scaines called me first and, following his voice, I found myself in what was obviously a study. Books lined three of the walls and an old oak bureau occupied the center of the room.

"Desk's locked, sir. I didn't know whether to force it."

"Quite right, Scaines. There's no need to damage property unless it's absolutely necessary." While I spoke, I was trying the doors. The top left one was locked, but all the others moved freely. I felt around inside the top right one until I came to a small metal lever under the bed of the desk. I pulled and the lid lifted at first touch. I smiled at his expression of incredulity. "My granddad had one, a secret lock."

We went through the contents together. All manner of receipts from odd jobs to the regular grocery bills which had increased, I noticed, by almost a hundred percent from a time about four weeks before. I nodded and continued: birth certificates, wedding lines for Amanda Holtby nee Cressington, house deeds and newspaper cuttings.

I opened up the deeds; there were four or five, one dating back over a hundred and fifty years. Each deed had a handwritten note paper-clipped to it detailing the date of purchase and the price. *Not a very safe place to keep documents like these; they should be in a security vault at a bank*, I thought and I flipped through them. The most recent were for this house, one in Haxby and another called Scar House at Lofthouse.

"What do you think about these?" I asked Scaines who was checking telephone bills.

He looked over. "This one is here, sir, where we are now. Houses owned by this Amanda Holtby? Perhaps they've gone to one or another of them."

"Hmmm. I don't know, they'll have to be checked. Where are they, do you know?"

"Haxby. That's about five miles outside York, sir. To the north. Lofthouse? I don't know, seems familiar. There's a Lofthouse something or other in Wakefield district."

One by one, my other officers reported back. No forwarding addresses left with local tradespeople, Amanda Holtby cancelled newspapers and the milk two days earlier for an indefinite period. Not an unusual thing for her to do by all accounts. I detailed a team to question the neighbors and a second one to visit the property in Haxby. The one at Lofthouse could be checked later, after we got back to Leeds.

"Sir!" Asquith who had just got into the car preparatory to going to Haxby rushed in. "There's been another murder, sir. At Masham Moor, North Yorkshire. Just heard it on the radio, thought you ought to know."

"The moors. Bit outside our current area of interest, isn't it? Is someone else going?"

"Harrogate's already there, sir. It's the M.O. which is interesting though. A strangling, a really vicious one."

"I see, right Asquith. Thanks. Find Sergeant Fearon, will you?" When she came, I called back to Control and asked them to relay the report to me. We both listened.

When it had finished I grabbed her arm. "Let's go, Shelly. Got to be Cleghorn, hasn't it?"

"Well, it could be, sir. It's a fair way though, out near Pateley Bridge, I think, just a few scattered farms."

I got them to patch me through to Pateley Bridge and eventually got hold of someone who knew about the reported murder. "How long would it take me to get out there?" I asked and was told it would depend on the weather. Maybe tomorrow, they said, if no more snow came down.

"Tomorrow? Get the helicopter," Shelly said.

"You feel okay to fly?" I asked, keeping my voice low.

Her eyes danced across mine. "Okay? I'd fly bareback on Pegasus if that's what it takes to catch this sick pig."

"Good enough, Sergeant. I'll call Leeds; get this show on the road."

Vincent Keoghan was on his way back stateside from Berlin. He'd just got the seat adjusted to a comfortable angle and was part way through his first Chivas Regal when the cabin attendant stopped by his seat and flashed him a smile. Vincent smiled back, his male model version.

"Mr. Keoghan?"

"Last of the line."

"Captain Jordan would like to see you on the flight deck."

"Is that so?" He stood up, keeping his head ducked until he was out from under the overhead lockers. "Mustn't keep the captain waiting. That's a keel-hauling offence."

The attendant took him forward around the stair head and opened the door through to the flight deck. Despite the size of the 747, it was a surprisingly cramped space and seemed even more so when he realized it was occupied by four men. All of them gave him a curious once-over as he entered.

"Mr. Keoghan," said the captain, twisting around in his seat and extending his hand. "Welcome to flight 2143. I'm Captain Jordan."

"Captain." Vincent—he had long ago dropped the Vinny diminutive—shook the other's hand.

"Captain Frazer here's my co-pilot, my flight engineer," he nodded to one of the men seated towards the rear then at the other one, "and our radio operator."

"Gentlemen," Vincent responded, nodding in his turn. As well as losing his nickname, Vincent had acquired a veneer of gentility over the years too.

"We've been ordered to redirect the flight to Heathrow, England, where you are to leave us. You'll be met when we land."

Vincent looked puzzled. "Me?"

"Message from the State Department, no less. Didn't know we had a diplomat among our VIPs."

"Well, I don't usually count myself as such, diplomat or VIP." He flashed his smile again. "Most thankful for your help, Captain. Sorry to have added to your problems." He took the message from the captain's outstretched hand. "Thanks again. Probably the First Lady wants me to pick something up from Harrods for her."

Back in his seat, he read the message. It was short and to the point. *Report to US Embassy, London, England.*

The captain came on the PA system a few minutes later to explain that they were being diverted around an area of stormy weather. They would be making a brief stop at London to take on further fuel. The 747 dropped down to the runway and taxied to an unused station at Terminal Three. A set of steps was wheeled up to the first class entry. Vincent stepped through and ran down the stairs, where a man was waiting for him. He could sense, though not actually see, curious eyes watching him from the plane.

"Mr. Keoghan? Mr. Vincent Keoghan?"

"Sure."

"I have a limo for you across there, sir." The man nodded towards the shadows beneath a passenger walkway.

He hefted his flight bag; it was heavier than it looked. "What about the rest of my baggage? It's still on the plane."

"I guess someone will take it off at the far end, sir. The embassy can provide whatever you need until you get back."

Vincent nodded. They got in the long black automobile with the dark tinted windows and sat back while the driver took him into London and Grosvenor Square. When he arrived, a secured line to Langley was opened, and he spoke in quiet tones with Deputy Director Hedges. He put the phone down and smiled at the picture of the president. He had just been ordered to call on an old friend. It wasn't a social call.

The same embassy car took him back to the airport an hour later to catch an internal flight to Leeds-Bradford airport. His flight bag was still firmly clutched in his hand, it required special diplomatic dispensation to by-pass the scanning equipment. There was a minor arsenal inside.

John Groves met him at the small local airport. They had worked together on several occasions and shook hands as he walked into the arrivals lobby.

At five o'clock it was fully dark and Amanda was just putting the finishing touches to the evening meal. She loved to cook and considered herself quite a chef when it came to preparing beef. Guests at her dinners were less convinced, however.

The last time she had cooked in this kitchen was when Paul had been alive, before she had decided the silence up here was just too much. A solitary tear formed in one eye… Paul had been… if only he hadn't liked solitude…

"Stupid, stupid cow," she whispered fiercely and wiped away the tear that had rolled down the side of her nose. Amanda picked up the tray and took it through to the living room where an enclosed wood burner was blazing away.

Stephanie sat cross-legged in a chair reading. Amanda could see she was feeling safe, at ease with herself. It showed in her face, showed in the way she looked. She was beautiful in a way that Amanda could only aspire to in her thoughts.

"What's that? What are you reading?" she asked, setting out the dishes on the pine table in the window bay.

"*Those in Peril.*"

"Ugh. Wilbur Smith, isn't it? I can't get on with him. Anyway, you can put it down, here's our dinner and tea combined."

They sat down opposite one another and ate. They were both hungry after last evening's drive and the business of getting settled in this morning.

"Well, what do you think? Peaceful?" Amanda asked, nodding at the snow-covered scene outside, where the room light illuminated it. "It's lucky we made the move when we did. We'd have never got here otherwise."

Her cousin smiled and finished her mouthful. "It's another world, isn't it? I opened the bedroom window between snow showers, and all I could hear was the wind. No sign of the village." She cut a piece of meat and built a forkful the English way. "The snow's good, it'll keep away visitors, oh." She stopped, hand to mouth. "I hope it isn't, er, too bad for you, Amanda. The quietness. I know you're a bit of a social animal."

"Hey. Don't you worry about me. As long as you talk to me I'm okay. Okay?"

Stephanie nodded.

"It was pretty awful up here with Paul. Both of us here but… um, apart. Never talked and wouldn't let me talk while he was working—which was most of the time."

"This is pretty good, Amanda." Stephanie changed the subject. "Really."

Amanda almost blushed; no matter how much effort she put into it, guests didn't seem to compliment her on the results. She lowered her voice. "Well thank *you*, ma'am. Thought we'd take the coffee through to the lounge and watch TV. The fire should have warmed the room through by now. Okay?"

The doorbell made them both jump, cutting off Stephanie's reply.

"Good Lord," said Amanda. "Who on earth is that? Some lost wayfarer, I suppose."

"I'll find out," said Stephanie. "You finish your meal."

She switched on the exterior light and put the chain on before unlocking the door. A man's head was framed in the narrow opening. The man was dressed in an anorak with the hood up, covered in snow.

"Yes? Can I help you?"

The man threw back the hood and she froze, shocked right through to the marrow in her bones. "Robert," she said at last. "What in the hell do you want?"

Robert Cleghorn gave her a smile, disarming and almost childlike in its innocence. "Hello, Steph. Er, are you mad at me? I just thought we really ought to talk, you know. Clear up these misunderstandings. Can I come in? Bit cold out here." He pushed at the door and noticed the chain for the first time. He pushed again and, without any apparent effort, one of the links in the brass chain parted with a *pop* and he was in the hallway.

"Who is it?" Amanda's voice came from the kitchen. The two dogs, huddled in their baskets, seemed reluctant to join in; one gave a half-hearted bark and the other a muffled whine.

If Stephanie heard her cousin, she showed no sign. Still in shock, she retreated a step or two, maintaining the distance between herself and her brother-in-law.

Getting no reply, Amanda dumped the dishes and pushed the door open between hall and kitchen. The man seemed vaguely familiar, standing there with a silly grin spread across his face. Stephanie stood frozen, like a mannequin in a shop window.

"Good evening," he said, his manner calm, composed. "Real sorry to call without warning like this. You must be Amanda, Stephanie's cousin? Hi. I'm Robert, Stephanie's brother-in-law. We're all family, hey?"

It was Amanda's turn to be shocked. This was the man they'd come all this way to avoid, turning up when snow had cut off the whole area. *How had he found the place?* Her mind worked overtime but accomplished nothing. "You'd better go through to the lounge," she said. "And close the door. I'll make some coffee."

Robert pushed the door closed and took off his parka, shaking it and showering snow onto the carpet. He hung the garment on a wall peg and smiled at Stephanie.

"Coffee sounds great." His voice held the sound of his smile, friendly, normal. "Care to show me the way, Steph?"

Stephanie shook herself and turned towards the lounge, moving ahead of him on rubbery legs. In the room, she sank into an armchair and just like that, her mind started to work again. *What did he want? Can I get the shotgun if I pretend to powder my nose? What's he doing here?* Her thoughts ran in ever faster circles. *Will he become aggressive if I tell him to leave? Will Amanda bring the dogs through?*

Robert was happy, as happy as he had ever been. Here he was in front of a roaring fire just across from the woman he loved. *No more problems, all gone, all over now. Straighten things out; put her right about Alan's lies.* He was happy just to sit there and look at her.

After a couple of false starts, Stephanie managed to start a conversation. "How's Alan? Last I heard, he was thinking of asking you to do some work for him."

"Alan?" Why was she asking about Alan? Robert searched his memory, he could not remember when he had seen his brother last. There had been something about a tree falling onto the house but quite genuinely, he couldn't recall the details. "Seems a while now, Steph. Can't say exactly. Guess he's well enough."

Amanda came through then, with a tray of cups and a pot of coffee. She put them on the low table between Stephanie and Robert. "Look, if you two have things to discuss, don't mind me. I know it's terribly silly of me, I just love this soap, *Home and Away*. Never miss a day. I'll just put the TV on quietly. Okay?" It was the best she could think of on such short notice, but the American didn't seem to mind, he virtually ignored her. She switched the TV on.

"So, tell me, Steph, what lies has Alan been feeding you while I've been away? Must have been quite something to make you stop loving me." The question was blunt and to the point.

Stephanie felt herself flushing with anger and fought to keep herself under control. Why did Robert think they'd been in love?

"Hell Stephanie, it was only a few months and I'm back now. What's he been saying?"

He must be mad, she thought, *really mad only you shouldn't say that nowadays, mentally unbalanced was how you said it.*

This was how the last conversation had gone, on the phone. It seemed he was living in a make-believe world where he forgot the bits he didn't like. Somehow she had to humor him until he could be got rid of without upsetting him.

"Alan said a lot of things Robert, over the years. What exactly do you think he said?"

"Lies, Steph. I'm only talking about the lies. The other things don't matter."

"Now..." Her voice cracked and she tried again. "Now what lies would they be? If he told me lies, how would I know that's what they were?"

Robert was flustered. He had imagined her falling into his arms, now that Alan was out of the picture. She would spill out all of Alan's stories and he would point out the lies. Then she would say that she never believed Alan and, well, he hadn't expected her to be so distant.

Robert cleared his throat. "Well, he must have said I didn't love you anymore. That was a lie, how could I stop doing that? Maybe he told you I'd gone off and left you when I had to go to the Gulf. Something like that, was that what he said?"

Stephanie clasped her hands, interwove her fingers to stop them shaking. "Alan never said anything of the sort. You probably don't know this if you haven't seen Alan for a while, but I've left him."

Robert was exultant. It didn't matter what lies Alan had told her, she'd seen the light and left him and now he was here with her. Had Stephanie sent for him? Yes, she must have sent for him. "Well that's just great. We..."

Stephanie unclasped her hands and held them up. "I left him because he used to hit me." She nodded to emphasize what she had said and sniffed; she was close to tears. Even so she was pleased with the way she had switched the subject.

Robert's face went through several color changes, each shade of red deeper than the last. "He hit you?" He clearly found the idea unthinkable. "He... why the dirty bastard! I'll break his arms, I'll kill him." His expression, which had started out as disbelief, had hardened into anger.

Amanda was watching them now; Stephanie seemed to be handling him although the last remark had stirred things up.

"I'm sure you would have stopped him if you'd been there, Robert." She tried to smile at him.

"You bet, Steph. You wouldn't ever get hurt with me around."

"I know you'd protect me. You wouldn't hurt me or Amanda, would you?"

Robert nodded, then watched, puzzled as her gaze went past him.

Amanda gasped.

He followed their gaze and saw his brother's face looking out of the TV screen.

"... the Strangler, as he is being called, has now been positively identified as Robert Cleghorn, a native of Florida, USA. The police are now adding a third victim to the previous two—P.C. Harrison of the Harrogate District Police. These pictures are shown courtesy of Sky TV and are coming live from their news helicopter."

There was an image of the slightly damaged police car.

"This is the car where P.C. Harrison was found, strangled and hidden in the boot. The murderer may still be in the area and people are warned to stay home and not to open the door to strangers…"

Robert was as stunned as the two women. He watched as Alan's picture reappeared on the screen. Was Alan here? Why had he killed a policeman? In the few seconds that he stared at the screen and then turned back to Stephanie, she was gone. He could hear her feet on the stairs.

Robert ignored Amanda, and raced after Stephanie, taking the steps three and four at a time. He met her just coming out of a bedroom with a shotgun in her hands. She tried to lift it but it was a heavy piece, and Robert had his hand on the barrel before she could get it anywhere near pointed at him. He pulled it from her and threw it aside before bundling her back into the room and back onto a bed.

"I can explain," he told her, "just give me time, and I can explain. I think… I think Alan is here…"

"No," she was weeping uncontrollably now. "Get away from me, keep away." Frantically, she pushed herself across the bed away from him until she was half sitting, leaning against the wall.

Robert stood up. From somewhere had come the cold calculating part of him, the part that looked after survival. He looked around the room. It wasn't large; it was a spare room with boxes of things against the wall and a pair of suitcases on the floor at the foot of the bed. There was no phone. He crossed and looked out of the window. There was nothing below, no convenient garage roof or porch. Robert went out, there was a key in the lock and he turned it, tried the door. From the other side of the door there came the sound of Stephanie crying.

He picked up the shotgun and checked for cartridges as he went back downstairs. Robert found Amanda in the kitchen with a cell phone in her hand. He backhanded her across the mouth and the phone dropped, clattering to the quarry-tile floor.

Robert was panting a little, not from exertion but from the effects of warring emotions. He took a great breath and pushed Amanda ahead of him into the lounge where he stood and watched the remainder of the news flash.

A man was being interviewed. *"No. None of my officers has personally been to the scene of P.C. Harrison's death as yet. I should say, too, that it is too early to be certain Cleghorn killed P.C. Harrison though everything we know so far points to that. I'll issue a further statement as soon as we have all the facts."*

Robert thought for a moment. Did he know the man? He might, but before he could be sure the newscaster's face returned to the screen.

"That was Detective Inspector White of the Ridings Regional Crime Squad, the officer in charge of investigating this case. The number on your screen is for the incident room which has been set up in Harrogate. If you have seen this man," Alan Cleghorn's picture came up again, *"or see anything suspicious, please ring this number. The police have*

asked us to stress how dangerous this man is. If you see him do not approach him under any circumstances."

A low growl came from the back of Robert's throat. *Nothing was working out as it should. Everything was going freaking wrong. If he could just get Stephanie away from all the liars…*

He reached out and grabbed Amanda by the arm. "C'mon, bitch. I know you've been poisoning her mind." He dragged her upstairs, unlocked and opened the door and pushed her roughly inside. "Now you tell her it's all a load of shit. You hear?"

He went downstairs again and began to look through the cupboards for some whisky—something, anything to calm his nerves. He needed to think, and his head was starting to hurt.

John Groves fought his way through the evening rush hour traffic on the Leeds ring road, and talked to Vincent about the forthcoming job. Groves was a thickset man; his mohair jacket barely encompassed the barrel chest and the huge arms. He spoke from the side of his mouth. A pale scar at the corner which gave him a permanent lopsided grin, stiffened the features on his left-hand side.

"So we're here to take out Cleghorn?" His voice was a deep bass; the words were spoken slowly, as though they'd been rattling around inside that huge ribcage before finding their way out. His tone was matter of fact, like he was talking about nothing more important than the price of steak.

"Uh-huh." Vincent gave nothing away.

"That give you a problem? Heard you worked with the guy."

"No problem. Just a job."

"Heard he's been strangling people around here."

"Yeah. Me, too."

"You're not saying a lot."

"I'm thinking." Vincent's acquired polish was wearing a bit thin. Pretty soon he would be just Vinny again.

Groves turned left at the Seacroft roundabout onto the A64. "Hate these things, these circles. Cannot get used to them." He gunned the gas pedal and overtook a slower car driven by a female in the fifty yards of dual carriageway. "Bitch's got all night, we ain't. Heard Cleghorn was pretty good."

Vincent—Vinny—showed his perfect smile and swept his fingers through his hair. "All right, John. I c'n see there's goin' to be no peace till I tell you." He eased his tie and leaned back. "Rob Cleghorn—only don't call him Rob less you want him goin' berserk—Cleghorn and I trained together. We got split when they sent us out to the Gulf then afterwards, when I joined the CIA. I persuaded Robert to join up, too. He was one of the best, was Robert. One of the very best 'til one night in Prague."

"Out of the way, sucker." Groves used a right turn only lane to overtake a lorry. "What happened in Prague?"

"He was sent in to deliver a package to a contact. The contact had been turned and Robert found the KGB waiting for him. He went through them like greased lightning, but he got hurt in the hand-to-hand. Got a head wound on top of an old injury he'd taken in Iraq or Afghanistan, helluva busy guy was Robert. Hospitalized for a helluva time after that."

"So, he obviously got better. Why didn't he carry on?"

"Well that's it. He didn't get better." Vinny yawned. "The director or someone fairly high up the tree got pretty worried about how unstable Cleghorn was. They ordered scopolamine to be used on him."

"I know the name, but what does it do?"

"Makes you forget things, sometimes imperfectly."

"So Cleghorn loses his memory, then what?"

"I don't know. Killed a nurse I believe. Escaped. The Company's been looking for him ever since."

"And how long's 'ever since'?"

"Years, or so I hear."

John was silent for a while, scorching the tarmac until he had to turn off the trunk road onto narrow country lanes. "Reckon you can take him, Vinny?"

Vinny chuckled and stretched like a cat. "I can take anyone."

"If you know where he is."

"Just get us to this place, John. There's someone there who knows."

"And they'll tell you if you ask?"

"It's this woman. Robert's got a thing for her. No," he added as Groves vented a dirty laugh, "not the hots. He worships her, thinks the sun shines out of her ass, but his memories of her have all been planted."

"How do you mean?"

"Scopolamine and barbiturates, they don't just make you forget, they also make you susceptible to suggestion. They let the doc put anything he liked into Robert's mind."

"So Cleghorn thinks he loves this broad and it's all a crock of shit? Why, for Chrissake?"

Vinny smiled the kind of smile a cat wears when it considers a fish in a bowl. "Just seemed the thing to do when the doc said Rob needed something rock solid to cling to. He had a wedding photo of his brother and wife in his wallet, always carried it around with him. I just tore off the part with his brother on and gave it back to him." Vinny shrugged. "Between her and Jerry Lee Lewis—he's a big fan of Jerry Lee Lewis—between them, there wasn't a great deal of room in his brain for anything else. Reckon I'd have saved him a lot of heartache and us a lot of work if I'd just blown him away when I had the chance."

"What chance was that?"

Vinny was tired of talking. "Just shut the hell up and drive."

CHAPTER 28

My father, who is a strong yet gentle man, once said that I would make many acquaintances in life but very few friends, only enough to count on the fingers of one hand. I was beginning to think him right. Instead of going in the helicopter to the site of the latest murder, I was ordered to make a statement to the press. In my place I sent Sergeant Shelly Fearon (whom I would have liked to have as my friend) and Venables from forensics.

It wasn't long since I'd thought Superintendent Flowers might also become a friend, a few days, that was all. How quickly things can change. I understood the pressure he worked under and understood, too, that the pressure had to be passed down the chain. There were other ways to do it—better ways. Shouting, slyness and forgetting loyalties were not the ways I would have chosen.

Still, budget or no budget, we had to take on several temps to help collate the information coming in from the public, to return telephone calls and liaise with other police forces and civic bodies. There had not been this level of interest in a murder since the "Yorkshire Ripper" twenty-five or so years before. As a direct result of the Sky TV broadcast, the newspapers were already calling Cleghorn the "Yorkshire Strangler" though how they had learned the manner of Harrison's murder was beyond me. We had ordered a news blanket immediately after the Harrogate police had called Flowers with the report. I suspected that somewhere there was a policeman tipping off the newshounds. Was this person—or persons—revealing facts about our work for money? I resolved to keep an eye open for above-average lifestyles both in the Regional Crime Squad and other forces I worked with.

Considering the number of officers out of the office and on the job, I was lucky to still have anyone left to address in the incident room. When I went in, I noticed DC Scaines sitting on a corner of a table taking a few last drags from a cigarette. Government legislation on smoking had come into force in 2007 and the offices had been no smoking areas ever since. Only the Old Man, Flowers and Scaines actually flouted the rules; Scaines did not have the clout of the other two and extinguished his cigarette before I had taken two paces into the room.

I ignored the infringement for the moment and turned on an overhead projector. The slide was a photocopy of an ordnance map for the Pateley Bridge area; I dropped it onto the projector and looked around at the company. "Okay, what have we got, lads?"

"Bad weather everywhere."

"The snow?" I asked and he nodded. "How tightly can we define the area of Cleghorn's whereabouts?"

DC Asquith said, "If we knew how long the victim had been dead, we could be more precise, sir. I'd say an educated guess would place him on one of those two roads: Pateley Bridge up to the reservoir or the one that goes up over the moors. That one's been blocked the longest so he wouldn't have got very far. We've got, say, fifteen miles of road."

"And what's on the road?"

"Well, there's Pateley Bridge at one end." He put a finger up in the air and its shadow on the screen pointed to the place. "Small town; rural, picturesque. There's Ramsgill there and Lofthouse." He pointed again. "That's a small village, and then there's maybe a hundred farms and holiday cottages."

Lofthouse. A name on one of the deeds in Stephanie's cousin's home? "And that's it?"

"There's a hotel here at Watt, with maybe six houses around it."

"Still got a lot of houses to cover with the few men we're going to be able to chopper in." I was musing really, just vocalizing my thoughts.

"Certainly is a lot, sir." Asquith was a typical Yorkshireman, no beating around the bush. "Point is, sir, I was born around there. Know it like the, well, the back of my hand. Know a lot of the farms. Lot of them are quite a way off the road—we could maybe give those a miss on the first sweep, because of the snow, you know, drifting."

I nodded. "I get the picture but at least he can't get out of there in a hurry. Okay—Scaines, I want you to organize road blocks to go in if and when the weather up there changes. I want us to concentrate in a circle around Lofthouse. Cover every road, bridle path in and out. Asquith…"

"Sir?"

"With me." I shooed him ahead of me and as I passed Scaines, I spoke in a low voice. "No smoking area, you do know that, didn't you?"

He nodded.

"If you've got to have a drag, use the bog."

"They're patrolled, the Old…"

"Exactly."

In my office, I grinned at Asquith. I had rather taken to him. He had impressed me before with his willingness to take whatever job he was given and get on with it.

His summing up of the conditions on the moors was sound and coupled with his good luck in knowing the area made him the ideal choice for the team.

Scaines had tried to impress me on several occasions. However, he was a bit too clever—good if things worked out, a disaster when they didn't.

"Asquith, your file says you're a dab hand with computers. And being a computer nerd myself, I guess it can't be wrong, can it?"

"I guess it *could* be wrong, sir, but it isn't. I've done a bit of surfing."

For me, my university education had made it easier to join the force and get a couple of speedy promotions. My main difficulty had been convincing the long serving coppers I wasn't a jumped-up college boy. According to his file, Asquith was my exact opposite. Comprehensive school until sixteen and then tea boy and laborer on a building site. Next, he'd fed cardboard sheets into a case-making machine and then started at a local hotel as barman and later bar manager.

Since then, Asquith had spent six years with the force and been given a commendation for bravery when he had taken the weapon from a man who had knifed another in a drunken brawl. He transferred to the plain clothes section a couple of years before I came to Leeds. He'd seen drugs undercover work, building society and bank robberies and a multitude of felonies and misdemeanors—all part of the learning curve.

"Right, computers it is then though not surfing. Collating." I pointed to my office machine. "I'll show you how it's set up and what I want doing. I want a full back-up after every session. Okay so far?"

"Yes, sir. Cracking machine. Thought you'd have the latest in Microsoft operating systems by now, though."

"Nothing but the best for Stewart White, Asquith. That's what they said. Anything he wants, he gets," I joked with a smile.

"Really?" He didn't seem to know whether I was joking or showing off.

"No, I'd rather the latest OS be out of beta before loading it up. Now, poke that switch there and get the thing booted. If things work out as planned, I want you with me on a helicopter trip. You can show me the delights of these Yorkshire Dales I've heard so much about."

My cell phone warbled at me, cutting any further conversation off. "DI White," I answered.

"Definitely Cleghorn's work, sir." It was Venables. "Exact copy of the bruising in the earlier cases. I'd swear to it."

"Body count's getting a bit high." I grumbled.

"Guess so and, something else, sir."

"Yes?"

"Sergeant Fearon, sir. Had a bit of a fall getting out of the helicopter."

"Oh hell. Is it serious?"

"I don't know, sir. They took her out in the chopper again, to the hospital in Harrogate. I don't know what it's called now that it's a trust; seem to change it at every verse ending."

A dozen or more images flashed through my mind, none of them pleasant. "What are the roads like between here and Harrogate?"

"Main roads are no problem, sir. It's only the back roads that are affected down there. Up here it's still brass monkey weather and the wind's doing nasty things with the snow."

"Okay, Harry. Get everything you can and get back here. I want a full report, soonest. Pleasant journey."

I broke the connection and put my scattered thoughts in order. When I came out of it, I found I was looking at an oil painting on the wall, a woodland scene. Tomorrow was Saturday, supposedly my day of rest and I was meant to be collecting Pip. Not tomorrow though, not for quite a few days. I was going to have to ring Shirley and ask her to keep Pip for a little while longer.

"Something the matter, sir?"

"Oh—Asquith. Sorry, what was that?"

CHAPTER 29

Robert had heard no sound from the bedroom for some time. At first there had been one or other of the women sobbing but that had eventually petered out into silence. His thoughts had been in turmoil. Stephanie's reactions, her efforts with the shotgun, her expression which had suggested hatred and even loathing—all had been a revelation. *Where had her love gone?* It didn't make sense.

He knew Alan wasn't here, because… well, he wasn't here in England, that was one thing he did know for certain. And Alan hadn't killed the policeman; *he* had. Why? The TV news program brought back memories of the incident, but his motivation for the act was unclear. Revenge perhaps, retaliation? But for what? As Robert recalled the actual event his breathing became deeper, his mental vision narrowed, became crystal clear. Robert had the power of life and death; he could feel the pulse of blood racing beneath his fingers when he gripped the throat, his to decide—tighten the grip and stifle the pulse, relax and restore life. The act empowered him; anything became possible when a life was taken.

Robert's gaze was directed within. *Was this what it felt like to be God? Or what it felt like to be the Devil?* He searched for feelings of remorse and shook his head. There were none. Every one of them deserved to die, there were no mitigating circumstances, nothing to excuse them for trying to prevent him achieving what he wanted. Each one that he had dispatched deserved what they got; their deaths left the world a better place.

His fingers hurt and Robert looked down at his hands. A scarf, a thin, filmy chiffon thing, was wound around his fingers, cutting off the circulation. He had been holding it, knotting it, twisting it all while he had been thinking. He unwound it; it was Stephanie's, and it took his mind back to the two women upstairs. What should he do? Leave them there and get away from this place?

Perhaps, if he had another talk with Stephanie, away from the other woman… after all it had been she who had caused the problem, turning on the TV and drawing Stephanie's attention to the… execution.

Robert remembered the snow and the question remained unanswered. The snow cut him and this place off from the outside world; he was incarcerated here along with the women. There was no way to leave, so he would wait and see what Stephanie had to say for herself later on. But he'd better check the property over, make certain there was no way of escape from the bedroom where he had imprisoned them. There were some outbuildings at the back that he also ought to check.

The two dogs were safe behind the closed door to the kitchen, and he left the house by the front door, latching the slam lock into the open position as he went. The snow was only an inch or so deep at the front; the wind had scoured it away from the house and built it up into a four-foot drift along the line of the hedge bordering the front yard. Along the side wall, the snow was a little deeper but as soon as he turned along the back of the house, Robert was wading through knee-high drifts which soon rose to shoulder height.

A door led into what had once been a barn which lay some twenty feet back from the house. The snow was scoured away from the southeast facing wall, leaving the door clear. The door was a stout one and it was locked. Without some tools or a pry bar, Robert had no chance of getting through. He would have to go back and search for a key, or threaten the women into giving him one. He stopped as a sudden thought came to him—a memory of his father from childhood, a time when he was maybe six or seven. There had been a barn back of the house then, an unpainted wooden building with a door just as strong as this one and like this one, locked. He remembered his father, reaching…

Robert ran his hand along the concrete lintel over the door. Near the center, under the layer of snow, was a key covered in a thick coating of rust. Robert chuckled; it was so unlikely—so unbelievable—it just made him laugh almost uncontrollably. He stopped himself. It wasn't unusual to leave a key over the door; he'd been trained to check for keys around the door, under nearby rocks and flowerpots, under the mat.

The key turned with a protesting squeak, unlocking the door. The interior was dry and dusty, apparently from being unused for some time, otherwise it was clean. Workbenches lined one wall and a variety of hand and power tools were neatly shelved or hung on racks. A Workmate™ held a picture frame, all clamped up as though it had just been glued, a number of similar frames were leaning against the walls—evidently awaiting canvasses because several more were stacked alongside with canvasses stretched and stapled into place. *Quite the handyman,* thought Robert as he opened the door and went outside, *don't remember Stephanie painting, must be the other one.*

He frowned. *Had to be the other. If Stephanie was an artist, he would have known that. They had been—they were—in love.*

He passed along the back of the house, keeping clear of the snow drifts and looked up at the bedroom windows, identifying the one in which Stephanie and Amanda were locked. With no way down, anyone fool enough to try jumping was going to end up with a broken leg or worse.

The dogs started barking as he passed by the back door, flinging themselves at the glass, their great paws scrabbling at the wood. Robert ignored them and stopped outside a shed built from cinder block and closed with a galvanized steel roll-up garage door. He bent down and grabbed the handle, giving it an experimental tug. To his surprise, the door moved up easily and inside was a deceptively large space. He guessed that it must be built back into the hillside behind because there was no yard to speak of behind the building. A four-wheel drive Discovery occupied one side of the space, the vehicle he had followed from the old world village near York. *Interesting.* He looked back through the door, and realized that the steep drive led past the house and straight up here. He could see the Ford Fiesta parked at the bottom.

What was even more interesting than the four-by-four was a snowmobile painted in gleaming blue and white standing on a wooden duckboard to the right of the big vehicle. The key was in the ignition and he tried turning it. Nothing. He saw the reason almost immediately: two batteries were there on a bench, one of them coupled to a charger. The one under charge was large, much larger than the other and probably came from the Discovery. The other, smaller one, he guessed, would be from a lawn mower, motorcycle, or the snowmobile. Without consciously thinking about it or reasoning, Robert transferred the clips on the charger cables from the larger to the smaller battery. It began gurgling away at once.

There was a lot of unused space here, he realized, more than enough for another car. He went back to the snowmobile and tugged at the duck board until it was nearer the center with plenty of room down the side. A few minutes later, the Ford Fiesta was in the garage, hidden away from prying eyes. He switched it off and opened the door; the interior light came on and reflected back from the two-way radio he had taken from the dead policeman. He picked it up and after a moment's examination, flicked it on.

"… leaving the murder scene now Control. XK153l taking over this station. Am taking DC Venables back to Leeds, ETA at your location 1630 hours. Roger and out."

Robert may have had memory problems but there was nothing wrong with his thought processes. He jumped out of the car and went outside onto the driveway, looking up into the darkening sky. A few moments later he saw what he expected to see: a helicopter moving west, its flight lights strobed brightly against the sky's dark gray. *The cops have started looking for me.*

Stephanie cradled Amanda's head against her chest and rocked her to and fro. She had wiped the blood from her cousin's swollen lips and had tried to console her with silly, soothing words despite the fact that her own worst nightmares had come to visit.

She stared vacantly over Amanda's head at the window, trying to come up with some plan, some way to get out or get to a phone. The window was far too high to jump. With a rope… for a minute or so, she toyed with the idea of sheets knotted together, but they were in a spare room, only a thin cover over the mattress, and not strong enough. She made a wry grimace. Amanda had always been the tough one, the one who comforted, gave strength, and now here they were with the tables turned. When Robert had struck her, Amanda had collapsed, both physically and mentally.

Perhaps the years of abuse she had put up with from Alan had toughened her in this respect. He had slapped her, hit her with his fist, knocked her down and dragged her around by the hair for the most trivial of imagined reasons. After some time Stephanie had learned to endure it. She had been in a foreign country with no relatives to support her, no close friends from whom she could seek advice. At first she thought the fault was hers, that she was always doing something wrong. But under the guise of going to the bookstore, she had learned about battered women. She brought home the golfing books her husband had ordered her to purchase, but she snuck looks at books in the self-help section. The bookstore owner had noticed, and would casually leave a book at her elbow when she came into the bookstore. It took years, but she'd found the information, the strength, and thanks to Amanda, the means to get away from Alan.

Looking back, she wondered how different the two brothers actually were. Robert was physically stronger than Alan; he had been trained to kill, if his stories could be believed. Perhaps it was inevitable that one should abuse his wife while the other murdered. Both seemed to solve—no, settle—their own internal problems with violence.

Her thoughts wound down, and eyelids heavy, Stephanie closed her eyes and presently, fell asleep.

Vincent was out of the car almost before John had turned off the ignition. He stood at the gateway to Holtby House in Brideswell and looked from right to left and back again. He was aware of John Groves coming up behind him. "I can see two cameras from here and the telephone cable is armored. Standard home security over here, I guess. Can we avoid setting it off?"

"Can a mouse eat cheese?" John snorted over his right shoulder. "Just a thought, how do we know there's no one home?"

"I don't know for sure. Look at the snow on the driveway though. One set of tire tracks. I'm betting that's from a car leaving here after the snow settled rather than someone coming in." He nodded at the path alongside the driveway. "A lot of foot traffic though. Think the neighborhood soccer club came to visit?"

"Cover your face until we get under the porch. Don't want to be on camera, do we?" John put his hands up to brush back his hair and walked rapidly up to the front door. Vincent followed, using his knuckles to rub vigorously at his eyes.

With their backs to the camera, which covered the front door, they rang the bell. There was no reply. The front door was heavy wood with a window oval at head height. John looked through into a large hall and chuckled. He winked at Vincent and pointed to the left. "Control panel's there, right out in the open. They're usually set at a minute and half to two minutes though anything up to forty-five seconds will get us in without a peep."

He felt through an inside jacket pocket and brought out two different screwdrivers, a pair of wire cutters, and a penlight which he switched on. "Okay. Ready when you are."

Vincent smiled his wide white smile and tried first one then a second lock pick on the Yale. He had the door open in seven seconds and stood back for John to go through.

John focused the light on the two crosshead screws which held the cover on and then put the penlight in his mouth. The cover came off in less than fifteen seconds. Inside there were four wires to choose from, he made one quick cut—another ten seconds. A second, slightly longer check and a then second cut, a further fifteen seconds or so. "Isolated," he said and replaced the cover, slid the tools back into his pocket. "Why the hell go to all the expense of having this stuff fitted if it's crap gear they're putting in."

"Flippin' cowboys, John. Let's look around."

Inside the study, Vincent went straight to the desk, its roller cover still open. Ignoring the contents of the top for the moment, he tried all the doors and found the locked one. He looked thoughtfully through a bunch of small keys and tried one; the key turned partially and stopped. He tried a second and the little lock clicked open.

The only thing there was a large page-per-day desk diary and Vincent wondered why it should be locked up. He opened it and the name *Amanda Holtby* was printed in the ID section. He flicked through the pages until he came to the last couple of entries.

Two days before, Amanda had written: *Stephanie doing well, recovering from recent traumas. Getting to be cheerful again and rather good company. Introduce her to the bridge club ladies?*

Over the page, Vincent read the next entry. *Steph's had a weird phone call from brother-in-law. Frightened her to death. Going to Kiln Hill. She's always liked lakes, think Scar House reservoir will do her good. Good food, some music and scenery. Got to do her good. Hope I can stand it though, haven't been up there since Paul died.*

"Heard of Scar House reservoir?"

John came in with an ice cream he'd filched from the ice box. "No, why?"

"Because I bet that's where they've gone." He showed John the diary entries. "If that's where they are, it's a safe bet that's where our Bob Cleghorn has gotten himself to."

"I've got maps for the whole country in the car. If it's in England, we can find it."

Vincent sat looking at the ice cream for a moment and then used a handkerchief to clean the polished wooden drawer handles. "Not left any prints out there have you?"

"Is a duck's ass watertight?"

CHAPTER 30

It was ten-thirty on Friday night when I reached home. I had made arrangements for Asquith and myself to leave for Harrogate the next morning. I had tried to speak with Shelly earlier on, but I was told that she was under sedation so my first task was to visit her in the hospital, see how she was, no matter what Joe Flowers thought. After that, I was going to fly out to the site of Harrison's murder.

There was no time to go to the store and get some fresh food. I opened up the cupboard and looked at my store of tinned food, one unappetizing label to the next. At least Pip, poor little bugger, would be getting something nourishing, and he would have company, too.

Okay, was it going to be meatballs with beans, or stewed steak and beans? I chose the steak—and the beans, of course. My mother, had she still been alive, would have been ashamed of my present eating habits. As it was, she was probably spinning in her grave. *Five types of vegetables or fruit every day*—I could imagine her lecturing me and I smiled at the thought.

At least tinned stuff doesn't take long to heat through; I transferred it from the pans to a plate and made myself comfortable in front of the TV in the sitting room in time to catch the SKY news at the top of the hour to see if they were still covering my murders.

My murders. I was getting possessive. It wasn't as if I had anything in common with the killer—I still couldn't weigh the guy up, get under his skin. Okay, so it was becoming more and more apparent that Cleghorn enjoyed his work or was certainly starting to, as was often the case with serial or multiple killers. But what was it that had kicked him off? What had Alan Cleghorn said or done back in Florida that had led to his being murdered by Robert? Did Robert have a history of mental illness? Had his mother locked him in a dark room or had his father beaten him? There were so many possible causes for violence, so many questions to be asked and so few answers to be found.

The news finished and I was lost in my thoughts, I hadn't heard a word of it. I switched the set off in disgust and took my plate through to the kitchen, dropped the plate and the spoon and fork into the sink and ran some cold water to cover them. I poured a glass of water from the fridge and went towards the stairs.

Bedtime beckoned.

Not for long, though. I had one foot on the bottom step when the doorbell rang. I yawned and crossed the hallway and opened the door. There was a huge shape standing there, about the size of a yeti; he peered down at me from between the raised lapels of a thick fur jacket.

"Hi," said the figure. "Stewart ? That you?" The accent was American and vaguely familiar.

"That's the name. Hey! You're John Merrick."

"Damn right I am. Pleased to meet you."

He stuck a huge gloved hand out towards me. I took it and got shaken pretty thoroughly. I was knocked sideways, and it must have shown.

"Kinda surprised you, eh?"

"Well yes, John. Look, I'm forgetting my manners, come on inside." And I put the water glass down on the hall table before it got spilled.

"Boy, this is one cold place, ain't it?"

"Sort of brisk, you might say." I closed the door. "Come through here. Haven't been in long so there's no fire going, but the heat has been on for a few hours. We'll thaw you out pretty fast. Fancy something to eat or drink?" I pointed him at the settee since I couldn't see him fitting into a chair.

"That's real nice of you, Stewart. No food, thanks. I ate well on the plane but I'm cold outside, guess a cold beer inside'll kinda even things up a bit."

"No problem," I said breathing a sigh of relief that John wasn't hungry. I went out to the kitchen while he shrugged out of his outdoor clothes and brought in a pack of Carlsberg.

"Try one of these, John… my God, John, you surprised me, I'm only just beginning to believe it."

John Merrick pulled the tab and took a huge swallow, maybe half the contents of the can went down in one go. He grinned and wiped his mouth with the back of his hand. The grin was infectious, and I returned it knowing I liked this man in the flesh just as much as I had done on the phone.

"Well, Stewart," he said and finished the can, "you told me come over for a few beers anytime I felt like it. But that isn't the reason I came." He pulled his coat across the settee and felt inside, pulled out a manila file which had been folded down the middle and stuffed into the inside pocket. "Been carrying this close to my heart for the past twelve hours. It might stop a bullet if I got shot at." He straightened it out and looked at it thoughtfully. "File on Robert Cleghorn. Thought it best you should see it and the safest, quickest way to get it to you was person to person."

"You going to charge us for the personal service?" I joked.

John grinned again. "Ain't had a vacation yet this year so I decided to do a bit of driving around. That's what I told the customs feller, *Tourist*. Things in Highlands County are getting a bit boring. Had a four-car fender bender in the main street the other day and Alan Cleghorn getting himself killed, that's all."

He passed me the file and I pushed the remains of the six-pack towards him as I opened it.

The military service record was on the first sheet with dozens of doctor reports behind it. Between the military record and the medical stuff was a handwritten note—actually, a photocopy of a handwritten note. It confirmed Cleghorn's treatment was being paid for by the Chuckaluck Canning Company and was signed by a J.D. Klein, MD. I wondered what the significance was, and asked John about it.

"CIA, if that means much to you, Stewart."

"It does."

"One of the many names they use when they have to interface with the real world. It tells me that Cleghorn—Robert Cleghorn—was one of theirs. Before you read any further, I'd better warn you the CIA has very long arms."

John then explained how he had been warned off the Cleghorn investigation, and told me that he had called in a lot of favors to get hold of a copy of the file.

"So you see, Stewart," he finished, "the material in there is very sensitive. Far too important to trust to the mail."

I nodded and pulled a can of Carlsberg from the pack, then pushed an armchair nearer to a wall light before I started reading more thoroughly. "If you need any more beer, John, there's some in the fridge through there." I nodded to the kitchen door. "If anything else in there takes your fancy, it's yours."

I glanced briefly through the service record and saw he'd served with the special forces, which suggested where his unarmed combat skills came from. However, it was the medical reports that I was really interested in.

It appeared that Cleghorn had been treated for psychiatric disorders for over a year following a blow to the head which had aggravated a previous cranial injury.

That explained a lot, and I remembered the further injury Cleghorn had sustained in the York fracas. The cumulative effects of the blows to his head were likely to be unpredictable.

I skimmed through the medical notes.

He'd been treated for psychosis with both haloperidol and chlorpromazine—which I recalled from somewhere was pretty standard treatment for violence and antisocial behavior.

Then I came to the next memo and couldn't really believe what I was seeing. *Extended treatment with scopolamine and sodium metholinctus over the course of thirty days!* Were they trying to fry his brain from the inside out? Small amounts of both drugs could be used as disinhibitors; they relaxed the patient, but God knew what the quantities mentioned here over such a time span would do.

Next was a photocopy of another handwritten note; it appeared to be a doctor's memo. I deciphered it: the note suggested there was a degree of amnesia present. However, there was no date on the note so I couldn't say if that was before or after the bizarre treatment mentioned on the previous page. A footnote in a second and clearer hand suggested that these were Cleghorn's final problems—*and hardly surprising*, I thought.

A final typewritten letter on headed paper was included, from a Dr. Lim in the Neurological Unit—the name of the organization and the address had been neatly blacked out before copying. The letter diagnosed Cleghorn as suffering from temporal lobe epilepsy; it listed possible symptoms: white mist and other visual effects, bad taste sensations, uncontrolled muscular spasm, followed by one or two other less likely events and then recommended action. Four Tegretol® (carbamazepine) a day as long as the symptoms persisted. In other words, as long as Cleghorn survived.

I put down the file and glanced at the clock on the windowsill. It was just short of one in the morning. I tapped the folder. "This explains a lot, John. Robert Cleghorn is one very mixed-up man. He should never have left hospital without additional in-patient therapy. Even so, it appears that he would need a handler. He's supposed to take prescription drugs; I doubt very much he's doing that, maybe never did it. I'd guess he doesn't remember much if anything at all about these killings once they're over. Maybe he's not even aware of what he's doing at the time."

Merrick agreed, "I got that part. What I don't understand is how a guy can kill like this guy has and then not remember it. These killings aren't just a moment's work; it takes some time and a lot of effort to strangle someone."

I nodded. "You read the bit about the 'fugue' state?"

"Yeah. Didn't understand a word of it."

"No, me neither. I don't think anyone does really, not fully anyway. I've read about cases where epileptics have had a seizure, come out of it, made a cup of tea and sat down without any recollection of what they've done or been through."

John shrugged. "That's a long ways from murder."

"I heard of a man who killed his mother and couldn't remember it—denied it bitterly. Under treatment later, he was found to be suffering from multiple personality disorder. Two personalities, the one that killed his mother only in control during the 'fugue' state. Sufferers say it's like losing time; seconds, minutes, even hours."

John lifted his hands, let them fall again. "Words, Stewart. Just words describing what happens, not why or how it happens."

"True enough, though every little bit helps to build a picture of what he might do and when."

My guest blew out a great gust of air. "Whatever you guys do, it's my guess the CIA are after him. They usually manage to clean up their own dirty linen."

"I think you said something along those lines before, John, but this time they're going to be out of luck. This is my bailiwick here, and I've got him bottled."

"You've caught him? Hell." John's expression was one of incredulity.

"No. Not yet. Two days ago he added another murder to his list, and this time it was a copper." For John's benefit, I added, "A uniformed policeman." I noticed the beer had gone. I walked quickly through to the kitchen and got two more cans and brought them back, throwing one to John.

I opened the other one and took a long swallow. "He's up in the Dales—rough moorland country, and he's snowed in. Just a matter of time now. One day, two at the maximum. In fact, I'm going up there by helicopter in the morning to visit the murder scene and to see how the search is going."

"Well here's luck, Stewart." He held up his beer can. "I don't suppose that there's room for little old me in that helicopter?" He stretched his arms out a little, making himself look even bigger. "I'm a helluva good guy to have in your corner." He flexed his biceps at me, nearly bursting his shirt sleeve.

I was at a loss for words. My bosses would not only object, they'd have me on the carpet and back to directing traffic.

"You wouldn't be an expert on the Dales, would you by any chance?"

John smiled slowly. "Alan-a-Dale, Chippendale, know 'em all."

"I'll take you up to the guest bedroom. Hope you're not too jetlagged; we'll be up and away before seven."

Several miles north of Harrogate, Keoghan and Groves were becoming very aware of the vagaries of British weather. From the four inches or so of snow which had hardly hindered them at all along the main roads, it suddenly changed to banked drifts of snow higher than the car. They had crawled with spinning tires along a minor road to the top of a hill and as far as they could see there were blinding white fields and frosted trees and hedges.

"Hold it." Vincent put a restraining hand on John's arm. He pointed to a set of flashing blue lights. "Does that mean the same as it does back home?"

John nodded. "Police. A road block."

"I wonder why?"

John shrugged. "I can check the police bands, see if they're on the air?"

"It all takes time and it won't necessarily help us get through. Let's try the direct approach. What's the next place on the map?"

"At least we know it's not us they're after. Hmm, next is Pateley Bridge."

"Okay then. We're tourists, okay? Researching our family tree?"

"Family tree?"

"Our ancestors came from round here." Vincent explained in a tired voice. "We're checking out church documents and gravestones."

"If you say so."

In any event, there was nothing to it. The policeman who came up to the window explained they were there to check cars exiting from the area rather than entering. "Where are you bound for, sir?"

"Pateley Bridge, officer."

"Checking grave stones," John added.

Vincent looked across at his companion, his expression neutral, then back to the policeman. "Looking up our family tree, officer."

"Fine sir," said the policeman. "You may get searched on the way back. Don't pick up any strangers and it'll all be okay."

"Thank you, officer."

They drove on into the town, then through it, and turned off onto the Lofthouse road. The road had been cleared of snow over the first five miles; in evidence of this were the huge piles pushed to one side or the other of the road every hundred yards or so. It came to an end quite suddenly. Tractors with great snow blades were still at work attacking drifts six or seven feet in height.

Vincent banged his open hand against the dashboard and cursed. "What a cluster fuck this is turning out to be. What do we do now? Wait for the stuff to melt?"

John scowled although the facial scar turned it into a grotesque grin. "Looks as though that's it, Vinny... Vincent."

Vincent threw his head back and closed his eyes. "You're certain there's no other way?"

"Only across the high moors, and it's going to be a damn sight deeper there. So, short of sprouting wings, no."

Vincent drummed his fingers against his chest for a moment and then sat up and opened the door. "Stay here," he ordered.

He was gone four or five minutes and then came back smiling. He opened the door and pointed at the diplomatic bag on the back seat, . "Get your tool bag, John, and put your coat on." Vincent leaned in and pulled his own coat out.

"Where are we going? And what about the car?"

"Leave the car. It's all arranged—oh, and leave the keys in the ignition."

They walked across the cleared road to one of the huge tractors. Groves followed Keoghan up the steps and into the roomy cab.

"Right, my friend," said Vincent to the driver. "Whenever you're ready."

The snowplow backed out into the middle of the road and then set off between the just-discernible gate posts into a field.

Vincent knew money was the answer to most problems. Enough of it could move mountains; a modest amount would take them to their destination.

CHAPTER 31

Hours had passed. Amanda had spent much of the first few of them sobbing quietly and had said hardly a word since being locked in the bedroom. Quite suddenly, however, whatever had been going on in her brain lost its hold on her. She sat up. "I'm hungry."

Stephanie had spent the same hours staring out of the window. She looked at her cousin and then turned back. "What do expect me to do about it? Go and knock on the door and say, 'Pretty please, we're hungry'?" More than a touch of anger crept into her voice.

"Well, he's got to feed us. He can't be meaning to kill us or he'd have done it by now." Amanda chewed her lip. "Don't you think?"

Stephanie breathed out noisily, relieving some of her tension. "Well, you might be right, but I wouldn't bet on it. He's more than a nut case, you know. He's a murderer, killed whoever got in his way."

"Aren't you forgetting something?"

"And what's that?"

"He's in love with you."

"He thinks he is."

"That's good enough."

Stephanie nodded. It was good enough if she could think of some way to use it. *I tried to shoot him, could I convince him of anything after that? If she tried and it didn't work, they were no worse off than before… probably.* "All right," she said. "We'll give it a try."

She got up and went to the door, began to bang on it.

Below, in the lounge, Robert had been watching the news. Over and over, the same story with minor variations, interviews with people whom he had never seen, never spoken to. A barman and his wife, a blond youth who spoke about his friend… every fifteen minutes, something different.

Robert tried to remember them, the people that the news report had blamed him for killing. *There was the policeman, the one with the car—but he had… he'd done something.* He shook his head, tried to clear his mind. *Pills. I used to have pills, kept me… going but you can't get them from the drugstores. Guess that's why I keep forgetting. Anyhow, lots of those things got nothing to do with me, bad memories, bad… dreams. No. Don't want those.*

A pounding kept going on and for several minutes, Robert thought it was a migraine, and he searched through his pockets for ibuprofen before realizing that it was outside of his head.

He got to his feet and went to the door of the lounge, stood at the foot of the stairs; the noise was coming from above. *Hell, Stephanie was up there with that friend of hers.* He stumped up the stairs on legs that felt like a robot's.

"Robert."

That was Stephanie. "Coming, Steph. I'm coming." There was a lock, a key in the keyhole. He turned it and almost fell forward as Stephanie pulled the door open. She smiled at him uncertainly. "Robert?"

He smiled back. "Steph."

"Do you think we could visit the bathroom?"

"Why did you get that gun, Steph? You know I love you—I wasn't going to hurt you."

She kept the smile fixed on her face. "You scared the daylights out of me. They were saying you'd, um, hurt people, Robert. It was just for protection."

"I scared you? You need protection, Steph? Against me?"

"I wasn't thinking too clearly, Robert."

How far did she play this? She now knew that Robert could be distracted with a mention of Alan. "And there was Alan; he'd said things about you. I just didn't know what to believe."

A flash of anger crossed Robert's face. "I knew that brother of mine was spreading poison." It was the only word he could think of. Robert's expression softened and with surprising tenderness, he stroked Stephanie's cheek with the back of his hand. "I wouldn't hurt you Steph. You've got to believe me. What did he tell you?"

Stephanie stood rigid as his knuckles brushed her skin. This is how it started with Alan: a caress, then a slap, or worse. But she had learned to be a good little actress. She kept her face soft, even though she could feel goosebumps lifting on the skin of her arms. "He, um, he said you'd beat me. Said you had this terrible temper. If I ever went with you, you'd get, er, fed up with me and go after other women."

Robert hit the door with his fist and the oak panel fractured. "The fu… sorry, Steph. I just knew he was poisoning your mind."

Before Stephanie had time to react, he put his arms around her, pulled her close. "He talked you out of marrying me, didn't he? It doesn't matter now, just tell me the truth." Robert held her away from him, his thumbs pressing into her biceps and his eyes boring into hers. "What did he say?"

"Yes, Robert, you're right. How did you know? He called you a beast, I shouldn't think of marrying you."

Robert released her and shook his head from side to side, looking like a great bear in the room. "I knew it. Knew it. I'll kill him for that; I swear I'll kill him."

Stephanie massaged her bruised arms and desperately tried to hold herself together. "Can you see now why I thought I couldn't trust you? I mean, if your own brother says that sort of thing, how was I to know what was truth and what was lies?" She spoke the words like lines in a play.

"Yeah." Robert sighed. "I can see it all." His face underwent change after change as emotions came and went: hate, disgust, worry and finally, triumph. In his mind, he played out the confrontation with his brother: the grappling, the blow to Alan's throat, dragging him to the lake and watching the body float away.

All at once, Robert realized it was not imagination, that it was all real, that Alan was already dead, he'd killed him. He staggered with the shock of it; he sought a chair and collapsed into it.

"Goddamn."

Stephanie took deep breaths, composed herself, waited a few minutes, and then went to him and looked into his face. Robert was quite unaware of her; his eyes had become glazed and saw nothing in the present. She beckoned to Amanda who had watched in almost disbelief as the tableau had played out. Together they went out, closed the door quietly and went downstairs.

"Shouldn't we have locked him in?" she asked Amanda at the foot of the stairs.

"It wouldn't have done any good. You saw how he broke the door panel. It might only make him cross again."

In the kitchen, they got milk from the fridge and some biscuits from a tin on the dresser. "I'm going to see if I can talk him into letting us go," Stephanie said between mouthfuls.

"God no." Amanda looked horrified. "Let's go now, while he's out of it."

"We've no idea what's going on in his mind. If he comes to and hears us getting the car out of the garage, he could turn murderous again. No. I've got to try."

She finished the glass of milk and ran up the stairs again.

The BMW seemed a lot smaller with John Merrick crammed into the passenger seat. I wasn't complaining. His overpowering size would make a copper or a villain take notice. Again, I mentally rehearsed the excuse for taking him with me. He had a good knowledge of the criminal and was very well acquainted with his background; his help would be of enormous value.

There was no use in explaining the debt of gratitude I felt. Merrick had brought me the files at considerable risk to himself and invaluable help to me.

Six forty-five at the offices and pretty well deserted. "Come on up, John. See where it all goes on."

He followed me up. "I was going to say how much better furnished your place is than mine."

"You were going to?"

"Yeah. Before I saw the state of your, what do you call it? Your squad room. Real home away from home. Ah, who's this? Someone working late?"

It was Alec Bell. I nodded to him. "Morning, Sergeant." He nodded back and got up from his desk to follow me to my own office. Inside, I pointed to an arm chair for John's benefit and looked across at Bell. "What can I do for you?"

Alec glanced at my visitor then back again, held up a plastic evidence bag. "Sorry about this, sir, but as long as you're here, I wondered if you'd care to comment on this."

"And this is?"

"Another note from the bomber. Know you've got a lot on your plate…"

I cut him short. "Has it been to forensics yet?"

"Not yet, sir. It's only been handled by one person at Philibuild and we've got her fingerprints, maybe the postman, too. I can run him down. Envelope, too, in a separate bag. I'd just like your opinion before I take them down."

I took the plastic bag and saw the note had been made up in the same manner as the previous one, cut-out letters from magazines and newspapers glued onto coarse white paper.

YOU WERE WARNED TO
STOP THE ROAD. YOU
SAW WHAT HAPPENED
WHEN YOU DID NOT.
CONTINUE AND FACE

MORE SERIOUS
REPRISALS.

Naturally, there was no signature, no identification. I spoke my thoughts out loud.

"Not your usual type of blackmailer, is it? No demands for money, literate. Neat, too. Look how he's centered each line. I'd look for someone middle class and middle-aged, doesn't seem to be a young person or an eco-warrior. No mention of the environment or harm to rare species."

I stared at Bell as I collected my thoughts. "This is what I'd like you to do. Check Philibuild's personnel files. Look for someone sacked or made redundant in the last couple of years—management, upper office echelons, something like that. Get down to the local newspaper offices and check the back numbers for letters to the editor, check the road's planned route for properties recently purchased. Oh yes, and when you get it down to forensics, get them to do a number on possible DNA traces from saliva on the envelope gum, and postage stamp."

I waited for a comment but got a thoughtful nod of the head instead. "If the DCI asks about any of this, don't mention my name. Understood?"

Bell nodded again then spoke. "Yes, I do understand, sir, and thanks for the ideas. Good luck with the murder hunt. I know the pressure you're working under." He scuttled out of the office.

"One of my team." I explained to John. "At the moment, he's attached to another senior officer because of this Cleghorn business. Relieves me of the responsibility."

"What's the problem? Poison pen?"

"Bomb threats. We're trying to find a man who knows how to blow things up."

"Hell. What's he using for explosives?"

"Fertilizer and diesel fuel, I'd guess."

"Ha. Used to use it to blow stumps out of the ground back on m'daddy's ranch. Any high school student knows how to do it."

"Exactly. Easy to get hold of so there's no clues there. Got to cover the psychological ground instead."

"Morning, sir." DC Asquith put his head round the door. "Ah, um. Sorry, didn't realize you had company."

"Come in, Constable." I made the introductions and explained how John would be going with us, Sergeant Bell's bomber already gone from my mind. I took a road map from the top of my desk and opened it up. "Can you show us where we'll be going, Asquith?"

"Sure." He looked at the map for a minute, got his bearings and pointed. "The murder site is right here, bottom of Brown Ridge on Masham Moor. Must be the only stand of trees in the area, mainly heather and gorse otherwise—and grassland." He grinned. "Only mountain sheep survive up there, sir."

"Hell. You mean it's even colder up there than here? Should of worn m'fur lined pants as well as a coat."

"Freeze your um, freeze you to death up there, sir. Anyway," he pointed again, "There are road blocks here, outside Pateley Bridge and at Healey across t'other side of the moor. There's just no other way in or out and no one answering to the description has come through the blocks."

"How recent is that information, Asquith?"

He checked his watch. "Up to half an hour ago, sir. The snow's still falling on the high moors so I wouldn't expect anyone through from Healey at all."

"Okay. Are we expected at Harrogate?"

"Oh yes."

"Good. Great. Let's go."

The drive up to Harrogate was uneventful. The usual packed line of traffic and the inevitable queue-jumpers were absent at this time of the morning, and the road surface had been cleared of snow. It took us just short of twenty-five minutes, city center to town center.

I took the opportunity to explain that one of my officers had been hurt in a fall from a helicopter and I was going to call by the hospital to see her.

We arrived there at 7:40 a.m. and the ward sister was not inclined to let me in. She had breakfasts to see to and the patient in question had to bathe. I flashed my warrant card at her and uttered sympathetic words and namedropped various detective inspectors and chief inspectors until she relented.

"How is she?" I asked as she led me along the corridor from her desk.

"As well as any woman can be who's just suffered the trauma of a miscarriage; she's in an anguish of self-blame and her hormones are running amok."

Which, of course, was news to me.

The sister stopped at a doorway and knocked before looking in. "All right, Inspector. Don't expect too much and don't go upsetting her."

I promised not to, holding my hands up. "Nothing could be further from my mind, Sister. She's a friend as well as a colleague."

"Hmm. Well." She looked into the room again. "You have a visitor, Mrs. Fearon. An Inspector White? Do you feel up to seeing him?"

I couldn't hear or see anything, though. Evidently the reply was favorable.

"Okay, Inspector. In you go. Five minutes."

Shelly looked unwell, which was to be expected. There was no smile for me, only to be expected, too. I reached down and picked up her hand and she squeezed my fingers. "How soon do you think you'll be out of here? I've got this great recipe for fish gumbo that I can't wait to try on you."

A ghost of a smile formed on her lips. "What are you doing here, Inspector White? I thought you were out catching that maniac Cleghorn." She tried to move and winced a bit. "Suppose you've heard?"

"About the baby? Yes. Yes, I've heard, and I'm really dreadfully sorry, Shelly. But I'm more concerned about you. You okay?"

"I'll survive, Stewart. Just give me time."

"All the time in the world."

"It's just that… the poor little bugger's never going to get a chance now."

I held onto her hand. "It's no use dwelling on what might have happened, you know. I'm sure you do know it just can't be helped. Used to worry about my tongue growing so long and look at it now." I stuck it out and touched it to the tip of my nose.

Shelly gave a weak smile and started coughing. "How on earth do you do that?" she asked when she had recovered.

I bent down and whispered. "I can do all sorts of things with it. You'll have to get better before I can show you."

I felt the brush of Shelly's lips against my cheek. "Don't worry. I'm sad because the little thing never had a life, but I'm pretty good at the 'what will be, will be' thing." She started coughing again and held on tightly to my hand.

The sound of the coughing had obviously attracted the sister's attention. She came in just as Shelly said, "Now get out of here and get the job finished, Inspector." Still gripping my hand hard, she shook it up and down to emphasize her words.

I leaned over and kissed her gently on the forehead. "You just get yourself better, you hear me?" And without looking back I left the room with the tears running down my cheeks.

CHAPTER 32

Vincent Keoghan was unhappy. The job was becoming more of a mess by the hour. Snowdrifts had slowed them drastically, and while it was warm and dry, even comfortable in the enormous cab of the tractor, daylight had already gone.

In darkness, things went from bad to worse. The vehicle's headlights—adequate for plowing fields and finding a way along narrow lanes—were more or less useless in snow-covered country where ditches waited to snare the wheels and stone walls had to be searched yard by yard for gateways.

After the driver had managed to claw his way back out of the second ditch, it had become obvious that their lightning-fast dash across country was not and never had been anything more than a Yorkshire man's imagination. At close to midnight they found a barn with bales of straw inside and horsy-smelling blankets. The hours between midnight and dawn were long, freezing, and miserable.

Vincent occupied his mind by cataloging the places where he had spent grim intervals of waiting. A week-long period in Somalia in torrential rain, sheltering beneath a rockslide and warmed by the smoky flames of a fire fuelled with animal droppings. Bosnia. Four days in a roofless house with shells whining overhead without letup, the explosions shaking the stone walls every two minutes—almost to the second. Sleep was impossible. Consecutive thought took an immense effort because his brain insisted on counting the seconds between detonations. And yet, Vincent could not remember being colder and more frustrated than he was right now.

Dawn did arrive eventually. Jim, the tractor driver, woke first. He was a farm worker, used to being up before the sun, and he woke the others. Snow was falling. Sometimes it was possible to see the boundary walls at the edges of the fields where snow had banked up into mounds, at other times visibility was limited to a few yards.

Jim wanted to keep the five hundred pounds Vincent had paid him to take them to Kiln Hill House up by Scar House reservoir. He put a jolly face on things. "Right gents. We can see where we're going now. We'll be able to make it all right; I'll start the tractor up."

"I hope you're right, feller," said Vincent with a scowl at the snow coming through the doorway.

"Piece of piss. No problem."

Just what a piece of piss meant was beyond Vincent. They did make it, though it took them a further two hours before the Americans were dropped off at the toll bar at the foot of the valley. Jim left with instructions to bring the hire car through as soon as the drifts had been cleared or to take it back to a garage in Pateley Bridge. Vincent didn't care what actually happened to the car, the job was the only important matter. They would figure out how to get away afterward.

Vincent smiled grimly as he trudged through the snow in shoes ill-suited to the conditions. He'd been flying from Berlin to Washington DC, and wasn't prepared for a winter survival exercise. Presumably Cleghorn got here in a car, the sister-in-law too; neither of them was going to need transport for very much longer.

John Groves had folded his largest scale map to show the area immediately ahead of them. "It's got to be up this way."

"Very good, John. Is there another way you can see?"

"Well, no. Not yet."

They slogged on for another thirty-five minutes until they came to a wooden bridge to their right. Beneath the covering of fresh snow, it was just possible to see the ruts left by several vehicles which had turned right.

"That goes up to a dam at the end of a lake. It must be straight on."

"Reckon that's right. We've got one set of tracks going straight on. Wonder how long they've been there?"

"Hard to say." He looked up at the sky from which a light snow was still falling. "How much snow fell last night?"

"I don't know, but I'm going to guess the tracks are no more than twelve hours old. Come on."

They passed a few dwellings. Oak Farm, the Pines, a rambling house half hidden by trees had a sign covered in windblown snow. Vincent went up to it and cleaned it. Dunroamin. "What the hell sort'f a name's that?"

"Dunroamin. Done roaming around," John explained. "They've quit roamin' around."

"Yeah I get it. But hell, what a name."

The next sign pointed right and said Kiln Hill House. A house huddled in against the hillside a quarter of a mile away. The partly obliterated tire tracks turned into the lane and ran as far as they could make them out; there was no vehicle to be seen.

"Here we are, John boy. We'll keep to the side here, where we've got a bit of cover, and reconnoiter."

Robert lay back in the armchair and dozed.

The fire had died back yet still threw out comfortable warmth, like the sort of heat you got in late spring, in the evening. It was like putting your hand near a wall that had been soaking up the sun all day and was now giving it back again. The ground could do that too, if you laid down on it, feeling the heat coming back at you.

His dreams took him outside. Overhead the sky was an impossible deep blue which changed infinitesimally to yellow and then to a dusky orange at the horizon. The sun sat crimson and oblate, a fraction above the long line of black hills, black clouds hung in front of it like meager curtains stretched across a long window. On the far side of the sky, blue was gradually swamped in sable and new leaves glowed green against the darkness.

It was warm. Late spring when the air is still fresh enough to taste like wine. Early evening when the first stars blink furtively along the eastern skyline. Stephanie was there in the corner of the field with him, holding him against her nakedness. He watched entranced, his hair as red as the sunset sky against her pale skin. Robert could hardly bear to watch as he made love to the willowy form alongside him, watched his head dip to kiss her breasts, and watched his fingers caress her waist, her hips.

For a moment he looked up, as though he might have heard breathing—and just for that moment, it seemed that it was Alan who was holding Stephanie. Yet how could that be? She loved *him*, not Alan. So what was his brother doing holding her so tightly? Then he turned away again and watched once more, confident that he *was* the one who held the girl; she was clinging to him. Robert's eyes lost their focus and his vision turned inward; he was there now, with her. He slid to the ground beside her. He could feel the warmth of her hands on his body, feel her breath against his cheek and they made love together.

The warmth had gone from the grass bank. Robert was cold and damp and the sun had long since vanished though a three-quarter moon rode the sky. He stood up, his heart beating like a hollow drum in his brain, and the touch of his shirt felt like barbed wire round his neck. Absently brushing at the grass and twigs that had embedded themselves in his clothes, he turned and looked across the paddock, which was bare and empty. He climbed the fence and walked across to the place where he had seen them together.

The grass was flattened there, with a small patch of color just visible in the moon's silver light. Robert bent down to touch it, then picked up a sapphire earring. He smiled at the memento, a souvenir of their first love-making.

Stephanie watched him; he hardly seemed aware of her. She wondered if she and Amanda could make a run for it but his eyes were sometimes closed, sometimes open and when they were open they seemed to stare at her.

She was looking through the sitting room doorway, and her line of vision was restricted. Stephanie could just see the barrel of the gun and visions of him chasing after them with the shotgun eventually decided her against running. Instead she went to the kitchen, closed the door and busied herself with breakfast: toasted pikelets and a pot of tea. She looked at the cutlery in the drawer and even though she wasn't sure what she could do with it, she slid a steak knife inside the waistband of her jeans. Its presence would, at least, give her a feeling of added security.

As Robert eventually returned to the here and now, he was shivering violently. *So cold*. His eyes focused slowly, first on the fire which had died away to ashes and left the room to go cold, then, as a movement caught his attention, he turned to the doorway where Stephanie was standing.

Stephanie. He smiled.

"Would you like a cup of tea?" she asked.

"Great," he said.

"There're some buttered pikelets, too, if you like."

Pikelets? He thought of little pike, small fish, maybe like little kippers, smoked. Robert was ravenous. *Christ, I could eat anything.* "Great, Steph, Whatever's on the menu." He shook his head, his smile became a grin. "It's really great to see you again, you know? Like a new start at life. Really."

Stephanie smiled uncertainly and went to pour tea and bring him the pikelets, which turned out to be English muffins... no, crumpets, that's what they were. Robert wolfed them down and drank half a cup of tea, his immediate needs filled, he looked up and caught the girl looking at him again.

She realized she had been staring at him and looked away. "You were really hungry, weren't you?"

"Sure was, Steph. And thank you for breakfast. You know, Steph, we really do have to talk about what we're going to do. Would you consider coming back to the States with me?"

How she retained her composure, Stephanie never knew. She had been playing a part ever since Robert had unlocked the bedroom door and it seemed as though the real her was buried under so many layers of *pretend* that, apart from an unnaturally long pause, there was simply no sign of her on the surface. "Well, that's one option I guess, Robert. The truth is, though, I've been away from England for so long I really want to stay here."

There was a fractional change in Robert's features, a tightening of muscles, a narrowing of the eyes. Anger, it suggested.

Stephanie smiled. "Just for a while. I could show you around."

He relaxed again and again the change was so slight that Stephanie wondered if it was just in her imagination. Robert's smile came slow and easy. "That sounds..."

A voice came from outside, a voice from the past.

"Goddamn. Goddamn it to hell."

Robert stood up and looked through the window where he could see a tall figure, a male, in the early morning light. The man was standing on the drive, his head turned to the side so that the face was in profile.

The figure was fuller, the face a little older than he remembered, but there was no doubt in his mind. "Goddamn. Crispy-both-sides." The flood of memories which accompanied the recognition made him stumble with shock. They seemed to erupt from every crevice and recess in his brain, memories long forgotten: painful, evil; death and maiming. Robert put his hands to his temples and screamed at the sudden knowledge of what he had been. No human sound of pain, but a feral scream of fear and hatred, primeval, an animal cornered and in fear for its life.

Stephanie clapped her hands to her ears and stared at the gaunt figure with crooked fingers and wild, frightened eyes.

Robert stood to his full height, his hands dropping to his sides. Something had changed. His stance was that of an athlete, every slightest movement had the grace of a stalking animal, the readiness for instant action of a mountain lion with dinner just a leap beyond its claws.

He retrieved the shotgun from beneath the settee and went out into the hall, opened the front door and blocking its further movement with one foot, he shouted out into the snow. "What do you want, Vinny?" His voice was perfectly flat, betraying neither pain nor pleasure at the meeting.

In contrast, the voice which answered him was rich, persuasive and filled with bonhomie. "Why Robert, hello there. What do *I* want? I want you to step out here and we'll swap a few stories."

Robert could feel his muscles growing rock hard; the door handle creaked where his fingers clutched it. He'd control the anger, hold it in check until the time was right. He could almost feel the muzzle of an unknown pistol pointing towards him from the relative darkness outside. "No, no Vinny. Too damn cold out there. Step inside, buddy. It's warm in here."

Vinny's voice changed its timbre slightly and Robert, keyed up, heard the tiny difference as though it was a shouted warning. "Won't take a minute. Got a cab waiting down the end of the driveway and I've got this message from Hedges. Wants you back in the fold. Look, I've got his letter with me." Vinny's hand went towards the opening between his coat lapels.

"Careful, Vinny."

"Slow and careful, Robert." He reached in and brought out something square and white. "Now, come and get it for God's sake." The note of impatience was about what you might expect from someone waiting in the snow with a taxi meter running.

"Bring it here then, Vinny."

Vinny seemed to lose all restraint. "Come on out, damn you—and it's *Vincent*," he shouted.

Has he really lost his cool, wondered Robert, *or is he just faking*? He applied more pressure. "Vincent? Vinny not good enough? Well, well Vincent. Slip the letter through the door and be on your way. Don't forget your cab." Robert started to ease the door shut but stopped as Vinny shouted again.

"Okay, I'll slip it through the door, if that's what you want."

Robert moved swiftly back behind the door, going down on one knee expecting a hail of bullets to come through at chest height. He pulled the shotgun to him and swung it round, ready for the rush which would follow the bullets.

Neither came.

What did come through the door was a small, gray, pear-shaped object: a grenade. Robert had used hundreds of them in the past and instinct took over. In the corner of the hall was a heavy, leather-covered chair; handling it like a feather pillow, he tossed it over the grenade and flung himself backward into the sitting room. "Get down, Steph!" he shouted, wondering where she was.

The grenade exploded with a roar which, in the confined space, sounded like Armageddon and looked like the reddest flames out of the inferno. The armchair blew to bits, shreds of fabric and splinters of mahogany flying like shrapnel, plaster showered from the ceiling, some of the oak paneling in the hallway was ripped off the wall, broken into strips and sent scything into anything less solid than timber.

Three seconds of absolute silence followed and Vinny, preceded by his favorite weapon, entered. The gun's barrel peered one way and then the other, searching through the wreckage and smoke for any sign of movement.

He stopped. The sound of sobbing came from the kitchen and Vinny's eyes flickered towards the splintered door, the pistol following his gaze. It was all the time Robert needed, before Vinny could react to the slight sound, a chair came through the sitting room doorway too fast to dodge. It hit his right shoulder and arm and as Vinny lost his balance, it fell and struck him on his outstretched ankle. He crashed to the floor, yelping with pain and surprise and, suddenly chilled, he watched a man-like shape materialize from the cloud of hanging dust. A blackened mouth opened in a grin which revealed teeth startlingly white against the dusty and dirty face.

"Hello, Vincent," he said softly. "I gotta say, I'm surprised you came all this way just to see me. After Prague—when I killed your friends from the Russian Mafia, when I thought I'd killed you—I never expected to see you again. I guess Hedges never found out who the mole was after all, never tumbled to those twenty kilos of cocaine that used to go everywhere with you in the diplomatic bag. Obviously he didn't know, or you wouldn't be here, alive, would you?" Robert chuckled. "I'll fix that shortly."

Vinny's eyes searched around, looking for the gun which had fallen from his fingers. It was lost, somewhere among the debris, not that he was worried about it. He knew he was the better man. This old has-been had been away from training for years, his reflexes would be shot to hell. Vinny grinned and Robert ignored it.

For the moment, he was relishing this vision of his past. *Hey, he told himself, I was on the side of the great and the good; this loser was a weevil, needed stamping on then, needs stamping on now.* "Remember when I was in that facility, recovering from the beating I got from those Czech guards? Did you enjoy shoving the scopolamine into my arm? Hmm?"

A hint of surprise entered Vinny's eyes. *How did the schmuck know about that?*

Robert grinned again as he saw the expression and knew what was going on in the other's brain. "Oh, it nearly worked, Vinny. Full marks. I'd forgotten until seeing you today, you brought it all back, just like that." Robert snapped his fingers and a little cloud of dust came off them. "If Hedges had sent someone else, he'd probably have got to me, someone I didn't recognize. So now you've got to kill me, Vinny. Just in case I ever say something to Hedges."

Vinny had been steeling himself for the effort as he let Robert whine on. His right arm was useless, weakened by the earlier attack. He worked himself around and now he was poised, ready to take whatever opportunity presented itself.

"Gotta kill me?"

"Yes," said Vinny as he lunged with his left arm straight, knuckles forward, to strike the other's Adam's apple. There was no impact, nothing where he'd aimed except for empty air and his arm was suddenly locked in a vice-like grip.

Robert's face filled his vision, the whites of his eyes glowing like white hot steel, the pupils as black as the blackest night. "Gettin' slow, Vinny. All that good living and not enough bad guys to keep you up to scratch. And look at the flab, Vinny. Goin' to hell in a handcart."

Vinny's right hand suddenly shot out, going for the eyes as fast as a striking snake despite the weakness, but the strike was blocked and a split second later the arm was broken. Robert had turned the arm palm upward, had snapped it down over his shoulder and broken it at the elbow. Vinny shrieked and clamped his mouth shut.

"Never learn, do you, Vinny? Never as good as me, not then, not now. And now, hell, you're going to suffer."

Now Vinny *was* frightened. His erstwhile friend was mad, insane. Already the pain from his injuries was indescribable. Robert moved the arm and the broken ends of the bone grated together, pain piercing to the very essence of his being. "Listen Robert," he said desperately, "this isn't my doing. You've got it wrong. It wasn't me who was the traitor in the department, it was Hedges."

Robert didn't seem to hear.

"Robert, how the hell do you think I could afford four mil of coke?"

Robert looked at the arm he was holding, clinically, as though it was a specimen of some sort. He put his head on one side and pulled.

"Robert!" screamed Vinny. "For Chrissake! The best I ever pulled down was a hundred grand. Hedges. He ordered you to Prague to be killed away from American… Rob… Oh God, freakin… Robert…" Vinny whimpered as the pain eased fractionally. "Hedges, he had you locked up in that freaking hospital and ordered the scop… no, freaking no, Robert."

Robert's grip never relaxed. He could feel the bones separate and the broken ends grating as he sank his fingers into the flesh between the two. He could hear Stephanie still crying in the kitchen and wanted to get this over with. How much was true and how much fabricated on the spot, he did not know. He would separate that out later but for now, he wanted to hear everything Vinny was going to say.

"We were friends, Vinny. You could have said no, you were too close. Plenty of excuses you could have thought up. You just wanted to be better than me and when you couldn't be better, you wanted me dead."

"No. Oh God Robert, no I couldn't. Hedges had me cold, had to do what I was ordered." Robert shook the injured arm a little. "Stop, Robert, please. Freaking stop."

It was the "please" that did make him stop. "Okay, Vinny." He rammed his right hand against Vinny's windpipe and squeezed it hard. This time there was no hallucination, no misty vision. He smiled fiercely as Vinny's struggles weakened, as he went limp.

Robert was omnipotent. *I can do anything.*

Long seconds after Vinny's life had gone; Robert dropped the body and stood up. He was about to go into the kitchen to comfort Stephanie then froze when he saw a face through the side window. A gun was held at the side of the face, the barrel pointing vertically upward. The gun-carrying hand came forward, the knuckles brushing against the glass pane, wiping the melted snow.

Robert was covered in dust, immobile, all but invisible to a casual observer. The man outside the window moved on, towards the front door. Robert went back to Vinny's body and searched through the plaster and broken furniture until he found the handgun. He picked up the Glock, wiped some of the dust off it and went to stand behind the door.

John Groves reached the door which was still ajar and squinted carefully through the narrow gap into the vestibule. He saw his colleague's body, the blue parka making it easy to recognize. If an operative needed back-up, John was a good choice. If he needed something with which to stick a microphone under a table, John would already be chewing the gum; if a fuse had to be lit, John would have already been lighting a cigarette. Brains were not John's forte; his immediate response was to go into the hallway to see how badly the grenade had injured Vinny. He pushed at the door, pushed harder as it fetched up against some fallen plaster. He bent, intending to drop to one knee at Vinny's side.

Robert brought the barrel of the heavy hand gun down hard at the base of the man's skull. John dropped without a sound, falling across Vinny's body.

Giving the matter no further thought, Robert ran into the kitchen to find Stephanie. She was slumped down against a set of cupboard doors, blood staining her fair hair, seeping slowly between her fingers where she held them against the wound. It seemed a contradiction that a man so given to violence could at the same time be so tender. He gently pried Stephanie's fingers away and separated the strands of hair to see that the wound was entirely superficial. There was no sign of foreign matter; it was a clean cut, probably made by a piece of shrapnel, a fragment from the grenade body.

It took every ounce of strength Stephanie had not to scream at Robert to get away from her. She took a deep breath and calmed herself.

Robert asked in a perfectly normal voice, "Gotta first aid kit around here?"

She nodded and pointed out the white box with its green cross on the top of the kitchen dresser. Robert cleaned the wound with antiseptic and applied a field dressing before half lifting her to sit on a dining chair at the breakfast bar. Leaving her for a moment, he went back out to the hall and shouted up the stairs.

"Hey!" *What in hell was the woman's name—ah.* "Amanda, come on down here. Your cousin's been hurt and needs some help." Then he thought of the taxi Vinny had mentioned. *Had the driver heard the grenade go off?*

He went outside, walked twenty feet down the track as far as the roadway, feeling in his pockets for some cash to pay off the driver. There was no cab, no sign of any vehicle and the two pairs of footprints backing off into the distance were quite plain. Robert followed them a little further, two hundred yards to the first slight bend in the road—still nothing. They had come on foot.

He turned back and stopped again as the sound of a helicopter filled the air. It swooped in from the east; the word *police* painted on its side and passed over at a height of a hundred feet or so. Robert waved to it, a bit of play acting would look natural and carefree from up there, in the cabin. It veered slightly and flew off to the north, in the direction of the reservoir.

CHAPTER 33

Andy Asquith was in his element, indicating landmarks and points of interest as they flew over his home area. A sort of proprietary tone crept into his voice as he pointed and shouted above the roar of the rotors.

"There's the road block at Healey, sir. See that, those stones? That's a Druid's temple, got to go back two thousand years at least. Across there, you can see the reservoirs coming up. First one's Leighton, then there's Roundhill. There are some ruins..."

"What's the village called, DC?"

"That's Lofthouse, sir."

I looked down, something beginning to worry at the back of my mind. Lofthouse, the name I had heard before. We were two hundred feet or so above the main street and police cars were moving along it. I hoped my instinct was right.

"Must have got the snowplows through then. They'll have enough people in for a house-to-house search, shortly."

The pilot broke in on the intercom. "We've come roadblock to roadblock now, sir. Where do you want to go?"

"Where to now?" I shouted at Asquith whose helmet didn't have an intercom set. "Any suggestions, DC?"

"The murder site, sir?"

I nodded. "Do a sweep around the houses we can see along that lane and then onto the murder site. Can you go forward and direct the pilot?"

We carried on along the length of the street and then followed a country road for a few minutes. The whiteness was beginning to hurt my eyes. The snow had stopped falling and the sky was a bright blue with a brilliant glare coming off the snow-covered ground. Someone waved to us as we came up to the end of the road which still had to be cleared here and then we followed a turn-off up towards the big reservoir.

"Enjoying the weather?" I asked John Merrick, squashed into a seat on the starboard side.

"Kinda nice now I can feel my pinkies." The Floridian chuckled. "Looks clean, don't it? All this snow?"

I chuckled, too. I could guess what he must be feeling, a man born to ninety plus temperatures coming to a place like this where the thermometer had not risen above freezing since he had arrived. Asquith backed away from the pilot's shoulder and squirmed back into his bucket seat and continued his travelogue.

"River Nidd and over there, that's Scar House reservoir. The murder was discovered just…"

"Scar House?" I almost screamed above the motor noise.

"That's right sir. Scar House."

"Christ Almighty." I thumbed the button on my microphone. "Pilot, when we get to the top, will you swing back round and make a slow pass over those houses again?"

"Right, sir."

"One of those houses is owned by Stephanie's cousin… Holtby, something Holtby. I saw the deeds, Scar House near Lofthouse. I thought it was the name of the house itself, not a place." I thumped the armrest. "Damn. How far are we from the place where they found the murdered policeman?"

"Six, seven miles."

"And the roads up here, were they blocked?"

"Not severely, sir. Not until last night."

"It's too much of a coincidence that Stephanie Cleghorn's cousin owns a house six miles from the murder site." I leaned over and explained the situation to John Merrick and then back to Asquith. "Cleghorn must be in one of these houses down here, I'll get the pilot to radio a message through to the police on the ground. Start the house-to-house out along here; leave Lofthouse until afterwards—if we still need to."

I leaned over to the American again. "Don't know how you work, John, but with me, it's often a gut feeling I have to go with. My guts are telling me Cleghorn's down there."

John grinned broadly. "We got a scientific term for it, Stewart. It's called a *hunch* and I learned to trust 'em years ago."

Robert returned to the house. Without really pausing for thought, he tapped a feebly moving John Groves behind the ear and carried on through to the kitchen. The back door was open, and he could hear the two dogs outside. Stephanie was still seated at the bar and Amanda was fussing round with a new pot of tea and thin cookie things. Ignoring Amanda, he took hold of Stephanie's wrist.

"C'mon, Steph. Get your coat on, we're getting out of here, now."

"What the bloody hell are you talking about?" snapped Amanda. "Where are you taking her? And what about that explosion? It's wrecked the place, wrecked it."

"Oh shut the hell up, lady," Robert lashed out, catching Amanda on the shoulder. It may have been a mere brush-off to Cleghorn but it staggered the woman. "I ain't got time for chit chat. I can't stick around here, the cops'll be thicker than wasps around honey."

Stephanie stood up and shuddered. The blow to the head and the explosion had shattered what self-confidence she had retained, and she knew better than to argue with Robert. Meekly, she allowed Robert to lead her to the hall; she slipped her arms into the torn and dusty coat he lifted from the hook. Then, back through the kitchen and out the back door, past the dogs which instinctively cowered away from him and across the yard to the garage.

Inside, he took just sixty seconds to transfer the battery from the charger to the snowmobile.

"That? We're not going on that." She cowered away from the machine as if it was poison.

"Damn right, Steph. The police have got to be watching the roads; the only way is over the hills. Don't worry, dear, I'm quite safe to ride behind—been miles on these things. Nothing here I haven't seen in Alaska, Norway. Spent time in both places, in the winter."

He checked the fuel and, finding it nearly full, he pulled out the choke and thumbed the ignition button. The two-stroke coughed once or twice and then caught, building up to its characteristic high-pitched whine. He pointed to the passenger seat and Stephanie got on; Robert stood astride the snowmobile, slipping the clutch to keep the engine revved up high while he walked it off the duckboards and out onto the snow of the backyard.

He put the machine into first properly and drove it across the backyard to a gate in the stone wall at the side and out into the field. Taking the steep scarp at a long shallow angle, he took them west and then northward.

Several police cars were parked along a short track leading up to a house set against the hillside. The pilot put the chopper down in a field next to the house. Asquith, John Merrick and I prepared to leave the helicopter and I remembered Shelly's accident. "Take it easy. It's further down to the ground than you think." We jumped out one by one into the snow. There was a gate leading to the backyard, and although I didn't take it in immediately, there was a fresh track through it in the snow leading back out into the field.

We went to the back door; a largish, rather buxom young woman let us in. She was so incoherent—with relief, perhaps, I wasn't sure—that she could hardly speak. I smelled smoke and something else, like the shooting range beneath the offices at work—explosives. I followed my nose through to the hallway where a scene of utter devastation met my eyes, devastation and two bodies—one alive, one very dead. I could see officers in uniform outside so I went to the door and pulled it open, bouncing it over the rubble on the carpet.

"Morning. Detective Inspector White from the Ridings Regional Crime Squad. You'd better come in."

I left them staring at the chaos and went back in the kitchen where Asquith had calmed the woman down somewhat. "Where's Cleghorn?" I asked bluntly.

She stopped in mid-ramble, and Asquith looked just a little put out. "Gone. He's taken my husband's snowmobile; he's got Stephanie with him."

I nodded. "How long ago?"

"Ten minutes? No more."

"Thanks. The uniformed police are out there," I nodded to the hallway. "They'll be through in a moment. We've got to get after them."

"Go," she said. "For God's sake, go."

"Which way did he go?" asked Asquith.

"This way, Asquith. John. Come on."

In the chopper, I pointed to the snowmobile tracks as the rotors were spinning up. "Just follow the tracks for now; we'll catch up with him in minutes."

Robert followed the slopes of the hills, angling gently up where he had to. This machine was not as high powered as the ones he was used to and needed nursing up the steeper inclines. However, stone walls and outcrops constricted the slopes and blocked his path. It became obvious very quickly that he could not get up to the dam and over the top with a direct run across the grade.

It seemed that back down the valley was their only route. The British police would be waiting for him and for the first time he had to admit the possibility that he was not going to escape. With the admission came the realization that the consequences of his recent actions would be incarceration. There was a distinct possibility he would be put somewhere very like the secure facility he had escaped from. Hell, he could break out again, but… no time to think about that now.

He started back down the valley in the hope that some other escape would present itself.

Robert found he was running parallel to the road, the hillsides and walls pressing him nearer and nearer to it and to the possibility that in addition to the helicopter, police cars might come in behind him. A mile or so went by and an opening in the hills to his right appeared. Without hesitation he veered away from the road and into the narrow valley. Behind him, Stephanie clung on for all she was worth as the snowmobile bucked and slithered in the increasingly wet and treacherous snow. Their general direction remained westward though constrained by the hills; it was also downward, away from the high moor-land and the cold.

Eventually, penned in by the slopes and trapped between dry stone walls, he emerged onto a narrow road. It was covered in virgin snow; no one had come this way since the snowfalls had begun. Robert gunned the motor and turned right onto the road; left would take them back towards Lofthouse, where the police were present in force so, right was his only choice.

The road came to an abrupt end. Robert almost dragged the machine across the middle of a square of stone walls and just stared around him for several moments.

The cold stream of air had revived Stephanie and she looked around, as perplexed as the American. "It's over Robert," she said. "There's nowhere else to run."

He turned off the snowmobile's ignition and stepped down in to the ankle-deep snow. "No. You're wrong, Steph. It ain't over 'til I say it's over. Come on, kid, this way." He pulled her with him along a narrow path; besides the way they had come, it was the only other way out of the enclosure.

They passed a sign as they went, the snow only partially covering the lettering and already melting and dripping away. *How Stean Gorge.* Stephanie read as she was hurried past it.

She knew about How Stean Gorge, a popular place to visit in the summer. It was a natural gorge which had once been a series of underground waterways. The waterways had collapsed and gave the gorge a twisting, ravine-like appearance. Pathways ran along the edges and white-painted timber bridges crossed the rushing water at intervals. Children loved its dark eeriness and the way the water mingled with their shouts echoing along the confining limestone walls.

Now it was deserted except for Robert and Stephanie stumbling along the paths, almost splashing through unstable banks of melting snow. "This is getting us nowhere," cried Stephanie, as she tripped and clung to her abductor's arm to prevent herself sprawling in the mud and snow.

Robert knew she was right though he could not admit it, not even to himself. "Come *on*," he shouted, more roughly than he had meant to, trying to be gentle again when he saw her recoil. "We've got to keep going, Steph. There's a way out, there's bound to be." At least she was with him. Just her being there made him feel strong. He wouldn't leave her even if she did slow him down some. He couldn't, not now.

The path broadened out, split into two. Another sign, dripping wet but otherwise quite clear told them the caves under Nidderdale were open from April to November between 9:00 a.m. and 4:00 p.m. Robert glanced at his watch, which said 10:30. "At least we got the time right, Steph. Wrong month, right time. Let's check them out."

"For God's sake, Robert, not in this weather. They've got to be flooded out with all this snow melting. There'll be raging torrents down there."

"Look, Steph. You're the only thing that's keeping me going. If it wasn't for you, girl, I'd be holed up back there waiting for the police with this." He reached inside his windbreaker and half pulled a gun into view. "Now please, come on. If there's too much water there, we can come back up."

They went on until an iron gate blocked their way; Robert put his hands on Stephanie's waist and simply hoisted her over it. He leaped up, putting a foot to the top and was over. The opening to the caves was not large, just a cleft in the rock wide enough for one person at a time to pass through. Inside, a wooden cupboard was secured to the rock wall; the words *Emergency Only* were stenciled on the doors. "I guess that means us." Robert smashed the small pressed steel padlock off with the butt of his gun. Inside were blankets, flashlights and ropes. There was food, too; Robert recognized the British version of MREs. Robert filled his pockets and then tossed several blankets to Stephanie. "It might get cold in there. These'll help." He took a coil of rope and four flashlights, three of them he tucked into pockets and held the fourth ready to use.

He flicked on the heavy waterproof light and shone it around the small vestibule. "That way, I guess, Steph. Let's go exploring. You know, I feel lucky with you along. I guess we'll find our way under these hills and far away, huh?"

There was no response.

CHAPTER 34

I saw the tracks left by the snowmobile as soon as we were high enough to see over the house. I was about to tap the pilot's shoulder and point the way, but he was ahead of me, swinging round and plunging after them.

John Merrick nudged me. "Those suits back there? I'll give all my next month's pay to the Sisters of Mercy if they're not Agency."

"CIA?"

"The same. Looks to me like one of them threw a grenade into the house. Can't have been too particular about who it killed or maimed."

"Didn't work, though. Clumsy, weren't they? Cleghorn got the both of them."

"That guy is some piece of work." There seemed to be a note of admiration in Merrick's voice, I grudgingly had to concur. Cleghorn was a consummate professional, unstoppable: he'd be a valuable ally under other circumstances.

"Yeah, well. He's done enough killing. It's time we put a stop to it."

"Ain't that the truth. Do we do it or do you pull in a SWAT team? How do you work it here?" John was a happy as a sand-boy, beaming at the thought of a shootout.

"Depends on the circumstances when we get him cornered." I turned to look him squarely in the face. "If I do decide to go after him myself, I want you well back and out of the way. It's me that's armed, me and DC Asquith. If you get injured I shall be out of a job faster than you can say Gordon Bennet."

John Merrick continued to beam at me. He reached inside his sheepskin coat, just below the neck and pulled out a small cannon. "Now don't you go worrying about me, Stewart. Me and Slim, here, we've been through a lot together, we know what it's all about and we don't want keeping away from the fun."

"Bloody hell, John. Put that away, will you?" I was both amazed at the huge handgun and alarmed. "How the hell did you get it into the country?"

Merrick dropped the gun back out of sight. "When this is all over, we'll go and have a few more beers. Maybe I'll tell you then. Okay?"

And maybe I really didn't want to know. I *did* know I should not let him get involved any deeper in the business, but what could I say without appearing ill-mannered? I settled instead for a curt "We'll see." I paused a little as we covered another mile. I noticed he wore a wedding ring. "Got a family, John? Won't your wife be missing you?" And I knew instantly I'd said something wrong. John's smile vanished like a lightbulb turned off.

"My old lady died two years ago last summer." He paused a moment, his gaze drifting away from my eyes and out of cabin. "She'd gone shopping at the Florida Square Mall." He chuckled, though it didn't sound humorous. "One thing she was *really* good at, was shopping. Used t'visit the Beall's outlet stores, search through those racks of fifty-percent-off items, y'know. She'd come back with enough stuff to keep herself in clothes for a year. Never wore half of them, left them there hanging in her closet. Hell, she surely loved shopping."

I reached out and put a hand on his shoulder. "Sorry I asked, John. Only wanted to know if there was someone waiting for you."

"Don't mind me." His grin started to come back, sunlight coming from behind a cloud. "Just ignore me, a sentimental old fool."

I wished there was, or even had been, someone I could feel that way for.

"At least Emmeline went quick. Heart attack. Doctor said she never knew what hit her."

"Guv," said the pilot in my earphone, "he's turned away from the dam, maybe he couldn't get up the slope. Looks like he's heading back to Lofthouse."

"What the hell's he going to do?" I asked of no one in particular. "It's crawling with police between the house and there."

No one replied. The pilot followed the tracks and we kept our eyes skinned as we travelled above the road, the snowmobile traces alongside. "Breaking right here," said the pilot.

I nudged Andy Asquith and pointed. "You're right. He's had to come this way because the machine won't take him up the hills. Maybe would if it was just himself, but he's got the girl, too. Extra weight."

"He's not going anywhere here, either. That'll take him down to the gorge, no further."

"What's that?"

"How Stean Gorge. Sort of a small-scale canyon; quite a tourist attraction in the summer. Not been there since I was a kid."

We continued on for a few more minutes, the helicopter's roar altering frequency as we flew low between the hills, changing direction along the winding valley. We saw the abandoned snowmobile then and the pilot spun, rose a little as he killed forward speed and set us down in the patch of snow next to the machine. Merrick, Asquith and I left the chopper and started out after the footsteps left by Cleghorn and his sister-in-law. A little further on, the helicopter's noise had diminished sufficiently to hear each other without shouting. I paused and told Asquith to let the uniforms know where we were.

"C'mon, Stewart, he's on foot. He can't be far ahead of us now." John Merrick was chafing at the delay and, fearful he would go on without me, I followed on. "Catch us up when you've let them know the score," I told Asquith. It seemed a long time before he did catch us up at a gateway with a sign about the caves and opening times.

"If he's gone in there, can he get out some other way?" I asked him. "You're our expert, don't forget."

Andy Asquith shrugged. "Don't know, sir. It's been too long since I was here; I was only a youngster at the time."

"The uniform lot coming? With guns?"

"No, sir. Couldn't get through, poor area for radio. Went back to the chopper and the pilot tried too. No dice."

The caves were neither large nor spectacular: merely a series of linked, low-roofed spaces with small stalactites depending from the gray and sometimes mud-encrusted ceilings. A faint pathway where feet had compacted the dirt wound around rocks and a few mounded stalagmites until it came to the end, a five-minute walk. In front of them, Cleghorn saw a white and black painted barrier surmounted by a sign reading, *members of the public not allowed beyond this point.*

"I don't think they mean us." Robert said and pushed the barrier aside. He swept the beam from the flashlight on the ground in front of them, and presently found a cast iron grill covering a sizeable hole in the ground. The grill was not fastened down, relying—it seemed—on its sheer weight to deter anyone from opening up the hole.

It was heavy all right, but to Robert it might as well have been balsa wood. He lifted one corner and dragged it round in a half circle, leaving the more-or-less square hole uncovered.

Stephanie stood back several feet from the black opening. She looked bored, though really, she was watching from a place far back in her mind, the place she'd gone when Alan was hitting her.

"Look," said Robert and she looked.

"What is it?" she asked and with a seeming faint effort of will, added, "You're not going down there, are you?"

"We are, sweetheart. You don't think I'm going to leave you now we're together again, do you? Can you hear the water down there?" He tipped his head. "It means there's a way out and we're going to find it."

Somewhere in the back of her mind, she rebelled at the idea of climbing down into this filthy black hole, but what could she do? Stephanie was too tired to resist.

"There're metal steps set in the wall, see? Now get yourself over the edge and it'll be just like climbing down a ladder."

Stephanie did as she was told, putting her feet where Robert said, moving a foot down to the next cleat and the next. A musty smell rose up from below, damp and faintly mushroomy.

The smell evoked memories of childhood. The first house she could remember, a run-down, rented place; her father had locked one of the bedrooms permanently because the roof let in rainwater. There had been mold on the wall, great curtains of the evil-smelling stuff. She gagged. coughed, shook her head.

She finally reached the bottom and stepped onto a stony floor with puddles of water reflecting the light from Robert's flashlight. He flung down the coil of rope and came down the metal steps to stand next to her. He put an arm around her waist and back inside her mind she flinched away from the touch. But there was no physical movement, nothing to signal her revulsion.

A short tunnel, about ten feet high, led onward, and he shepherded her along until it opened into another cavern. This was a sizeable one, its roof perhaps sixty feet high with the flashlight only just illuminating the ceiling above them. The sound of rushing water was plain, and they walked carefully towards the noise. They were eventually stopped by what seemed to be a deep chasm running from one side of the chamber to the other.

Robert grunted. A small sign of stress when it appeared they could go no further. The flashlight glinted off an iron ring set into the floor, an aid to professional cave explorers—spelunkers—he guessed. He bent to tie the end of the rope to it, throwing the remainder over the edge. "C'mon, Steph. Water. What did I say? Running water means a way out."

It sounded glib and Stephanie knew it was stupid. She had to say something. "Robert… these underground waterways often fill up completely, no airspaces. And with the run-off from the melting snow…"

"Trust me, baby. This is our way out," Robert said.

Stephanie nodded. She was dead if she ran and dead if she climbed down the hole. She was out of choices. Robert told her how to use the rope and Stephanie got down on hands and knees and backed her way over the edge. Rope climbing was something she had not done since her schooldays; she had hated it then and still did. She felt numb and frightened; nevertheless, she slowly let herself down into the darkness, feeling for footholds in the rock wall before sliding her hands lower on the rope one by one.

"Well done, Steph. Take it nice an' easy. Shout when you touch bottom, it ain't far."

Robert's idea of *not far* was different from Stephanie's. She had descended thirty feet or so; her arms felt as though they were coming out of their sockets, her muscles were on fire. She wasn't strong enough to climb back up so she continued down, feet feeling for purchase. Abruptly, her foot slipped free from a water-slick toehold. Her hands slid against the rope, taking the skin off her palms, her knees banged against the wall, shredding her jeans and gashing her legs. The fall took her another fifteen feet. She landed awkwardly, one leg giving away as it took her weight and pitching her head first at the wall. Stephanie cried out.

"Stephanie!" Robert screamed and flung himself flat on the ground at the top of the precipice. He shone the flashlight down and saw her lying supine on the rocks below him. "Stephanie baby, can you hear me? Are you all right?"

There was no answer and panic-stricken, he took hold of the rope and half slid—half climbed down after her, not feeling when he skinned his own hands on the rope.

"Oh God, Steph. Wake up, hon, wake up. I'll get you out of here."

The two sets of footprints led us through the gate and onward. I was suspicious. It was too easy. I could imagine being set up and searched around to check every bit of cover from which he might have planned to ambush us. There was nothing, however, and it left me feeling high and light-headed, primed for a confrontation.

We climbed the gate and went inside, saw the ransacked cupboard of emergency supplies. "I'm sorry, Andy," I said eventually. "You're going to have to go back to the chopper and get the pilot to lift off so he can make radio contact. I want a caver or a potholer who knows this place. I want climbing gear and some firearms, too. Okay?" DC Asquith, looking slightly rebellious, nodded. "Okay. Go."

When he had gone I shrugged. "I know he wanted in on this but hell, safety first. We really ought to wait here until we get support."

"Maybe we should, but the man's a killer, and we don't know what's going on in there. And if there's a river down there or a stream, we don't know what's happening with that either. Goddamn, the girl could be drowning now."

"Okay," I muttered. "You've made your point. Don't overdo it." With that, we each took a flashlight from the cabinet and went on.

We came to where the barrier had been pushed aside and almost tripped over the grid which, from the marks on the ground, had obviously once covered the hole next to it. I thought John would stop here for he seemed far too big to get through the opening, but he passed through without any problem. He was more limber than I'd expected and I followed him down.

There was a tunnel below—the only way to go—and we followed it until it opened into a much larger space. John took hold of my shoulder and said, all trace of his usual smile gone, "I'm sure I don't have to say this, Stewart, but I'm going to anyhow. This Cleghorn's one tricky devil." John had already taken out his Colt and was using it to add punctuation to his sentences. "You be careful, friend. I don't want to stand at your graveside tomorrow or the next day. Okay?"

I nodded. "Thanks for the concern, John." I took my own 9mm Beretta out from its unaccustomed shoulder holster and we continued on.

"Running water," I whispered and saw John nod in the light from my torch. We reached the edge of a crevice or a chasm of some sort, and our lights reflected back from a wide stream of racing water, maybe forty, fifty feet below us. "Christ. Have they gone down there?"

"If they have, I reckon they're dead as… what was that?"

I heard it, too. A high keening sound, more animal than human, though somehow, instinctively, I knew it was the latter. With nerves on edge from the weird noise, we made our way towards it and found the ring set into the edge of the ravine and the rope going over. We shone our lights over the edge and there below was the man I had been hunting every waking hour of the last week. He was kneeling on a ledge thirty feet below me holding the hand of a woman I assumed to be Stephanie.

Cleghorn's head was flung back, his mouth open, emitting that unnerving racket and his eyes were gazing into somewhere I had never been and dreaded the thought of ever going. I turned to my companion and shrugged. He smiled grimly.

"Cleghorn. This is the police," I shouted at last. I thought he hadn't heard me, too taken up with his own grief to notice us. "Cleghorn," I shouted again and he gradually came back, looked up, staring straight up into the light beam. "Is she still alive? Is Stephanie still alive?"

He shook his head. "I don't know. Maybe."

"Have you tried to move her?"

Another shake of his head. Almost too quietly to be heard. "S'my fault. I made her come with me."

"Okay Cleghorn. Forget all that." I didn't want a guilt trip adding to his genuine shock and grief. "Come on up here. We've got specialists coming. They'll be able to get a stretcher down to her, take her to hospital. Now, come up, take it slowly."

Cleghorn stood up, his shoulders drooping in resignation, a dejected, forlorn figure. He wound his foot into the rope and started to climb.

I almost didn't notice John Merrick as he took a small handgun from the left-hand pocket of his sheepskin coat—at least it looked small compared to the gun in his other hand. He moved a little way along the edge, away from me. I was quite aware that he kept the Navy Colt in his right hand trained on Cleghorn's head while he climbed the rope and put an arm out to the ring where the rope was secured.

"Son of a bitch...Watch it, Stewart, the swine's got a gun." He thrust me violently aside and pointed his own gun down at the climbing man.

Cleghorn's face tilted up, looked at Merrick's towering figure. He opened his mouth. "Jo..." The 44 bullet took him in the side of the head, just forward of the ear, almost a grazing shot, a few millimeters to the right and it would have left no more than a bloody furrow. Nevertheless, the force of the impact knocked Cleghorn from the rope, and he fell like a rag doll, narrowly missing Stephanie's limp body and bouncing off the rock face into the swirling water.

The shock of the icy water brought a moment's clarity to Robert and incongruously, it was not Stephanie's receding form that occupied his clouding consciousness but a song of Jerry Lee Lewis. The first few words from *Great Balls of Fire* went through his mind, the lyric that ended, *too much love drives a man insane.*

As I pushed myself to my knees and from there to my feet, I frowned. *What had I just seen?* I think I saw Merrick drop the small gun on the floor at the very edge of the chasm. I'll swear his hand was shaking and the pistol almost slid over the edge. It had happened very fast: did I really see it?"Thanks, John. I didn't see he had a gun." I looked down at the weapon curiously, then over the edge. "Where's Cleghorn? His body?"

"Hit the water and disappeared. He's gone for good now, God rest his soul. No," Merrick seemed to mentally shake himself, "you wouldn't have seen his gun, I was just better placed. I don't think he'd noticed I was here."

I guess I nodded. Merrick was smooth, no doubt about it. *Should I say something, or not?* I shrugged and said, "Well, it's over with now, I guess. We'll have a stretcher party in here soon and once the girl's out, we can go. I'll have to report in to my superiors but there's no chance of his being alive; once you go underground in one of those streams it's good-bye."

"Need me to help with the explanations?"

I shook my head. "Somehow, I think that'll simply make matters worse."

Stephanie Cleghorn was taken off to hospital in the helicopter which left us having to go back to Leeds in a police car. We dropped John Merrick at the railway station where he would take a train to Manchester airport. That left me with the unwelcome prospect of reporting back to Flowers.

CHAPTER 35

After writing up my report and facing Flowers, I took of a couple of days off. I drove round to the vet's and picked up Pip. It seemed odd, Pip was a bit of a stranger—a one-eyed, three-legged dog who nonetheless was tickled pink at being with me again and back in his old haunts once more.

Shirley Kelly had been perfectly correct about how quickly he would adapt to his new condition and thankfully, I adapted, too. A few hours after picking him up, I hardly noticed his lopsided gait and his new habit of turning his head slightly to look at me. I was just pleased to have him back with me again. The thought of having so nearly lost him brought home to me just how much I loved the little scoundrel.

On the Tuesday, the second of my days off, I got out my fishing rod and walked with Pip through the orchard. Pip carried a large knuckle bone I had brought home from the butcher's. At the river's edge, I cast my float into the water and sat down on a convenient log while Pip began to gnaw at his brown bag lunch.

The weather was still cold yet bright, the clouds high and just thick enough to turn the sun hazy. *A morning for thinking.* I might even sort out a few priorities, given enough time, I thought. So I sat there while my bottom turned numb and tried to decide what I really felt about my beautiful black sergeant. Was it just a case of hormones hijacking my brain or was there something deeper at work?

I was not to find out. A movement off to the right caught my attention; I turned and saw a figure walking along the river bank from the stile on the boundary fence. Shapeless in bulky clothing, I could make nothing out except for the height and the shotgun broken open and crooked over his right arm. It was definitely a man; the height, the way he walked made it obvious, and for a moment he seemed to resemble Richards, the man I had almost instinctively blamed for Pip's injury, the one I had sent to prison in Birmingham.

Only for a moment though. As soon as I saw the green wellingtons and the waxed jacket with the cloth cap I guessed it was my neighbor. The *gentleman* farmer I had not yet met. He was red-faced, red-nosed and carried an obvious chip on his shoulder. Despite the fact that I took an instant dislike to the man, I nodded as pleasantly as I could.

"Nice morning."

I might as well have remained silent.

"That your dog?" he said, his tone bullish.

I nodded.

"You let him come near my sheep again, and I'll finish the job I started. Understand?"

I laid the rod down carefully and stood up; Pip left his bone and backed up until his rump was pressing against my legs. My own height of six feet was easily four inches more than the other's although that would not have mattered just then. I would have done the same if I'd been a garden gnome.

I glared down at the farmer. "My dog was reared on a sheep farm and brought up on sheep's milk. He'd no more worry a sheep than he'd try to fly. Now with me, it's a different matter. I was reared in a concrete jungle and when I bite, I break bones. Do *you* understand? You go anywhere near my dog again, and I'll skin you and nail your hide to my back door. Now get off my land!"

"You can't threaten me like that." His face couldn't get any redder, but it started to take on a purplish tinge.

"Can't I?" I took a step forward and got a good grip on his waxed collar. I turned him about and frog-marched him on the double to the stile and with a final shove, pitched him halfway over it. I stood there as he picked himself up and retrieved his gun from the bottom of the fence. He mustered a little dignity and climbed back onto his own side.

I think he was about to say something, but presumably thought better of it and hurried out of sight. I turned and nearly fell over Pip who was standing right behind me. I bent and stroked him behind the ears. "Deserves a good deal more than that," I told the dog who always listened to every word I said, "still every bit helps, eh?"

We walked back to where I'd left my rod. "Another hour, I reckon, and then we'll go and cook some dinner."

We finished the next hour and I reeled the line in and started to walk back to the house. Just before I reached the graveled backyard, the hairs on the back of my neck rose. I could feel them prickling. Somebody was watching me, waiting for me. Cleghorn? Had he survived and tracked me down? My mouth dried up. On top of the earlier business with the neighbor, I felt quite disconcerted, unnerved.

I turned a complete circle, trying to spot who and where the watcher was, another careful step and I saw Shelly Fearon leaning against the back door with her arms folded.

"Well hello, Stewart." She grinned. "They let me out last night so when I found out this morning that you were at home, I came round and cooked us dinner."

I licked my dry lips and grinned back at her. She looked a little tired but was just as beautiful as she had been in my thoughts earlier in the morning. I took in a great breath and exhaled, dispelling the last shreds of the fright that I'd given myself. "Shelly. Hey, you're a sight for sore eyes. Welcome back."

At the back step, I put my arms around her and gave her a quick and heartfelt hug. "And thanks. It's cold out here, let's get inside and see if there's a good bottle of wine around to warm us up."

We went inside and I breathed in the smells of cooking; I was pleased I had given her a key. "What's on the menu then, Sergeant Fearon?"

"Sausage Creole done in my own spicy stew. Just something I invented. How does that sound? After that, there's tangy mince tart with brandy sauce. That grab you at all?"

"Sounds good to me. Hope there's enough for you, too."

A little later, we were doing justice to Shelly's cuisine. After the first few mouthfuls, Shelly looked at me across the table. "I hear Flowers has made it public knowledge that he supported your appointment over the Old Man's objections."

"You hear a great deal for someone on sick leave."

"I work at it. I also hear Alec Bell has caught his bomber."

"That so? I'm really pleased about that."

"He didn't say anything about it being your ideas that led him to the man."

I ignored that bit. "Did you hear who the bomber was?"

"A former employee of Philibuild. Apparently his back garden is due to become part of the new road."

"More than enough reason to bear a grudge then."

"It sure is, but now it's your turn, Stewart."

"Sorry ? How do you mean?"

"Cleghorn, of course. I've heard the official version of his pointing a gun at you and you shooting him to protect both yourself and Mrs. Cleghorn."

"Well, that's the only version I can tell you at the moment, Shelly. It's as true as it gets."

"Somehow, it all seems a bit flat. As in *made up*."

"Ouch! I got knocked down towards the end and I was a bit groggy. A potholing expert…"

"A speleologist."

"Pardon?"

"That's what they're called. Potholing experts."

"Right. One of those told us there are miles and miles of caves and tunnels under the moors up there. Cleghorn's body might never be found."

She pushed her food around the plate for a moment. "Does that mean that if they did find him, it might not tally with your story?"

I looked up at her and not for the first time told myself this was not only a very desirable young woman but an extremely astute one, too. It could make for a very interesting future and our past together was not yet a fortnight old.

"Let me think about things a little more, Shelly. I'll tell you what I can if I think you won't be compromised by knowing, I'll tell you. Okay?"

"Okay."

It was way past midnight when I thought we should call it a day; we had finished the bottle and a second and most of a third by then so I called a taxi for her. It hurt like crazy to see her leave, though tonight had not seemed the right occasion to talk about serious matters. I sighed, hoping there would be other times and went through to the kitchen to do the washing up. While I was putting the plates away I heard my fax machine chattering in the study. I dried my hands and went through and started reading it as it was coming off, but the writing got a little shaky and I had to wait for the page to come all the way through before I could read it.

Dear Stewart,

I had to write and let you know what really happened back there in the caves because I like you and don't want you to think I was trying to flimflam you in any way.

I was never quite sure you believed me when I said I'd come to England just to deliver the files and of course, you would have been right. You see, I was fairly sure I recognized Alan Cleghorn the moment we fished him out of the lake. He went to high school with my son when we lived in Fort Myers.

Later, when he was older, Jim, my son had been smoking pot and I reckon he was getting into cocaine and maybe crack when he got in debt with a bunch of lowlifes who were pushing the stuff. They were going to teach him a thing or two with knives when Alan Cleghorn intervened and saved my son's life, not to mention his career.

Alan also helped in other ways. I told you my wife died of a heart attack a few years ago. I lied to you Stewart. She had a stroke and it took two years of very special nursing before she died. That was very expensive; I was in hock up to my neck. Jim had maintained his friendship with Alan Cleghorn and through him, I was able to obtain enough money to pay for the treatment. Again Alan Cleghorn had come to my family's rescue and when it became clear that his brother had killed him, I wanted the swine.

I'm sorry I had to deceive you, Stewart. Believe me when I say it's not my usual style.

Well, that's about it except that I got what I went to England for and I hope that wherever Alan is now; he knows I paid my debt to him.

Don't forget, if you're over in my neck of the woods, call round and we'll have more than a few beers together. And by the way, the bed in my guest room is a whole lot bigger than yours.

Try and have a nice life, Stewart. Bye now.

John Merrick

The fax answered questions I hadn't really wanted to ask. Should I let sleeping dogs lie or show this to Joe Flowers? It might mean the end of my career, almost certainly the end of it at Leeds if I did.

I needed to talk with someone, and despite the lateness of the hour I rang Dad. "Hello, Dad. Sorry to wake you up at this unearthly hour."

"Don't worry about it, pal. Couldn't sleep tonight anyway." Which was almost certainly a lie. "Glad you called. I've been wanting to call you, but I reckon you've been pretty busy. Anyhow, see you got him, eh?"

The death or disappearance of Robert Cleghorn had received full media coverage. Dad had probably been watching every bulletin.

"Did you doubt me?"

"Not for a minute, son." I could hear the pride in his voice, bless him. "When they chipped you off the old block, they took the best bit they could find. Now, what's the story, eh? How did you catch him?"

"I'll save that until I see you. It would be a long night if I told you now."

"Well, okay then. But make it soon, won't you?"

"Sure will, Dad. Hey, what do you think of someone who steals half a pair of cufflinks?"

"I don't know. This a joke?"

"No. I had to change my shirt at the office the other day, put my cufflinks on my desk and went out to the gents to wash. When I came back, one of them had gone."

"Maybe you've got a lady admirer. Taking a souvenir."

"Maybe we've got a lunatic thief in the offices. Had three pound coins stolen a few days ago, too."

"Certainly into big-time crime up there. I did warn you."

"I know, but I'll have him."

"I'm sure you will, son. Goodnight and God bless… Oh…!"

"Yes?"

"Any jackdaws roosting round your offices? Or magpies?"

Dectective Inspector White will Return in

"Damage Limitation"

ALSO FROM
DAVID COLES & JACK EVERETT

The Diamond Seekers

1/1: Jihad Britain

The Hand of God

The Last Free Men

Last Mission

COMING SOON FROM
DAVID COLES & JACK EVERETT

Damage Limitation: An *Inspector White* Caper

Damaged Souls: An *Inspector White* Caper

WWW.ARCHIMEDESPRESSE.CO.UK

Author Biographies

JACK EVERETT is author and coauthor of a number of fantasy, science fiction, crime and thriller novels. Some are published, some are in progress and others are still in gestation. Jack also handcrafts stunning snooker cues and award-winning modern *objets d'art* from exotic and magnificently figured timbers. He collects books and playing cards though there is little space in a much-overcrowded home. He dreams of having a bigger library, and hopes to one day have the extra room he dreams of.

DAVID COLES began writing fantasy and science fiction longer ago than he can now remember. His works have explored the local stars, killed off huge numbers of Roman legionaries, uncovered what happened to King Arthur and the Round Table—and hatched a few thriller plots. A founding member of the international Historical Novel Society, he has attended workshops run by Terry Pratchett and the late David Gemmel. David lives with his wife and a pet laptop in God's own county—Yorkshire in the UK—where he also designs and builds websites for friends and programs for fun.

About Barking Rain Press

Did you know that five media conglomerates publish eighty percent of the books in the United States? As the publishing industry continues to contract, opportunities for emerging and mid-career authors are drying up. Who will write the literature of the twenty-first century if just a handful of profit-focused corporations are left to decide who—and what—is worthy of publication?

Barking Rain Press is dedicated to the creation and promotion of thoughtful and imaginative contemporary literature, which we believe is essential to a vital and diverse culture. As a nonprofit organization, Barking Rain Press is an independent publisher that seeks to cultivate relationships with new and mid-career writers over time, to be thorough in the editorial process, and to make the publishing process an experience that will add to an author's development—and ultimately enhance our literary heritage.

In selecting new titles for publication, Barking Rain Press considers authors at all points in their careers. Our goal is to support the development of emerging and mid-career authors—not just single books—as we know from experience that a writer's audience is cultivated over the course of several books.

Support for these efforts comes primarily from the sale of our publications; we also hope to attract grant funding and private donations. Whether you are a reader or a writer, we invite you to take a stand for independent publishing and become more involved with Barking Rain Press. With your support, we can make sure that talented writers thrive, and that their books reach the hands of spirited, curious readers. Find out more at our website.

WWW.BARKINGRAINPRESS.ORG

Also from Barking Rain Press

VIEW OUR COMPLETE CATALOG ONLINE:
WWW.BARKINGRAINPRESS.ORG

Made in the USA
Charleston, SC
10 February 2015